RIDER IN THE RAIN

WILLIAM ALTIMARI

IMPERIUM BOOKS

"Rider in the Rain," by William Altimari. ISBN 978-0-9728726-6-9 (hardcover). ISBN 978-0-9728726-7-6 (softcover).

Published 2014 by Virtualbookworm.com Publishing Inc., P.O. Box 9949, College Station, TX 77842, US. Copyright 2014, William Altimari All rights reserved. No part of this publication may be reproduced, stored in a retrieval system, or transmitted in any form or by any means, electronic, mechanical, recording or otherwise, without the prior written permission of William Artimari.

Manufactured in the United States of America.

ACKNOWLEDGEMENTS

I thank Veronica Altimari and Ana Rizzo, two very special people, for employing their editorial talents in the preparation of the manuscript.

FOR MY MOTHER, AND FOR ALL MOTHERS, WHO
WERE THE FIRST TO TEACH US THE DIFFERENCE
BETWEEN THE GOOD GUYS AND THE BAD GUYS.

ARIZONA TERRITORY

THERE'S NO GREATER FRIEND THAN A
HORSE THAT'S SADDLED AND READY TO GO.
– Texas Bix Bender

PROLOGUE

Caravaggio touched the soul of Father Gallo more profoundly than any other painter. His fearless use of light and shadow shocked the viewer at first, but then allowed the inner self to be transformed to where it felt at ease communing with God. As with everything else in creation, it sounded even more evocative in Italian, and chiaroscuro was a perfect term for this most haunting of effects.

Father Gallo kissed the embroidered cross on his purple stole and hung it on the nail of the confessional door. On this Saturday evening, he again took justified pride in the way in which he had arranged the flickering lamps at Mater Dolorosa Church in San Miguel to help uplift the souls of the faithful in the manner of the legendary master. So effective was it, though, that he almost missed the last penitent sitting in a pew before the side altar. He would never rush anyone out of church, no matter how weary he was after hearing Confession, and so he settled into a rear pew to wait.

"You don't have to sit back there, *padre*," said a compelling voice with a Sonoran inflection.

Father Gallo went forward and sat at the end of the pew. The man was dressed in black, and his hat lay on the pew beside him. Caravaggian shadows obscured his face.

"Can I help you, my son?"

"May I have a moment of your time?" he said while still facing the altar.

"Of course."

"I want to know if there's such a thing as an unforgivable sin."

Without hesitation, he answered, "God's mercy is infinite."

He had been asked that question countless times, so his answer was always ready. Yet tonight, with this man, it seemed weak and thin. He did not know why.

"Are you sure?" the man asked.

"Yes." He gestured to the confessional. "I always have time for one more."

"I'm not ready."

"I understand."

"I wish you did."

No priest was accustomed to being rebuked, but he thought it best to say nothing. He was not sure why.

"I've committed many sins against God and man, but none greater than driving another to despair. Would you agree this is the worst sin of all?"

"It is very grave."

"Forgivable?"

"With penitence."

The man said nothing.

After a long silence, Father Gallo said, "If you confess to a crime outside of Confession, I cannot shield you. In there" – he pointed – "it's between only you and God."

"*Padre*, you're a fox."

Father Gallo touched him on the arm and smiled. "Don't share that."

The man laughed softly, which seemed amazing under the circumstances. "Thank you for your time."

"Is this a dismissal?"

"Oh, no. I was just being merciful. Isn't this the place for it? Go and enjoy your supper."

"I cannot leave a man in pain."

The man's laugh was harsh now. "Then you'll have to stay by my side forever."

"I have as much time as God will allow me."

The man turned toward him for the first time. Although his face still lurked in shadow, the candlelight reflected in his eyes, and Father Gallo could just make out a heavy dark moustache and perhaps a scar on his left cheek.

"I'll leave you now," the man said but seemed reluctant to leave.

"Where will you go?"

"Far away."

Father Gallo laid a hand on the man's arm again. "Flight is rarely the answer. Have you heard of the Roman poet Horace? He said, 'The sky, not the soul —.'"

"*Caelum non animum mutant qui trans mare currunt.* The sky, not the soul, they change who run across the sea."

Father Gallo was stunned into silence.

"That's a strange crucifix," the man said, pointing to a side niche in the church.

"Yes."

"I always thought Christ was nailed to the cross, not tied to it."

"That isn't Christ."

"A crucifix without Christ?"

"Yes."

"How can that be?"

"His name is Dismas. Most people call him The Good Thief. On the first Good Friday, Jesus promised that he would be with Him that very day in Paradise."

For the second time, the man looked at the priest.

"God works mysteriously," Father Gallo said. "To bring you here. Before Dismas."

The man turned away.

"May I get my stole?"

"Not yet. I have to atone first. Before I confess."

"You have it backwards. You should atone afterward."

"My whole life has been backwards. But I have to suffer more before I can ask for forgiveness. Possibly when I return . . . ."

"Do you really believe you can suffer more than you have?"

"Oh, yes. Never doubt that."

When the man picked up his hat and stood, Father Gallo saw at his right hip a long-barreled revolver tucked butt forward into a black sash circling his waist.

"Good night, *padre*."

But the priest was not so easily put off, and he followed the stranger down the nave. When they reached the heavy mesquite doors, the man stopped.

"I've never understood why church doors are so tall," the stranger said, looking up. "Men are small. Smaller than they think. But these doors . . . *Por qué?*"

Father Gallo smiled. "Perhaps they're tall to let in the Holy Spirit."

"Or the Four Horsemen of the Apocalypse. Don't let down your guard."

Startled at those words, Father Gallo stood there in silence as the man pushed the doors open.

"You know of the Horsemen?" he finally asked.

The man seemed not to hear. "*Padre*, do you know who I am?"

"I believe I do. Many have claimed you're only a legend."

The man said nothing and walked through the doorway.

"Before you leave, *señor*, please remember one thing. The man tied to the cross behind you is the only person in all of human history who was ever promised Heaven. . . . And he was a bandit."

But the stranger had already vanished into the night.

PART ONE

The causes of my horror lie deep.

—De Quincey

1 SOLITARIO

Writhing masses of rattlesnakes high as a horse's hips are what Easterners often expect when they lope into Arizona. Yet the desert grasslands south of Tucson speak of rich cattle country and fat horses lazing in the sun.

The girl sat on a low rise with her arms wrapped around her drawn up knees. Her gray Stetson was pushed back, and her black hair dipped down below the sweatband. She gazed at the horses in the rope corral below. A Mexican *remudero* with his hat pulled low against the sun sat outside the corral on a camp chair, and his horse grazed nearby. She had counted twenty-seven horses in the remuda, mostly sorrels and bays. But it was the black and white pinto that had lit a spark in her.

"Looking for a mount, my dear?"

She turned to her right and saw a pear-shaped man waddling toward her. She stood up respectfully.

"Good morning," he said, tipping his hat. "Colonel Buxton at your service."

"Hello," she said and held out her hand like a man.

Startled, the colonel took it gently, but she gripped his with assurance.

"I have many fine steeds down there."

"You're the auctioneer, sir?"

"Auctioneer, proprietor, man of letters."

He wore a long coat that had been the height of style around the time Grant had taken Vicksburg and a hat with a brim wide enough to shade a Virginia plantation.

"And you are?" he asked.

"I'm sorry, sir," she said. "Colleen Callaghan."

"Ah, yes, of course. The Celts have always had the finest eye for horseflesh."

"You're a flatterer, colonel."

"It's my business. Has one of those animals caught your fancy?"

"Yes, sir."

"May I sit? These old wheels of mine. . . ."

She smiled. "Make yourself easy."

He lowered himself to the grass and she did likewise. Although she was wearing denim trousers, she kept her knees down this time and drew her legs beneath her in a more ladylike fashion.

"Which one will you steal at a shameful price?"

She looked back down the hill. "The overo."

The colonel smiled. "My most handsome horse. But why is it that young women always buy for color?"

"I'm not, sir," she said, still gazing down at the herd.

The pinto stood apart from the rest of the animals. While they grazed at one side of the corral, he stood at the other end and stared off into the distance.

"He's a loner, Miss Callaghan. I never recommend a loner to a young person. How old are you, if I may ask?"

"Sixteen, sir."

"I have a red bay down there perfect for you. A seven-year-old gelding. His name is Buddy. A little over fifteen hands, not too tall for you. He's even Indian broke. Sweetest temperament this side of a litter of puppies. Cowy, too, if you want him for ranch work. Can turn on a five-dollar-gold piece and throw you back four and ninety-nine in change. At one time a few years back he was owned by a Texan Ranger. Laughs at gunfire."

"How do you know you're right, colonel?"

"Right about what, miss?"

"Maybe the pinto isn't a loner."

"Just look at him."

"Maybe he isn't ignoring the other horses. Maybe they're ignoring *him*. No, colonel, I don't think he's a loner. I think he's alone."

"Perhaps you understand him better than I do."

"Will he go high?"

2

"He might. He's only seven. Good feet. He's not a ten dollar horse."

"Over a hundred?"

"Can you afford that?"

"Colonel," she said, smiling with the wisdom of someone twice her age, "you don't expect me to tell you my top bid, do you?"

"No, I expect you to tell it to yourself. Always know going in how you're going out."

"Thank you. I'll do that."

"He might even go higher. Look down there."

A young man had come up to the corral and was speaking with the wrangler and pointing to the pinto.

Colleen slowly wrapped her arms across her chest.

"Do you know him, Miss Callaghan?"

"Yes."

"With no liking . . . ?"

She said nothing.

"Time to get ready for the auction." He stood slowly. "I'll have my man haul some benches from town." He hesitated. "Young lady, I don't know why I'm doing this because it won't profit me a cent, but I'll offer the pinto first."

She looked puzzled as she stood up.

"People are usually reluctant to bid high early in the auction," the colonel said. "They hope they might get a better deal later. Sometimes the first several horses don't sell."

She smiled. "You're a gentleman, colonel."

"All men of the South are gentlemen."

"And are they all colonels? It seems like they are."

"Each one over fifty. And now I must take my leave."

"One more thing," she said quickly. "Do you guarantee soundness?"

"Miss Callaghan, I start the bidding so low I don't guarantee these horses even have lungs."

He touched the brim of his hat and walked away.

As the colonel headed back toward San Miguel, Colleen noticed at the far end of the rise a man standing with his arms folded. His back was toward her, and he was staring down at the horses. He seemed as alone as a solitary saguaro on a desert slope. After the colonel passed him, he turned and came toward her. The assertiveness in his stride made her uneasy.

When he was about twenty feet away, she began to make out a face she would never forget.

"Hello," he said in a voice as resonant as an ancient philosopher's must have been.

"Good morning, sir."

"I have my eye on that pinto."

"He's a loner," she said without thinking. "Not a good choice, the colonel says. There's a nice bay gelding that he recommends."

"I'll have to look him over."

The man wore a black shirt and black *calzoneras* with small silver conchos down the sides of the legs. A silver silk bandana was knotted around his neck and flowed halfway down his shirt front. His flat-brimmed black hat hung down his back by a stampede string. A black silk sash encircled his waist.

Collie wondered as she studied him if there were such a thing as restrained flamboyance.

"Looks like we have a competitor." He pointed to the man examining the horses.

"His name is Stone."

"And might yours be Colleen Callaghan?"

"How . . . Have we met?"

"I'm intuitive."

"But . . ."

A smile brightened a face much in need of brightening. "Haven't you always wanted to meet a mysterious stranger?"

She suddenly felt at ease and smiled back.

"Besides," he went on, "whom else would you be? San Miguel is a small town and you have a face like the map of Ireland."

"Green and grassy?" she said, laughing.

He laughed with her. Somehow she felt that he had not shared a laugh in years beyond counting.

"Most people think a girl with a name like mine should be a redhead."

"Your mother must have kept that for herself."

"My mother?" she said in surprise. "Do you — ?

"Intuition."

4

"I'm what's called Black Irish."

"I've never heard of that."

"Dark hair, but blue eyes and fair skin and freckles."

"Ah. . . ."

"There's a story that it's because we're partly descended from sailors shipwrecked in the Spanish Armada."

"So you're part Spanish?"

"No," she said, laughing. "My mom told me it's just a legend."

He stared at her for a long time, and then he finally said, "Shall we go look at the horses?"

She turned and saw Stone still examining the animals. "Let's wait a spell."

"No need to fear him."

"Fear? Who said — ?"

"Brown eyes can lie, but blue eyes conceal nothing. At least yours cannot. I know — my mother had blue eyes. They're too pure."

"He's the son of Harlo Stone, one of the big ranchers around here. Harlo owns the Lazy S. He wants to buy our ranch. Others, too."

"And?"

"And what?"

"There's more. I can hear it in your voice."

She hesitated and then said, "The old man isn't an ordinary rancher. Most of his stock is stolen or bred from stolen stock. He buys from rustlers who cross the border and steal from the *vaqueros*. Then he has his own brand artists work over the cattle with running irons."

"How do you know this?"

"Everybody knows it."

"Including the Pima County sheriff?"

"He's far away. We don't have any lawman here. We had a part-time sheriff last year. He owned our little newspaper, too. He took sick and had to resign. Sold the paper, too. He passed away just before last Christmas."

"Not even some sort of vigilance committee?"

"Just a group of the bigger *ganaderos* to settle little problems. Informal stuff, that's all. They're honest men. Mostly."

He gestured to the ground and they both sat down.

5

"Your father should be with you at the auction."

"My father passed away long ago."

She felt comfortable enough with him to pull her knees up and wrap her arms around them.

"I love Arizona this time of year," she said and inhaled deeply.

"So do I. But I prefer the desert to the grasslands."

"You do?"

"Yes."

"But it's full of sharp and harsh things and poisonous things." She eyed him mischievously. "Are you a sharp and harsh thing?"

"Poisonous, too."

"Stop it!" she said with a laugh.

He gazed out at the countryside. "Arizona is beautiful anywhere and anytime. I've been away, which is why I need a horse. I gave mine to a friend before I traveled."

"Back East?"

"Very far. But not half as far as my journey back."

She searched his face for some special meaning to that, but his eyes were too dark to read.

"You have another competitor," the stranger said, pointing down the hill.

A powerful looking man was making his way around the rope corral.

"That gentleman," Colleen said, "is Mr. John Racelyn Holden. He ramrods our little spread."

"Sounds like a British duke."

"I think his mother was English. He's one of the best cattlemen in the Southwest. He used to work for the Four Sixes ranch in Texas."

"Ah . . . . And now he works for you."

"Mother can pay him only half of what he's worth."

"But . . . ?"

"But he said he wanted less pressure. So here he is."

They sat quietly for a while, enjoying a cool breeze, and then she turned back to him.

"If you're a gentleman, sir," she said, half-teasingly, "you won't outbid me."

He pointed down the hill. "The pinto?"

"Yes."

He smiled. *"Pero ese potro es muy solitario."*

"So am I."

"Ah . . . . And the bay?"

"You'll love him."

"Don't you know that there are no friends at the auction block?"

"Pero usted es un caballero."

"My compliments on your Spanish—but I made no claim about being a gentleman."

"I'm making it for you."

He smiled at her again. "You're like a magician using misdirection—your blue eyes distract me while your hard fist gets hold of that horse."

"But I'm just a child," she said with mock innocence. "You're so much older and wiser."

His smile slowly closed inward on itself, like a flower at sunset. Without warning, his silence suddenly seemed sad as he stared off at nothing. Or at least at nothing she could see.

He was only about the age of her mother, and yet he seemed old beyond his years. It is an odd phenomenon that a person could seem a certain age but, at the same time, appear older than he should at that age. After all, if he appears older, how does one know he is not older? Yet somehow one knows, just as one can distinguish a worn old coin from a newer one that has been roughly handled.

The man was as stationary as a cat captivated by a candle flame. There was something unnerving about the way he stared far off. Collie felt that Heaven and earth could pass away and still he would not move.

For reasons she would have found hard to explain, the large head appeared too heavy for the body. As though overloaded with visions, it seemed weighted down with the certainly of its own unending ache. The dark face, empty of Classical beauty, exerted a pull that was more feral than fine. His left cheek was deeply scarred, split by a blow that would have slain almost any man. Half-hidden by his drooping moustache, his mouth seemed pulled down, drawn toward the earth by the weight of some unspeakable woe.

"Sir?"

7

He looked back at her.

"I was only teasing. You can bid on the horse."

He appeared to stir himself from his trance.

She smiled and held out her hand. "My friends call me Collie."

His hand seemed softer than it should have, and it enveloped hers with its warmth.

"Collie? Like the dog?"

"No," she said, rolling her eyes as only a young girl can. "Like Colleen. Or like the sheep. The dog was named after a sheep."

"Ah, so you're a sweet little lamb?"

"Yes, I am."

His deep-chested laughter startled the horses down in the pen.

"Shall we examine the animals?" she asked.

He stood up and extended a helping hand to her as a courtesy and she stood with him.

"Stone is still there," he said.

"But I'm with *you*," she answered without thinking and then reddened when she realized what an odd thing that was to say to someone she had met only minutes before. Yet he did not seem put upon or even surprised by someone he did not know seeking shelter in his shadow. He seemed to accept it as the natural course of events. Or, perhaps, the fated burden of his life.

The sun was low when Collie leaned her forearms across the top rail and stared at the empty horse pen outside the adobe bunkhouse. She felt as childish as a five-year-old for having assumed the beautiful pinto was destined to be hers. Who could have dreamed that someone would be willing to shovel out gold for an untried horse? And a loner at that. Her hundred and ten dollars now seemed like a sorry joke.

She heard Holden ride up and tie his mount, but she did not turn around. She was embarrassed by the tears in her eyes and dried them with the blue bandana around her neck.

Holden walked up beside her but remained silent.

"I didn't get the horse," she said without looking at him.

"I know." His voice was as gentle as iron wheels rolling across river rock.

"Bleeder Stone outbid me first, and then a stranger buried him with his bids. I left before it was over."

Holden put a massive arm around her shoulders.

"They both knew I wanted that horse," she said. "People can be so cruel."

"There aren't any friends at an auction."

"That's what the stranger said."

"You met him?"

"Beforehand. The odd thing is that he knew my name."

"It's a small town."

"But he even knew the color of mother's hair."

"And how many strawberry blondes are there in San Miguel?"

"He was a Mexican. Or maybe half. He seemed so kind. Frightening, too, in a way. I can't explain it."

Holden squeezed her shoulders.

"Oh, Rake, I feel like such a child. I was sure that horse would be in this pen tonight. Would you believe he nickered at me when I went over to him outside town? A horse I'd never seen before—how often does that happen?"

"Almost never."

"We understood each other."

"Intuition."

"I hate that word!"

"Why?"

"The stranger used it about himself."

"And now you hate *him*."

"No," she said with a sigh. "I've never hated anybody. But I've learned something about life."

"And it isn't even sundown. So much to learn yet today."

She gave him a puzzled look. "What do you mean?"

He made a sideways gesture with his head.

9

She turned toward the house. The pinto was tied to the hitching rail in front.

"Oh, Rake!" She threw her arms around him. "I didn't even know you were at the auction! I'll pay you back. I promise!"

"I ponied him out here," he said with a smile. "But you couldn't even bother to turn around."

"How much did he cost you?"

"Not a cent."

"But—."

"His withers are aching for your fingers."

Collie walked over to the horse slowly to avoid startling him. She approached casually at an oblique angle and avoided direct eye contact, like the seasoned horsewoman she was.

The horse nickered when he saw her.

Collie scratched his withers and inhaled his scent. She breathed lightly onto his nose, and he flared his nostrils. Then he sighed the earth-calming sigh only a horse can give and cocked a rear leg and relaxed.

"We're kindred spirits," she whispered. "I know we are."

Holden came over.

"What did you mean? About him not costing anything."

Holden stroked the horse's forehead. "After the auction, I stopped at *La Luna* for refreshment. Bert was behind the bar. He said someone was looking for a man named John Racelyn Holden, and Bert asked if he was a relative of mine."

"Bert didn't know your real name?"

"Guess not. I told him I was John Holden. Bert said the fellow was a Mexican and asked him to give me this." He pulled a folded piece of paper from a vest pocket and handed it to Collie.

Her eyes ran down a bill of sale for a seven-year-old pinto gelding. It was made out to Colleen "Little Lamb" Callaghan and duly signed by Colonel Barton Buxton. Final cost was two hundred and twenty dollars.

"Oh, Rake, how could he do this?" Her eyes were getting misty. "I don't even know his name. Did you find him?"

"Gone. Bert said he got into a card game with some of the hands from the S. Took a table, sat with his back to the wall, and asked if there were any children from the Lazy S who knew how to play poker. Bert said they fell over themselves rushing to the

10

table. He cleaned them all out. Bert said he was either a great card player or an even better cheater. Not one of those muck-snipes had a tail feather left."

"Did they try to hurt him?"

"Bert thought that if he'd been just some ordinary bean eater, the S boys would probably have biffed him. But there was something about him. They seemed cowed. He just stood up and turned his back on them and walked out of the cantina with every cent they had. Like licking butter off a knife."

"Where did he go?"

"I looked around, but a lounger outside the saloon said he'd bought a bay at the auction and rode north."

"You have to find him."

"What does he look like?"

"About mother's age. Fairly tall for a Mexican. He might only be half. Dressed in black. He has black hair and a heavy moustache that droops down low. His left cheek has a terrible scar. Not the kind from a slash, but as if someone had sunk a blade deep into his face. It's the kind of injury you can't imagine any person living through."

"Shouldn't be hard to find someone like that. Provided he's willing to be found."

"And he has very soft hands."

"What?! He touched you?"

"Oh, Rake, I shook his hand."

"Maybe a professional gambler. Or worse."

"You're starting to annoy me, cowboy."

He smiled. "Handsome?"

She thought for a moment. "Not in the usual sense. At least not to most women." She looked away. "Why on earth would he give me a two hundred dollar horse? Do you think mother will let me keep him?"

Holden pushed his hat back and gazed out toward the pasture where they grazed the horses during the day. "I don't know. She'll suspect less than noble motives. Can't afford not to. What mother could?"

"No, no, no! He wasn't like that. He was kind. And so gentle. . . . Especially after I told him my father was dead." She turned away.

"Collie."

She looked back at him.

He took her hat and let it drop down her back and hang by the string. He straightened a few stray hairs in the coiled black bun on top of her head.

"Your hair isn't on your shoulders these days. You're wearing it up—like a woman. You're not between the hay and the grass anymore. You *are* a woman now. Have to show more caution among unknown stallions. You know what I mean."

She nodded but said nothing.

"After you told me he was gentle, you hesitated. Why?"

She turned away and stroked the horse's neck.

"Collie . . . ."

Without looking at Holden, she said, "When I pointed out Bleeder Stone, I think he heard something in my voice. He knew I was afraid of Bleeder." She looked back at Holden. "I saw his eyes narrow. Very slightly. It scared me. But just for a moment. Please don't tell mother."

"Was he heeled?"

"Not that I could see. But I felt so safe with him. Like I do with you. How can that be?"

"Don't know."

"And yet I felt uneasy at the same time. I don't understand it."

Holden folded his arms and took a few steps away and stared into the distance. He was close enough to her that his broad back blocked out half of Arizona.

"I don't think . . . ." He paused but still continued staring off. "I don't think Colleen Callaghan will ever have anything to fear from this stranger." He turned back, grinning. "Whoever he is."

She jumped at Holden and threw her arms around him.

"I'll talk to your mother about keeping the horse."

She pressed her face against his chest. "Thank you, Rake." She hugged him more tightly.

"What's wrong?"

"I'm feeling foolish."

"Tell me."

"I'm not going to see him again, am I?"

"Probably not."

"I hardly know that man . . . and yet I can't bear the thought that he's gone forever."

2 RUMBLINGS

Kathy Callaghan hefted the blue enamelware pot from the stove and brought it to the kitchen table.

"Do you know why I love hot coffee late at night?"

She gestured at Holden's cup, and he slid it toward her.

"Tell me," he said, smiling.

"Because it's so decadent." She filled it with the dark brew. "Nobody who has to work for a living would drink coffee after ten o'clock."

"But we do have to work. I have to be up before dawn."

She filled her own cup and returned the pot to the stove. "Not tomorrow." She pulled a towel from a plate of sweet rolls left over from supper and placed them in front of him. "I want you to take an easy one tomorrow. Hire a couple of day workers in town. How many do we have at the moment?"

"Four besides our regular crew. Stone and Barbicane have sucked up most of the good labor in the area."

"Well, there must be a few chuckline riders around. Give them a day's wage."

"And the expense?"

"Let me worry about the cash flow."

She took a seat across from him.

"And who's going to ride the line?" he asked.

"One of the day men. Or tomorrow Harlo Stone's beeves can sample my grass if they want to."

"And if some of yours decide to chomp on his grass?"

"Then," she said, smiling sweetly, "he can offer up his loss for his sins."

Holden shook his head and sipped his coffee.

"Don't spill any," Kathy said. "It'll eat through the tablecloth." She savored some of the tarry elixir. "Good Lord, no one makes black jack like I do."

"A warning to be heeded and feared."

"Now" — she set down her cup — "tell me about this horse. And this man."

"Collie summed it up pretty well. Don't know much more than she does."

"And no one has any idea who he was?"

"No one."

"Not even my ramrod — whose wisdom rivals that of the Greek sages?"

Holden laughed. "Not him either."

"Seriously, Rake, do you think this stranger had designs on my daughter?"

Holden took one of the rolls and broke it in half and pondered it. "Don't believe so."

"Then what was it?"

"I think he just liked Collie. Everyone likes her. As they like her mother. Despite the hard look in her blue eyes at the moment."

"Two hundred dollars is a wagonload of liking."

"So? Let people attach value as they see fit." He took a bite of the roll. "You know, this bellywash wouldn't be legal without these sinkers to absorb the toxins."

She sighed. "You have such a dead palate."

"Is it any wonder?" he said, pointing to the coffee.

Kathy burst out laughing.

He laid a hand across her wrist. "What's wrong, Missy?"

"I worry about her too much, don't I?"

"Well, she's a wild card, so you have cause."

"She's so lovely and so trusting. . . ." Kathy stared into her cup. "I see every man as a danger."

"In other words, you're normal."

She remained quiet.

"I really do like this brown gargle," he said and got up and topped off their cups.

"Thank you. The aroma of Arbuckle's at midnight comforts me like nothing else."

Holden sat back down.

16

"You have crumbs on your moustache. There are some gray hairs starting to peek through that auburn brush. Did you know that?"

"Missy, I want to share one more thing with you about all this. Something Collie told me. She said that she teased him about being old and it seemed to make him sad. She said she thought she'd offended him about his age. But I don't think it was his age. At least not in that sense." He sipped his coffee.

"Go on. Please."

"I think maybe it reminded him that he was too old for some other reason. Too far gone. And that's why her innocent words cut him."

Kathy frowned but said nothing.

"And there he was gazing into eyes that could melt a slab of lead—and he saw his chance. To reclaim a little. What's two hundred dollars compared with that?"

"Reclaim what?"

"Don't know."

"But with Collie?"

"With innocence."

"But my little girl?"

"Kathy, I think we've been looking into the wrong end of the spyglass. It's not that this stranger did Collie a favor. I think she did one for *him*."

Kathy stared at Holden for a long time. "My God," she whispered at last.

"God indeed."

"But who on earth is he? Can we help him?"

"I suspect he rode away so we wouldn't even risk a try."

"Good Lord, why does life have to be so complex?"

"It isn't. Emotions are."

She smiled at him affectionately. "What makes you so wise, ramrod?"

"A life on the range."

"I need some more wisdom tonight."

"Tell me."

"I heard a rumor that Harlo is going to make another offer for the High C. And for Barbicane's place, too."

"So?"

"'So?' Is that all the wisdom I bought with my midnight coffee?"

"Not considering selling, are you?"

She turned away. "Maybe half."

"Half the ranch?"

"Half considering selling all of it."

She kept her eyes averted.

"Why?"

"I'm afraid, Rake. For Collie. And for you. Harlo is a man of iron."

Holden made a contemptuous grunt.

"Collie is my life," she said. "And you're my dearest friend." She looked back at him. "My conscience is tearing at me like a starving coyote on a corpse."

"Don't even think about selling."

"It's my ranch. I can—."

"It's your *dream*. And Collie's, too. It means the world to her. The High C doesn't stand for Callaghan. It stands for Colleen. Don't try to tell me it doesn't. I know it does."

"Oh, Rake. . . ."

Holden slid the lamp on the table closer to himself so she could see him clearly.

"Missy, there isn't a saddle tramp on the S who could take me down. And as long as I'm alive, Collie is safe."

"You always make things sound simple."

He smiled. "It's a gift."

She shook her head and looked away. "Why won't Harlo let me alone?"

"He doesn't really want your place. He wants the Bar Double B. And because you're atwixt him and Barbicane's spread, he needs the High C."

"But just to get access to Barbicane's creek? He doesn't really need that water."

"He does if the monsoons don't come, like last year. That little branch he has can't water his stock in a dry year. He had a bad die-up. Lost over four hundred head."

"I didn't know that."

"Terrible way for cattle to die."

"But he knows part of the creek runs through the High C. I'd have helped him. Why didn't he ask me?"

"Don't know, Missy."

"And he hates Barbicane."

"Probably good from Harlo's point of view. Adds some spice to the chili."

"Did you know that Barbicane asked me to dances a few times?"

"No. How's his dancing?"

"Oh, stop it. I don't know. I didn't go. He's attractive in a way, but . . . I don't know. He's offered to buy my ranch, too. More than once."

"I suspect he's thinking of a different kind of union."

"Mr. Holden!"

He smiled.

"Barbicane owned this land once," Kathy said. "He had to sell it."

"Why?"

"I don't know. I bought it from a different owner a few years later. Harlo was back east at the time."

"Well, be sure that if old Harlo hadn't been traveling, he would've snatched it like a hawk on a squirrel."

She gazed beyond him and seemed not to hear him.

"Kathy."

She refocused. "Sorry."

"What's the matter?"

She sipped some coffee.

"Kathleen," he said with a hint of sternness. "What is it?"

She set down her metal cup. "Harlo and I were friends once. Long ago. I was just a girl. He was a sort of an uncle to me. Did you know that?"

"No."

"Now he wants to take all I own. How on earth did it come to this?"

"That's a very handsome animal."

"Thank you," Collie said, smiling at Mr. Kelly. "And he has a sweet soul."

"And a name?"

"Diablo."

"With a sweet soul?"

"I named him that so people will think he's mean. Nobody steals a mean horse."

"Well, you could have tried Widowmaker," Pat Kelly said with a laugh.

Collie grinned.

"It's a cool morning and I have some cocoa on the stove. . . ."

Collie dismounted and tied her horse to the rail in front of *The Clarion*. She loosened the cinch a notch and flipped the stirrups up over the saddle.

"Why did you do that?"

"The stirrups? It's an old drover's trick. Out on the trail, flies are everywhere. If one bites him on the belly and he scrapes at it with a hind foot, he could get caught up in a stirrup. Then you have a wreck. And maybe a broken leg and a dead horse."

"I see."

They went into the newspaper office. Collie liked the smell of metal and ink. There was nothing quite like it, and somehow it seemed powerful and important. She took off her hat and gloves and sat by the stove while Kelly poured the cocoa.

In just the few months since he had bought *The Clarion*, he had become one of her favorite people. A young and clean-featured man, he was lean as a whip and fastidious to a fault. He favored dark suits, which made him seem even leaner. Nowhere to be seen in this office was the grousing old codger smoking bad cigars whom one read about in penny dreadfuls.

Most believed Kelly had been educated in the East, and a passing remark of his indicated that he had once worked for the Pinkerton Detective Agency. When he had purchased *The Clarion*, it had been a dull little sheet passing on meaningless gossip. Then some complaints from a few cowboys about being cheated by a faro dealer in one of the seven saloons in town had reached his keen ear. He had investigated, become convinced it was true, and the story had enlivened the front page of the next day's edition.

Like all faro dealers, this one worked independently under contract to the saloon owner, who collected a percentage of the earnings. The following Sunday morning the dealer had confronted Kelly while the newspaperman was leaving church. Since most residents of San Miguel were Catholic and so had just attended Mass, almost everyone was on the street and witnessed what happened next.

The dealer was taller than Kelly and twice as wide and loomed over him in the middle of Angel Street. He offered choice phrases on Kelly's drunken Irish ancestors and the lack of virtue of his mother. Then he dared Kelly to be a man and do something manly about it. Amid groans from a disappointed crowd, Kelly turned and walked away. No one had been more disillusioned than Collie.

Yet that feeling vanished when Kelly stopped in front of Collie and her mother and removed his hat and coat and vest and smiled and asked Collie to hold them for a moment.

Many stories took life from what was seen in Angel Street that crisp Sunday morning. Every witness had his own tale to tell of the lightning hands, the dazzling feet, and the eerie detachment with which the easterner had pummeled the dealer until he had sagged to his knees in the dirt. Only the blackest of hearts could feel no pity for the collapsed husk bleeding and openly weeping in pain and shame.

Later some would claim that Kelly carried a vest pocket advantage, but Collie figured that an excuse about a hidden pistol was just a story circulated by the timid who feared his fists. When he had come back to reclaim his things, he had offered Collie and her mother some hot cocoa, and now that had become the line he always used when he greeted her.

"So did you get the horse at the auction?" he asked as he poured himself some chocolate and sat at his desk.

"Well, no. . . ." Collie was unsure how to answer, so she told him the whole story of the mysterious stranger.

"Hmmm. That would make an intriguing piece for the paper."

"Oh, no, please don't do that. He seemed like a very private man."

"He told you nothing about himself?"

"No, not even his name."

21

"Or his occupation?"

Collie stared down at the mug cupped in her hands and shook her head no. After about a minute, she looked up. Kelly was gazing at her with the easy concentration he seemed to bring to everything.

"What is it, Colleen?"

She shrugged and lowered her eyes again.

"He was no altar boy, was he?"

"No, sir," she said, still looking down. "When he came toward me, I felt kind of all-overish. And his eyes—they went through me like swords. I said hello to him from a distance. Like that would protect me. It sounds silly."

"No, it doesn't."

"He . . . he seemed like a threatening creature from a far off realm. A dark archangel, completely alone."

"Fallen from grace."

She looked at him helplessly.

"An enigma," Kelly said with a smile. "Never tease a newspaperman with an enigma." He slid a piece of paper in front of him and picked up a pencil and licked the tip. "What did he look like?"

She described him, and Kelly jotted it down.

"Very detailed. You must have examined him closely."

"Yes," she said in a near whisper.

"And now he's gone?"

"Never to return."

"Why do you believe that?"

She hesitated and then said, "It's a kind of reverse magic, I guess." She blushed. "If I say that, maybe the opposite will happen."

"And you want to see him again?"

"Oh, yes. He's very lonely. Only a lonely man would do what he did for me."

Kelly set down his pencil and stood up and poured her more cocoa.

"Sometimes an enigma should never be solved," he said as he refilled his cup. "Sometimes it should be kept the way it is. Held fast as a special memory but thought about only in half-light or in darkness."

"I know what you're saying," she said, looking up at him. "But if that's true, then we're being selfish. *I'm* being selfish. My feelings shouldn't be the only things that matter."

"I don't understand."

"If we never *try* to understand . . . if we don't reach out to this man, who on earth will?"

"He sounds like he doesn't want to be reached."

Collie ignored that. "When he was speaking to me, you'll never guess who I thought of. Major Saxton-West. Do you remember him, Mr. Kelly?"

"The British officer who passed through last winter."

"Do you remember his face?"

"Of course. His bearing, too."

"Everything about him was incredible. I'll never forget how that silly cowhand from the Lazy S got mad at something. . . ."

"Just an offhand remark, as I recall."

"When he slapped the major's face, the world changed for me. I saw a manly ideal I've never been able to forget. I thought I was in love."

Kelly laughed.

"Mr. Kelly, there was so much power in the major's self-control. It was wonderful. He could have knocked that chucklehead galley west if he'd wanted to. And yet he just stared him down."

"I remember. I think everybody was impressed."

"After all these months I can see it like it happened a minute ago." She paused. "This week something changed for me. The man who bought me the horse was from a different world than the major was. I don't know if it's better. Probably it's not. . . . But that face. . . ."

"I heard that Saxton-West posed for several exceptional bronzes. Yet I don't think the face you're describing would appeal to very many."

"Oh, Mr. Kelly, you're missing my point. Don't you see? No sane man would *dream* of slapping *that* face."

3 BRANDING IRONS

Kathy sat astride her sorrel mare and gazed down the slope at her cattle grazing below. Holden was paying off the day workers in the pasture, and the cowhands threw long shadows in the late afternoon sun. He had told Kathy that they had done a workmanlike job, and she had insisted he give them a small bonus. That also ensured they would be back tomorrow.

The cowhands rode off toward San Miguel, and Holden trotted his horse toward Kathy on the low hill.

"You picked good men," she said.

He nodded but remained quiet.

She folded her hands across the saddle horn and smiled into the distance. "The end of another day in paradise."

"No less."

"Rake, have I ever told you about my father?"

"Never have."

"He was a sweet man and I was his princess. Like all Irish fathers, he had grand dreams. And as with all drunks, the dreams always vanished at sunrise."

Holden said nothing.

"He tended bar in Tucson. We lived down a back alley. We never had a cent. My two brothers died as babies, and my mother outlived my father by just a month. I promised myself that no child of mine would ever live in that kind of chaos." She turned toward Holden. "I'm not selling anything. Not an acre."

His weathered face smiled with a thousand creases.

"This was my father's dream. This life. And it was my husband's, too."

"You've rarely talked about him."

"He was bucked off his horse and hit his head on a fence post. It seems so long ago. Collie was still a baby. Sometimes it's hard for me now even to remember Brian's face. I know that sounds terrible, but it's true."

"It's not terrible. You should put out a picture of him."

"I had a cabinet photograph of him once. . . ." She turned away. "But somehow it got lost."

Neither spoke for a while, and then Holden said, "If we're going to make a stand, it would be nice to call in some markers, but there aren't any to call in. We have to think about that for the future."

"I don't understand what you mean."

"Can I speak bluntly?"

She looked back at him with a smile. "Nothing has ever stopped you before."

"Are you willing to grab the hot end of the iron?"

"Pull it out of the fire."

"Where were you born?"

That startled her. "Why — ?"

"Just answer."

"How do you know I wasn't born here?"

"Missy. . . ."

"The slums of New York."

"Figured as much. Do you know how I know?"

"Enlighten me."

"You make friends — most people do like you — but you don't make allies."

"What?"

"You act like you can rely on society for all you need. Like an easterner would. Call the engine company if there's a fire or the police if there's trouble. But there are no fire companies here. No police. Not even a broken down old sheriff. Just a wrinkle-horn like me. We're in the middle of Where-Am-I, Arizona. You need allies to stand by you when you're thrown from the saddle."

"I have friends," she said with an edge to her voice.

"I already said that. But they're all spooked by you."

"What are you talking about? I'm five foot seven. I weigh a hundred and twenty pounds."

"You're too critical of things. And of people. Too quick with a cutting remark. Your friends shy from you like a horse from a flapping slicker."

"Are you saying I don't have that right?"

"Right? Missy, the only right that concerns you is that you think everyone has a right to agree with you. Men are cowed by your beauty, and women are threatened by everything else."

"That'll be enough, Mr. Holden."

"There's the proof. You won't even argue. It's beneath you. Your eyes are like a slammed door."

"Stop it!"

Her horse spooked at her shout and she had to pull him back.

"Don't you realize you're being squeezed between Stone and Barbicane, and you're all alone? Except for me. People never live up to your expectations, so they hit the ice wall."

She just glared at him.

"I can't ride shotgun by myself, Kathleen. We're going to need help."

"I don't want anybody's help. I can't rely on it."

"There's too much at stake not to."

"Now here's something for *you* to understand, sir. I was surrounded by fools and drunks and cowards the whole time I was growing up. Day and night. So what do you expect? That I see people as princes?"

"See them as humans who'll care about you if you stop bullying them with a quirt. As *compadres*."

"I have to protect my daughter."

"That's exactly what I'm saying."

4 WHAT THE COWHAND TOLD

The Congress Hall Saloon drew its extravagant name from the fact that the large L-shaped building had once been the home of the territorial legislature. Now it gleamed as one the finest entertainment emporia in southern Arizona. To call Mr. Charles Brown's Tucson palace a drinking establishment would have been to compliment it with the back of one's hand. So important had it become to Tucson's identity that its home, *Calle de la Alegría*, the Street of Happiness, had been renamed Congress Street in its honor.

A massive mahogany bar dominated the sprawling central room. Behind it, a framed mirror five feet high and fully ten feet across reflected the perpetual delight of the patrons. Contrary to an Easterner's dime novel idea of a western saloon, the Congress Hall was not an asylum for drunken cowboys hurling insults across baize-topped tables at crooked card dealers. The main area contained only a single discreet faro table, and that served primarily as an advertisement for the games of chance available in the two gambling rooms at the rear of the building. Most of the central space was devoted to a large dance floor and elegant tables for discriminating diners. The finest spirits and wines arrived continually from San Francisco, along with carefully humidified cigars for those discerning smokers revolted by the usual scorched hemp stogies available in the Sonoran Desert.

Located down a well-lit corridor far from the keno and monte players in the gaming dens was a reading chamber furnished in a French Provincial style and housing the latest editions of newspapers from across the country. On the walls of this tranquil haven hung small pastoral scenes and soothing copies of the old masters.

Yet of all the enchantments offered by Mr. Brown, none was more prized than the billiard room. Two magnificent Brunswick tables had been hauled from Chicago, and money had rarely been more wisely spent. At any given moment, the hard chairs lining the walls of the room were occupied by impatient players waiting their chance at the green felt.

Occasionally Mr. Brown himself could be seen attending to his customers throughout the saloon and often chatting amiably with any so inclined. Now well into his fifties, he had come from New York more than thirty years earlier, when Tucson had still been part of Mexico, before the Gadsden Purchase.

Honored citizen though he now was, Brown had never attempted to shed some of the darker rumors about his past. The most enduring of them was that in his youth he had been in the employ of the governor of Sonora as a member of the Glanton band of scalphunters earning a hundred and fifty dollars per Apache pelt. According to some old-timers, the gang had been wiped out in an Indian attack shortly after Brown had left it, but not before they had buried jars of the silver *reales* blood money somewhere in the area. The most reliable accounts claimed that the fortune had been hidden not in the southeastern part of the territory but somewhere out near Yuma. In any case, young boys and bored old men could still be encountered roaming the borderlands in the quest for this tainted treasure.

As far as Brown was concerned, he seemed indifferent to such tales, as demonstrated by one of his most popular artifacts. Displayed behind the bar in a walnut case fronted with glass was the scalp of the Apache who had killed the famous frontiersman and miner John Stone close to Dragoon Springs. The Indian band was later hunted down and killed near Apache Pass by a detachment under the command of Captain Bernard. The hair on the scalp had remained shiny and sleek, but the attached ears with the brass buttons still hanging from the shriveled lobes took some of the sheen off the aesthetic experience.

Such were the entertainments surrounding Mateo Madero as he crossed the dance floor of the Congress Saloon. He set his bottle of *El Tesoro de Don Rodrigo* and two glasses onto a table in a dark corner of the main room. He flared a match on a thumbnail and lit the candle in the blue glass jar on the table and then stepped around and sat in a chair with his back to the wall.

The blue light cast an eerie wash all around him. He removed his hat and poured tequila into the glasses and set them to the side. The table was a formidable slab of battered mesquite that looked like it had been cut from a door salvaged from some colonial church. He ran his fingers over the gouged wood as if he could somehow discern a few of its secrets. Then he sat back and savored the aroma of grilled beef and fresh tortillas and waited.

Though the evening was young, the saloon was already packed with those seeking their own personal solace, befitting an establishment with tables that appeared to be hewn from cathedral doors. Tonight the saloon girls were busy.

Madero had always nurtured a special fondness for these women who wore out their feet dancing with customers, or who stood with saintly patience and listened to lonely cowhands desperate to talk and smell perfume and forget the stern monasticism of the trail.

Many years had galloped past since the last time he had been here. Now he gazed once more through the haze of cigars and half-remembered dreams. Near the right wall of the big room, a Mexican sat with his guitar and brought forth the melancholy tunes unique to the hill people far away in the Sierra Madre. Close by the Mexican, one of the saloon maidens was sitting alone at a little table and resting her chin on her hand while she studied Madero as though he were a painting she were analyzing in a strange museum. A satin dress lit her up like a swath of blue flame and was cut low enough in front to show more skin than a startled sheep at shearing time.

Madero smiled at the woman and she stood up. She was as tall as most men, and when she walked toward him with those long legs she did so with a self-confidence no one on earth could fake. The blue fire skirt extended to just below her knees.

As she approached his table, he rose.

"Hello, *vaq*—no, you're not a cowboy, are you?"

"No, miss."

He was looking into an exceptional face. She was easily several years older than Madero, perhaps approaching forty, and she seemed weary. Her eyes, toughened with life's cruel tempering, held him in their gaze. Pounds of lustrous black hair were pinned to the top of her head and set off her pink skin in an enormously attractive contrast.

"Would you like some company?"

Madero slid out a chair for her and she sat.

"Call me Kaney." She smiled and held out her hand.

He reached down and wrapped his fingers around hers. Her grip was confident and warm. Madero released her hand and sat back down.

"And you are?" she asked.

"A wandering seaman on an alien shore."

"Everyone is welcome here." Her blue eyes, despite their brittle patina, exposed a sincerity Madero had rarely seen in saloons, or anywhere else.

"Thank you," Madero said.

She idly slid some fingers around a silver locket hanging from a chain onto her breast. "Do you like sitting in the shadows?"

"Yes."

"Would you like to talk?"

"I always prefer to listen."

That startled her. "To me?"

"Of course. But I don't have much time. I'm told someone is looking for me. I don't want you here when that happens."

"Are you in danger?" She seemed genuinely uneasy for him.

"Who isn't?"

She hesitated and then said, "Well, handsome, are you heeled at least?"

"Barely."

She frowned.

"I have a dagger dozing in a boot sheath," he said.

Reflexively, she glanced down into the lush pink depths beyond her dress's black-trimmed décolletage. "I have a small pistol." She looked up. "Would you like to borrow it?"

"Nice home for it."

She smiled. "I like to keep it safe and warm."

"May I borrow it?"

She reached down for the pistol.

"No, only if I can retrieve it myself."

"You rogue!" she said with a laugh, and her fatigue seemed to vanish.

"I'll be fine. But thank you for your concern."

Madero slid a glass of tequila in front of her.

"No, thank you. I prefer rye. Will you buy me one?"

"What you mean is will I pay the price of rye for the small glass of tea that the bartender gives you." And then he smiled at this dark-haired Venus of forgivable sin.

"You *are* a rogue," she said, laughing. The well-earned creases at the corners of her eyes deepened with the kind of wisdom that can be acquired at perhaps an unimaginable price. Yet those eyes asked for no sympathy.

"But I *will* buy you supper." Madero pulled out a gold eagle and snapped it onto the table top.

"That's enough for many suppers," she said in surprise. "Good ones."

"Then we'll dine together."

She picked up the coin and then set it back down as gently as if it might break. "No. This is too much." She looked into his eyes. "Enough for breakfast in bed." She seemed disappointed and sad and slowly stood up. "I never offer that."

As she pushed herself away from the table, Madero softly pressed her hand down onto the wood. "Do you think I'm so ungallant as to suggest such a thing as that?"

Even in the unnatural blue light from the candle in the jar, Madero could see her face flush red.

"I . . . I'm sorry."

"No need for you to be. We'll have a couple of steaks—medium rare for me, with enough tortillas to stuff a mattress. No beans—I've had enough beans for a dozen lifetimes. And wine, if we can find any that won't cauterize our throats. I'm told Mr. Brown brings wines in from the Pacific Slope, so we should be safe. Then I'll take you to your door and bid you farewell."

She seemed dazzled by all this. "Why. . . ?"

"Why what?"

"Why are you being so kind?"

"Should I be unkind?"

Something caught Madero's eye at the bar, and then he looked back at Kaney. "How does that sound?"

She smiled, and this time the woman of the world faded off into time, and now only the expression of an innocent girl remained. "I'd be honored, *señor*. And may I know your name? Any name will do."

"Mateo Madero."

"You hold this." She handed him back the coin. "I'm done at ten."

This time she must have noticed him glancing beyond her shoulder, because she turned around.

"Is that the one who's looking for you?"

A big man with a shotgun was approaching their table.

"It is," Madero said.

She turned back to him. No woman had eyed him with such worry since the world was young.

"It's all right, Kaney. I'll see you here at ten. Please go now."

She studied the advancing stranger as she walked away, but he seemed not to notice her and came up to Madero's table.

The man extended his hand. "I'm John Holden."

"I know who you are — and I never shake hands with a man holding a firearm."

Holden laid the weapon onto the table.

Madero rose and shook his hand and sat back down. He nodded toward the other chair, and Holden removed his hat and sat at the table.

"Hunting rabid dogs?" Madero said, pointing at the shotgun.

"Possibly. And I've never been very good with sidearms."

Madero smiled to himself and slid one of the glasses of tequila over to him.

"I don't want to take the lady's drink."

"You're not. I was expecting you. The capable Mr. Brown has this restorative tonic carted here all the way from Jalisco."

"Why were you expecting me?"

"I have many acquaintances — even a few who care about my wellbeing."

"I see."

"I also have a supper engagement later and little taste for small talk."

Holden seemed uncomfortable. "I rehearsed what I was going to say a hundred times . . . but it's not coming. Just beating the devil around the stump."

Madero sipped his tequila. "I'm sure you didn't ride all the way up here to sample the latest journals in the reading room."

Holden smiled and pulled a battered tin case from a vest pocket and handed Madero a cheroot.

The two men lit up.

"Now," Madero said, "why am I being honored by a bow-legged old cowhand from the Four Sixes carrying a ten-gauge?"

"I know from Collie's description that you're the man who bought her the horse."

"You say that as if it's an indictment."

"It *is* a mystery."

"It's a desolate world, isn't it, where generosity is a mystery?

"So why did you buy her the calico?"

"Why not?"

Holden seemed frustrated. "Do you always answer a question with a question?"

"Do I?"

Holden rubbed the back of a hand across his thick moustache, as if that would soothe him. He had another sip of tequila and then went and got a cracked saucer that was masquerading as an ash tray. He set it down and resumed his place at the table.

"So you're not going to answer me?"

"My generosity is a concern of yours?"

"I care about that little girl."

"From what I could see, she's not a little girl."

"Exactly."

Madero had long ago mastered the task of concealing irritation. He took a draw on the cheroot and savored the smoke before he let it go.

"If you're implying an unthinkable act," Madero said, "I'd advise you to think a bit longer."

"I care for Collie."

"*Yo también.*"

"Why do *you* care for her?"

"She's a stranger to me."

"You'd never seen her before the day of the auction?"

"Of course not."

Holden reached for the bottle and poured both of them some more tequila.

"Don't try to get me drunk," Madero said. "Your liver will fail long before I even nod."

Holden set the bottle down and stared into his drink. "I've come here for nothing, haven't I?" he said, looking up.

"No. You've proven to me that you're an honorable man."

"Is that important?"

"More than you think. If you'd have come here for any other reason, they'd be carrying you out in a sheet."

That clearly startled him.

"Anything else?" Madero asked.

"How do you know what I was thinking?"

"I've lived many more years than you."

Holden seemed baffled. "I've got two decades on you or I'm a Dutchman."

"You do—*but I've lived more years.*" Madero just let that hang there.

Holden looked like was about to say something but then simply shook his head and downed the tequila.

"You're squandering the enchantments of the maguey, cowpuncher," Madero said. "That's worthy of being sipped."

Holden seemed not to hear. "*Señor*, do you know Mrs. Callaghan?"

"How could I?"

"A question answering a question again."

"It's an incurable ailment."

"I think Mrs. Callaghan and her daughter are in serious danger. From ruthless men with hearts of rock. And if you care about Collie, I thought you'd want to know that."

"How can I care about someone I don't know?"

"I'm not sure, but that's what I feel."

"You feel?" Madero said with a melancholy laugh. "*Solo el que carga el cajón sabe lo que pesa el muerto.*"

Holden stared at him with a look of surprise and alarm.

"Holden, all I did was buy a girl a horse."

"You touched her heart, too. Surely you know that. Maybe she touched yours?"

"Do the ruthless men include Harlo Stone?"

"Collie told you?"

"Anyone else?"

"I'm not certain. Possibly Lawton Barbicane."

"And he is . . . ?"

"Owns the ranch west of the High C. But I think he'd rather romance Mrs. Callaghan and make a different kind of merger."

"Does Mrs. Callaghan know you're here?"

Holden let out an easy laugh. "She'd try to skin me if she knew."

"Why?"

"She doesn't like favors."

"Why doesn't she line up with Barbicane if he's sweet on her?"

"Have you ever known the type of peculiar woman who never likes the men who like her? Or who always likes the men who don't?"

"I have."

"In fact, there's a newspaper publisher in town who puts a glow on her cheek, but he's never come calling."

"So she's all alone?"

"Except for a bow-legged old cowhand."

"She could do worse."

"Now *there's* a compliment I can graze on for a week," he said with a laugh.

"Go back to San Miguel and watch over them. That should be enough. Along with the ten-gauge."

"What if it's *not* enough?"

"Then I suppose you're in trouble."

Holden looked down and fiddled with his empty tequila glass. "Do you live here in Tucson?"

"I live everywhere. And nowhere. Tomorrow Buddy and I are on the trail to Magdalena."

Holden seemed disappointed.

"You're a worrier, Holden. It's in every wrinkle."

"Collie is a worrier about *you*. Do you know that?"

"No," Madero said, genuinely amazed. "Why?"

"I don't know. A man who'd euchered some of the Lazy S's toughest hands and best card players and walked away with his back to them—I'd say he's someone nobody needs be concerned about being hit in the face."

"Those *chavos*? They couldn't hit the ground if they fell off a horse. It looked to me like they were all studying hard just to be nitwits."

Holden smiled. "Collie worries about you just the same."

"Well, please give Black Irish my best. And someday, when she's older, you can explain to her that it makes sense to worry only about the living." He corked the bottle and pressed out his cigar. "Good night, *vaquero*."

5 WHO CARRIES THE COFFIN

Pat Kelly was enjoying the mid-morning air as he stood on the boardwalk outside *The Clarion* and saw a familiar rider coming up the street.

"Morning, Rake."

Holden nodded but said nothing. He looked ragged.

"Why don't you give that fellow some grain and rest and come in for coffee?"

Holden pulled his shotgun from the scabbard and turned his old gray over to a Mexican boy scrounging up business for the livery stable, and then he came inside the newspaper office. He tossed his battered buff hat aside and dropped into a chair in front of the desk.

"How do you stand the reek of that ink?"

Kelly gave his stained hands a useless wipe across the denim printer's apron and then handed Holden a mug. "This should uplift your soul."

Holden took it and savored the steaming black brew.

"So where did you ride in from?" Kelly asked. "Wyoming?" He poured some coffee for himself and sat on the edge of his desk.

"Do I look that bad?"

"Worse."

"Tucson. It's so damn dry up there the burr sage bushes run around behind the dogs."

Kelly smiled and sipped his coffee.

"Did Collie tell you about her horse?" Holden asked. "About the Mex who bought it for her?"

"She did."

"Well, I found him."

"The horse?"

"The Mexican."

"Was he missing?"

Holden gave him a sour look.

"Why did you go looking for him?"

"I had my reasons."

"Of course you had reasons. What kind of answer is that?"

"I was looking for help for Kathy and Collie."

"Against what?"

"The push on her ranch."

"Stone?"

"You know more than you like to let on. You were a Pinkerton man once, weren't you?"

"And Barbicane, too?" Kelly asked, ignoring the question.

"Maybe."

"You could have asked me for help. I adore Collie. And you know what people say—no one should pick a fight with someone who buys ink by the barrel."

"Or who can box."

"That, too."

Both men drank their coffee in silence for a while.

"So what did you find out?" Kelly asked.

"The Mex had never met Collie before the day of the auction."

"And you believe that?"

"As much as I believe the earth is round. This isn't a man who stretches the blanket. For some reason, I think he wouldn't lie if his life depended on it."

"What's his name?"

Suddenly Holden gave him a blank expression that made Kelly burst out laughing.

"You never asked him?" Kelly said.

Holden laughed with him. "I guess not. And he wasn't offering."

Holden looked away, but he seemed to be staring at more than the big printing press.

"So what was he like?"

"Strange." He turned back to Kelly. "But I'm not sure I can say why."

"You owe me something for that coffee. Try."

"Well, he was handsome—in a battered kind of way, I guess. He has a scar from a gash on the left side of his face. A sort of wounded beauty. Like a mesquite on the Santa Cruz that was struck by lightning but is still standing."

Kelly smiled. "Very poetic."

"He was pleasant. Friendly even, but offish, too. And he talks like he's had schooling somewhere. This is not an ignorant man."

"Did you speak Spanish or English?"

"We spoke English. He has an accent, a soft one. Mostly it's that musical undertone the Mexicans have."

"Anybody with him?"

"Looks to me like he plays a lone hand."

"What else?"

"There's something about him that just throws you off. There's this . . . what's the word for something that seems to contradict itself?"

"Paradox."

"That's it. There's a fire burning in him, that's certain. But it's far away. Like a blaze at the back of a cave. You can see it there smoldering in the shadows, but it's too distant for you to feel the heat." Holden shook his head. "Sounds kind of bizarre, I know."

"No it doesn't. Unusual, though. Was he armed?"

"When he stood to shake my hand, I gave him a quick look, and I didn't see a weapon. But I can promise you he's no monk."

Both men were quiet for a while.

"He was armed in other ways, though," Holden said at last.

Silence followed, and Kelly waited for him to continue.

"You wouldn't call me a timid man, would you?" Holden asked.

"Not in this life," Kelly said with a laugh.

"When you talk to this stranger, you're not explaining yourself, you're defending yourself. It knocks you right out of the saddle."

"He questions everything you say?"

"That's the damnable mystery of it. He doesn't. I never saw a man who was more relaxed. Almost uninterested. But that's just on the surface. You realize pretty quick that when you're

41

talking he's not looking at you, he's looking *through* you. Like a judge staring down from the bench at a man on trial for his life."

"Jesus. Sounds like you had a lovely time."

"I'll tell you, Pat, it's unnerving. . . . And yet . . ." His voice trailed off.

"What?"

"I'd say that if this man was your friend, you could sleep safely in a den of lions."

"And what if he was your enemy?"

Holden thought for a moment. "You could be inside a fortress behind a moat and live in nothing but dread."

"Well," Kelly said, setting down his cup. "Powerful words coming from an old horse breaker like you. Did he say anything about Collie?"

"Not unless I did first." Holden hesitated. "Do you speak Spanish?"

"Not so you'd notice."

"When I told him that I thought he might care about her, he seemed annoyed by the fact that I was assuming I knew what his feelings were. He quoted an old Mexican saying. 'Only the person who carries the coffin knows how much the dead man weighs.' It means that we can never really know how much feeling or how much pain another person carries in his heart."

"My God. He *is* strange. Where is he now?"

"On his way to Sonora."

"So you wasted your time."

"Completely. I was just barking at the knot." He swiveled around in his chair and gazed out toward the street.

"What is it, Rake?"

He turned back to Kelly with a look of absolute bewilderment. "There's something wrong with him, Pat."

Kelly could be as patient as a cloistered friar. He just remained quiet and sipped his coffee.

"Something off," Holden said.

"In what way?" Kelly asked with the casualness that had often gotten people to pour out their souls.

"I can walk out among two hundred head of cattle and tell right away if one isn't feeling good. I don't even know how I do it. But it's real."

"And the Mex?"

"He's not well."

"Physically?"

"He looks hearty as a buck . . . yet I swear there's something pulling at him. A sickness of some kind. There's a look in his eye that isn't right."

Kelly went to the stove for the coffee pot and topped off their cups. "How did he answer when you told him about the Callaghans?"

"Neutral. Like he didn't care."

"Well, why should he if he doesn't know them?"

"I guess he shouldn't—but goddam it, Pat, he bought Collie a two hundred dollar horse!"

"Diablo." Kelly sighed. "Maybe there's more of the Devil in this business than we think."

"When I was leaving Charlie Brown's place, I noticed a saloon girl watching me. She'd been at the table when I got there and looked daggers at me when I passed her on the way in. As I was walking out, she was leaning against the end of the bar. Her hands were hidden in the folds of her dress, but I managed to make out a nickel-plated ace in the hole in her right hand. Her eyes bored into me until I turned around and left the place."

"Loyalty like that from a saloon girl. Hard to figure."

"It says a lot about him."

"Maybe a lot more about her."

"Oh, one other thing. I almost forgot. Just before I left, I told him again that Collie cared about him, and he said one of the most terrible things I've ever heard anyone say about himself. He said that I should teach her that it made sense for her only to care about people who were still alive."

"Good God. What did that mean?"

Holden shrugged. "And there wasn't a bean's worth of self-pity in it. He seemed to be speaking about someone else far off. Talking like . . . how do you newspapermen put it?"

"In the third person?"

"Exactly."

Kelly stared down into his cup as he swirled it around. "May I make a suggestion?"

"Take the bit."

"Don't tell Collie any of this. She has this romantic notion about him, I think. Don't ruin it for her."

Holden laughed. "Romantic notion? She loves that horse so much that she calls the man who bought him *El Arcángel Oscuro*."

Kelly frowned in confusion.

"Her Dark Archangel."

"Heaven help us," Kelly said, shaking his head. "Hero worship lyrical. Why does a girl's life always have to be an opera?"

"God's own mystery."

"Will you keep me up to date on what's happening out there?"

"Why don't you come for a visit sometime? Maybe ask Kathy to a dance."

"Mrs. Callaghan?" Kelly said in surprise.

"Yes, indeed. The Rain Dance is coming up at St. Michael's Hall."

"What on earth is that?"

"A little festivity we have every year just before the monsoons."

"Well, I can't imagine going with Kathleen Callaghan. Good Lord, she's cold as glass."

Holden finished his coffee and stood up. "Funny about glass—it's brittle and it cuts, but once it's melted, it sticks and won't let go." He smiled. "Think about that." He went and got his hat.

"You're wrong about something, Rake." Kelly slid off the edge of the desk. "You said that when you mentioned your worry about the Callaghans, the stranger was neutral." Kelly handed Holden his shotgun. "I wasn't there and you were, but I'm certain about one thing. This is a man who isn't neutral about *anything*."

6 DREAMS

Collie crossed the big kitchen and wrapped her arms around her mother standing at the stove and then just rested against her.

"No, don't stop what you're doing," Collie said as Kathy was about to lay down the spatula. "I just want to hold you."

Kathy flipped over the slabs of ham and then set the spatula aside and turned around. "What's wrong?"

Collie laid her head against her mother's breast and slid her arms around her again.

"You feel cold," Kathy said and squeezed Collie to warm her.

"I had that dream again."

Kathy hugged her more tightly.

"I feel like such a baby."

"Everyone has nightmares."

"Over and over?"

"Over and over."

"I can still feel the rain hitting me."

"That's all right. Can you feel your mother loving you?"

Collie lifted her head from Kathy's breast and smiled. "Yes."

"Are you ready for some ham?"

"Mom, why do you go to all this trouble? Ernesto is a good coosie."

"*Cocinero*—let's be proper," she said with a smile. "On the trail he's the best grub slinger around. . . ."

"But?"

"Around the bunkhouse the men get tired of his fiery Sonoran flourishes and just need a good slab of ham sometimes. Or a dish of those mysteries." She pointed to the plate of sausages she had just finished frying.

"You spoil the men."

"I know." She turned back to her big iron skillet.

"Isn't it expensive?"

"They're worth it. And you let me worry about the cash flow. Besides, I love this time of day."

Collie went to the kitchen table and sat and watched her mother cooking breakfast.

"Want to learn a secret about how to get to know people quickly?" Kathy turned around and looked at her daughter. "At least part of them?" She went back to her frying.

Collie smiled. "Yes."

"Ask them what time of day they like the most. That'll tell you wonders about people."

Collie wrinkled her forehead. "I don't understand."

"You'll learn a great deal because they won't stop there. They'll tell you *why* they like that part of the day. For some reason, they can't not tell you. And then you'll suddenly be holding a candle near their soul."

"And why is this your favorite time? You haven't mentioned that."

Kathy paused at the frying pan but did not turn around. "Because these quiet hours before the sun comes up remind me that every day is a fresh start. No matter what happened the day before."

Collie thought about that but remained quiet.

"Please make sure you bring back a newspaper when you go in to get the mail today," Kathy said. "I haven't seen one in at least a week."

"That's because there haven't been any papers for the last ten days. Mr. Kelly is away."

"Oh . . . ?"

"He told me he was going on vacation. To Colorado."

"It's not much fun going on a trip alone."

Collie smiled at her mother's back. "I don't know if he's alone or not."

Kathy flipped the ham more vigorously but said nothing.

"Mom?" Collie said after a long pause.

"Mmmm?"

"Don't you think Mr. Kelly would make a good stepfather?"

The spatula clattered onto the edge of the skillet as Kathy turned around. "What kind of a question is that?"

Collie gave her mother her most innocent smile. She had perfected that long ago. "Just asking."

"Colleen Keira Callaghan, you never 'just ask' anything."

"I really like him."

"Everyone likes him."

"Then why isn't he married?"

Kathy went back to her cooking. "You'll have to ask him that."

"I have."

Kathy paused and then continued fiddling with the meat in the pan. "What did he say?"

"He smiled and turned away and mumbled something under his breath about not liking being burned by molten glass. I didn't know what he was talking about."

"He's like all these writers and wabblers," Kathy said in an indifferent tone. "Always trying to be clever."

Collie grinned.

"Keira, isn't it time for you to feed the horses?"

With its ambience of affluence and with its endless sprawl, the adobe ranch house of the Lazy S was every Easterner's dream of where a rich cattleman would live in the West. It looked big enough to barrack a cavalry troop, although the only residents were Harlo and his son and the servants. When Kathy rode up to the massive front door, a Mexican woman was waiting for her.

"*Hola*, Maribel," Kathy said as she dismounted her sorrel.

"Señora Callaghan," the plump woman answered with a smile. "I'll have one of the men water your horse. Señor Stone is waiting for you on the veranda."

"Waiting?"

"He saw you coming a long way off."

Kathy handed the reins to Maribel and walked around to the back of the house.

Harlo pushed his bulk from his chair under the shade of the latillas.

"Good morning, Kathleen." He held out a meaty and callused hand.

"Harlo, nice to see you." She shook his hand briefly and removed her hat.

"Please be comfortable," he said with a smile that seemed surprisingly genuine, and he pointed to a chair.

Harlo poured her a cup of coffee and offered her a plate of pastry.

"I have the apples for the empanadas brought all the way from Willcox. I'm glad I have them today—they were always your favorites, weren't they?"

"Yes," she answered softly.

Harlo Stone had one of those rare huge bellies that looked taut as a drumhead. No sag there. If someone flipped a gold eagle at it, the coin would almost certainly bounce back and gouge a chunk out of a bystander's forehead.

"How is Colleen?" Harlo asked, and he appeared sincerely interested.

"Very well, thank you. All grown now. And Willard?"

"As well as any lad is at that age."

Kathy hesitated and then said, "Harlo, Rake told me you had a four-hundred-head die-up last summer."

"Four hundred and fifty three."

Kathy lowered her gaze to the empanada on the plate in front of her. "Was it water?"

"No, Kathleen. It was lack of water."

"I'm sorry. Why didn't you ask me?"

"For what?"

"For water. You know what I mean."

"How could I ask for thousands of gallons of water from someone who wouldn't give me a drop of horse sweat?"

"But your animals!"

"They're dead. Leave them there."

The silence seemed to last a month. A soft breeze blew across the veranda, and the sudden squawks of a few wrens nearby seemed as startling as shrieks from Hell.

"I heard you want to buy my ranch," Kathy finally said.

"Is it for sale?"

"No."

"Then I don't."

"Well, that's what I—."

"I said I don't."

"Then how did the rumor start?"

"I've heard Barbicane is looking to expand." He tapped his belly and smiled. "This table muscle doesn't give me any room for expansion."

"That's all?"

"That's all."

Kathy stood up. "I'm sorry for bothering you."

"I'm not. I'm happy you came. We haven't spoken in three years and five months. And . . . six days."

She stared at him in disbelief. "You keep an exact count . . . ?"

A sad smile softened his sun-burnt features.

"Oh, Harlo, how did it come to this?" she said and turned and gazed blindly into the distance.

He brushed back the coarse gray hair from his forehead and folded his hands on the table. "You know how, I think."

She continued staring far away.

"To you," Harlo said, "the world isn't filled with people. It's overflowing with suspects."

Kathy said nothing.

"You take offense at anything and everything. You're always poised for a slight. Even people foolish enough to care for you get tired of it. So they walk away. And then you act like they've offended *you*."

"You don't understand. You—."

"Please. Spare me tales of your drunken father. I don't care about that. Nobody cares about that."

She sat back down. "I'm sorry. My life has never been the same since Brian died."

"You know, you never let me meet him."

"It doesn't matter now."

"It might have mattered then. I could have been there for you when he died."

Kathy said nothing.

"But you had to prove you could make it on your own. Has it made you happy?"

She looked away. "I can't remember the last time I was happy. I have the blue devils all the time."

"No point in that. We all end up in a box no matter what."

Kathy sighed. "I could never leave Arizona, though. Those stinking alleys of New York make me nauseated just thinking about them. When I'm sensible enough to reason like a human being, I realize I live in paradise. And Collie loves it here just as much as I love it."

"I know. That's always been obvious."

"She adores the Mexican people and everything about them. And she speaks the language better than I do. Everything about their way of life is just dyed in her wool."

"As if she was part Spanish herself," Harlo said with a smile.

Maribel came out with a fresh pot of coffee and refilled their cups and left after patting Kathy tenderly on the wrist.

"What is it, Kathleen?" Harlo said.

She shook her head. "I feel so uneasy and I don't know why. It's odd but somehow I feel it has something to do with the horse auction Collie went to."

"I heard about that. Willie lost the horse, too."

"I know. Collie was really angry that he bid against her."

"Collie is mistaken."

"What? I don't understand."

"He was bidding *for* her. Although she didn't know it. He was going to make a gift of the horse to her."

"What on earth for?"

Harlo smiled. "Because giving girls gifts is what boys do."

"But she's afraid of him."

"Of Willard? Don't be silly."

"All those stories about him and other girls."

"Those?" Harlo said, laughing. "That's just corral dust that boys stir up to impress each other. I doubt he's ever even kissed a girl. Now, there . . . that's the kind of Kathy laugh I like to hear."

"May I tell her about Willie?" she asked, still laughing. "I'm so glad to know that."

"Certainly."

"How did he ever get a terrible nickname like Bleeder?"

"He was beaten up when he was a boy and bled like a slaughtered hog. You know how cruel boys can be with their taunts."

"They've called him that all these years? Good Lord. I always thought he was called that because he beat up *other* people. I'm sorry."

Harlo shrugged. "So why were you upset by a horse auction, of all things?"

"Someone else bought Collie the horse. A stranger."

"Did you meet him?"

"He's gone. Never to return, I hope."

"Why did he do that for her?"

She just shook her head.

"I can look into it if you'd like. See if I can find out where he throws his loop."

"No, let it rest."

"But you can't rest."

"I know. It's the oddest thing."

Harlo eased his big frame back from the table and his chair creaked. "There's no chance he works for Barbicane, is there?"

"Barbicane? Why?"

"Barbicane softening up you and Collie before he makes a move. Maybe the secret gift won't be a secret much longer. And then possibly you'll look more kindly on him. He'll never stop hating the fact that he had to sell the land you own now."

"Then why did he sell it in the first place?"

"He got done up on the green baize. He's a degenerate gambler. And a bad one, to boot."

"I never knew that."

"And he'd like my spread as well. He's made some offers, but I've ignored them. Oddly enough, we got along once, but that was long ago."

"Did something happen?"

Harlo laughed but there was a hint of bitterness there. "Not really. Lawton is one of those people who enjoys making friends but manages to find a reason to dislike them eventually. Somehow they always disappoint him. The most trivial things wind up souring him and the friendship ends. If you're his friend, just buy a ticket and stand in line—your turn will come. And so he's a sad and lonely man."

51

"Has he ever been married?"

"Not to my knowledge. But he's always had an eye for you."

"Oh, stop it."

"I'm serious. He'd like his land back. I don't think he'd object to marrying it back."

"I know he's attractive, but he scares me. He's always scared me."

"Oh, I wouldn't worry," Harlo said. "Rake is there. He's a man you can tie to. Just tell him to keep that shotgun loaded."

"What if Rake isn't enough?"

But Harlo had no answer.

7 RIDING THE LINE

"This is the danger area," Holden said, extending his arm toward the grassland before him.

Collie scratched Diablo on the neck and shifted in the saddle a bit as she studied the intensity of Holden's gaze. The foreman said no more but simply let out a sigh, and his horse did likewise.

Collie and Holden were staring out across the northern boundary of the High C where it abutted both Barbicane's spread and Harlo Stone's Lazy L. Here cattle grazed in an irregular sprawl at the only spot where all three ranches bordered one another.

"If Barbicane or Stone are itching for a row, they'll start pushing each other here. Try to provoke something to justify the unjustifiable."

"But how will that help either of them?"

"It won't. But people do stupid things when they want what someone else has. Barbicane wants all the usable land around here simply because he wants it. And Stone wants a secure water supply that only your mom and Barbicane have."

"Look there." Collie pointed to a piece of broken wire on the High C's boundary.

"We don't want that," Holden said. "There can't be any excuse for wandering cattle. Your mother takes this too lightly. That's just the spark that could set off something. When you go back, ask her to get one of the outriders up here to fix this."

"Aren't you coming home with me?"

"I'll be along later. I want to ride the line for a while."

Collie laid a rein against Diablo's neck and turned south.

On the way back, she decided to ride the western wire. Soon she saw some of Barbicane's cowhands rounding up strays, and the boys shouted to her in their good-natured way. They were loyal workers who rode for the brand, but they always had a smile and a wave for an attractive girl, regardless of what side of the fence she rode.

A mile further on, she was surprised to see Barbicane himself, astride his black horse and all alone. With a posture as straight as a lance and hands folded over the saddle horn, he was gazing north toward where she had just been, but he seemed not to have seen her. As usual, he wore a white shirt and khaki jacket and trousers and a buff slouch hat. The wide brim concealed most of his prematurely gray hair, but his chiseled silver beard caught some of the sunlight. He always seemed to Collie like some sort of British colonial sentry guarding the outposts of empire. She thought about waving but then decided against it and rode on.

Most of her outdoor chores had been finished by noon, before the worst of the heat hit. She made sure she always began before dawn. The horses were her primary responsibility. She gave the entire *remuda* a quick visual inspection and then checked with each of the cowhands for any problems there might be with individual animals. Every hand was permanently assigned a string of three horses, and any bites or gouges or more serious health concerns had to be brought to Collie's attention immediately. If anyone failed to do so, he would feel the lash of an Irish tongue. Like most young people and some women, she hoped that sharp language was the way to impress tough men, although she was never really sure if it was effective. In fact, such salty words coming from a pretty sixteen-year-old girl often seemed comical to the seasoned ranch hands, and one of them had even jokingly christened her "The Profane Angel." Nonetheless, they always maintained serious faces and took the lashings with good grace. Sometimes Collie amused even herself when she cut loose, and she often had to struggle to remain imperious. She was certain that all the hands thought she was unaware of the handle they had given her, and she let them think it. And she was secretly grateful that each one of them was too much of a gentleman ever to mention it to her mother.

Should any horse present some serious issue, it would be quarantined for a visit from Doc Briscoe. The doctor was now semi-retired, if a doctor ever could be, and he had probably never even seen a veterinary establishment. Yet he was well-known for having often said that during the war he had treated as many equines as men, and he had famously remarked that he had always found the former far more agreeable than the latter.

After the horses at the High C had been fed their morning ration of hay, the fresh grass rarely being enough, Collie always supervised the cleaning of all the pens and corrals and also took on much of that work herself. In the late afternoon, she would check on the animals again before their late feeding.

As she made her way toward San Miguel, a heavy wind was blowing up from Mexico. The monsoons were looming. In a few weeks, they would slam into Arizona. Easterners never failed to be stunned by the savagery of rainstorms in the Southwest. Viewed from several miles away, they delighted the onlooker with God's own fireworks, but, experienced from within, they terrified like divine wrath.

And, as Collie knew, if they invaded one's dreams, they tormented without end.

Yet, to Collie, brutal thunderstorms were a trivial admission charge to pay to enter the gateway of Arizona heaven. The lush grasslands nourished animal and man with a bounty that always astounded outsiders when they were told that this was still really the Sonoran Desert. *Where are the dunes?* the Eastern soft-horns would always ask, expecting the Sahara. Yet, the dunes thrived, too, if only out toward Yuma. The saguaros, also, were missing here in the high grasslands, but those stately Sonoran sentinels could be seen at lower and sandier elevations not far off. In these upper meadows all was green, at least some of the time, since much of the grass was browning now in the June heat. Unlike July and August with their afternoon rains, waterless June seared without mercy. No one loved June in Arizona.

However, unlike the bald prairies elsewhere, these upland pastures were cupped in the protective hands of mountain ranges all around. Bleached out now in the midday sun, the heights would deepen in color as the day waned and led to Collie's favorite moment, that precious instant when the sun slid below the peaks and these montane guardians slipped into the night awash in lavender.

San Miguel came into view as Collie and Diablo descended out of the high grasses. She loved her little town as much as the wild land around it. San Miguel had sprung up to meet the needs of the cattlemen and *vaqueros*, and its Anglo-Mexican flavor was something Collie would have traded for nothing in the world. San Miguel even had a small Chinese quarter that housed mostly former railroad workers and their relatives. Like all young white girls in San Miguel, Collie had been warned to beware the haunts of lusting yellow men and their opium induced horrors. In fact, as with Chinese communities everywhere, the people kept mostly to themselves and earned a living laundering clothes or selling food. And, as always, Collie happily ignored her mother's strictures anyway and had several Chinese friends whom she cherished.

From the illustrated weeklies that occasionally made their way to San Miguel, Collie knew that her home was very different from the raucous cattle towns to the east. The wide, far-flung streets and acres of angular wooden buildings she had read about and seen in the engravings had no place here. In a land where a mesquite tree was considered big, there was little structural timber, so adobe usually did wood's work for it. And wide thoroughfares were unnecessary in a place without enormous herds of beasts or men that had to be shunted along. Collie liked the fact that San Miguel was a cozy little town of soft and flowing adobe curves that hugged its people with the same surety that the distant mountains embraced them all.

She rode down Angel Street to the livery stable to give Diablo some water and a rest in the coolness of the barn. Then she was about to walk over and pick up the mail when she noticed that the shades were up at *The Clarion*. She smiled and crossed the street. It was too hot for cocoa, but she wanted to pick up a newspaper and, more importantly, to see her special friend.

"Hello, Collie," Kelly said in a neutral tone from the back of the room as she shut the door behind her.

He had glanced at her but then went back to whatever he was doing at his desk at the far wall.

"Will there be a paper today, Mr. Kelly?"

"Tomorrow," he said without looking up.

He seemed distant and maybe even a bit annoyed. Collie had never heard him like that before. Suddenly she felt as uncomfortable as if she had stumbled into a monastery uninvited. She had no desire to stay now but felt it would look rude if she just turned around and walked out. So she took off her hat and sat at a small work table near the printing press and decided to wait a few minutes until it seemed appropriate for her to leave.

A thick green folder lay on the table, and she idly flipped it open. On the top of the stack of papers was some sort of file card. Pasted in the upper left corner was a picture of a remarkably handsome man with the heading **PHOTOGRAPH OF E. H. KELLIRIDE**. A description was printed to the right of it.

Name, E. H. Kelliride, alias Evan Kelliride, alias Evan H. Kelliride, alias E. Hardin Underwood. Age, 30 to 35 years. Weight, 180 lbs. Complexion, fair. Eyes, brown. Nose, straight. Nationality, American. Height, 5 ft. 10 inches. Build, stout. Color of hair, brown. Moustache, brown, if any. Occupation, unknown. Criminal occupation, bank robber and highwayman, train robber, horse thief. Marks, small scar back of left ear, large red birth mark thigh of right leg.

Beneath that, it said:

E. H. Kelliride is known as a criminal principally in Arizona, New Mexico and west Texas. In May, 1878, E. H. Kelliride and Wilt Corson 'held up' a Southern Pacific train near Tularosa, New Mexico. Kelliride and Corson were arrested and tried for this crime, convicted and sentenced to 12 and 8 years respectively. Before transfer to prison, both escaped from jail in Lincoln, New Mexico, June 3, 1878, and have not since been arrested. The Southern Pacific will give $3000 reward for the capture and identification of the men implicated in this robbery, or a proportionate amount for one, and $300 additional for each conviction. Persons furnishing information only, which may lead to the arrest of one or more of the robbers, will share in the reward. In addition to the above there are large outstanding rewards offered for the

arrest of these men, individually by banks, railroads and express companies robbed by them, and by Governors of States and Territories where they have committed murders and other crimes. These rewards offered aggregate upwards of $8000 dollars.

"Colleen!" Kelly shouted. "That's private."

Collie snapped her hand back as if she had just touched a hot stove. "I'm sorry."

Kelly came forward from the back of the room. He stopped at the table and took a deep breath and smiled down at her. "No, *I'm* sorry. I shouldn't have yelled at you."

Collie had the ability to stay angry at someone for about eight seconds. She smiled back.

"Did you have a nice vacation?"

"I had a tiring one."

That was obvious. He looked as exhausted as a prospector's mule.

"Cocoa?"

"On a day like this, Mr. Kelly?"

"Any day is a cocoa day when my friend Collie Callaghan comes to visit me."

"You're busy now, so I'll go." She stood and picked up her hat. Then she paused and brought a forefinger to her right temple and tilted her head as if she were thinking. "I was right. I think you *would* make a good stepfather."

For a moment Kelly was speechless. "You said that to someone? Not to your mother. . . ?"

She grinned and turned around and hurried out.

"Collie!" she heard Kelly shout after her. "Would you ask Rake to come in and see me?"

Lawton Barbicane stood up respectfully when Collie entered the small parlor.

"Good afternoon, Miss Colleen."

Collie glanced at her mother and then looked back at her visitor. "Good afternoon, sir."

The room smelled of coffee, or at least what her mother called coffee, but the pot and cups had now been set to the side on the tea table.

Kathy looked elegant in a pale blue dress and was sitting stiff as a fence post in a chair to the left of the sofa and facing Barbicane, who now stood before the opposite chair. The sofa beneath the window was vacant and seemed to form a barrier between them.

"I'm sorry, mom. I'll—."

"No, please stay," Barbicane said. He looked at Kathy. "Miss Colleen is old enough to be aware of these things."

Kathy gestured to her, and Collie set her hat aside and sat on the sofa between them.

Barbicane resumed his seat. He seemed too big even for the tallest chair in their red velvet parlor set.

"Mr. Barbicane is concerned about our cattle wandering onto his property," Kathy said. "Do you know if Rake has men riding the wire today?"

"He's riding it himself," Collie said.

"Does he usually do that?" Barbicane asked in surprise.

Collie shrugged.

"Answer, Colleen," Kathy said.

"I don't think so, sir."

Barbicane turned to Kathy. "Last year Harlo's men cut my wire in order to sneak in some of their stock to drink. I don't like to see any cattle die, and I let it go that time, but I'm finished with Harlo's arrogance. I'm taking measures to see that it doesn't happen again. These procedures are not directed against you, Kathleen. It's important to me that you understand that."

"Thank you for coming here to explain it," she said.

"I've offered Harlo access to water during poor monsoons, but we had a falling out long ago and he's an unforgiving man. So be it."

"I understand."

"Please tell your men to be careful not to ride onto my property. Strangers in the middle of my stock will be considered agents of criminal trespass. If any strays of yours wander in, just tell me. I'll have my boys round them up for you."

"Thank you. I will."

Collie thought Barbicane seemed suddenly uncomfortable, as if his sternness had not come naturally to him.

"I've offered Harlo a fair price for his ranch many times—we all know that the fire banked in him when his wife died. He could retire comfortably on just a portion of it. But he's an angry bull and I'm a red *muleta*, so I've given up. Please understand that."

Kathy remained as quiet as a nun.

"I don't want to appear to you to be unreasonable," Barbicane said. "I want you—."

"I understand," Kathy said.

The interruption startled him and seemed to make him uneasy. He looked as if he were about to stand up, but then he sighed and settled back again.

"All right. I'll try one more time. Let's have dinner at Don Luis's. My treat. Harlo and I and you. We'll see if we can settle this."

"Collie isn't just my daughter, she's my partner. She has to be there, too."

"That's fine. And bring your gentleman if you like. I want everything completely above board."

Kathy turned to Collie and nodded toward the coffee pot.

"Thank you, no," Barbicane said, standing up and reaching for his hat. "I'll be leaving now. I appreciate your hospitality." He smiled and it was not at all unpleasant. "And I need some time to recover from that stout brew of yours."

"Collie, get Mr. Barbicane's horse."

"It's always a pleasure seeing you, Kathleen."

Then Collie led Barbicane out the door.

When Collie came back in, her mother was sitting on the sofa and staring out the window.

"Mom, what did Mr. Barbicane mean by a gentleman?" Collie sat next to her and took her right hand.

Kathy sighed and stared back out the window. "I did something very stupid. . . ."

Collie squeezed her fingers.

"Mr. Barbicane asked me to the Rain Dance, but I declined."

"I don't understand. What's wrong with that?"

"It's the way I did it. He seemed so sincere. So needy. I couldn't just say no." She turned back to Collie with eyes desperate for understanding. "Could I?"

Collie just shook her head because she had no idea what her mother meant.

"I felt I had to have a reason, so I wouldn't hurt him. There's nothing wrong with that, is there?"

"I don't think so."

"Oh, Colleen, never tell a lie that anybody can disprove without even trying. . . . I told him I couldn't go with him because I was already keeping company with someone."

"Oh," she said softly.

"Sometimes your mother can be very foolish."

"So can her daughter."

"I didn't want to hurt that man. I don't want to hurt anyone. I've hurt too many people's feelings over the years."

Collie hesitated and then said. "There's more, though, isn't there, mom? More serious than the Rain Dance and Mr. Barbicane."

"Yes." Kathy gave her a sad smile. "Keira, if you learn only one thing about men and women in your life, remember this. Women will fight one another over anything, and men will fight each other to the death over absolutely nothing." She turned away and gazed far off. "There's a terrible storm coming, and it doesn't have anything to do with monsoons.

8 WE NEVER SLEEP

After dark, the atmosphere of the print room of *The Clarion* differed from its midday grind of metal and ink. At night, Kelly always kept the lamps lit late, and the door stayed unlocked until he went to bed. Anyone was welcome for a chat and a cup of cocoa or some coffee strong enough to float a horseshoe. Gradually the warmth and openness of this gesture had affected the mood of the entire area. In a town with no lawman, it counted for much that there was now a late night sentinel whose comforting presence was always to be seen, even from a distance, and who, apparently, retired for the evening only after everyone else had been tucked safely into bed.

Kelly led Holden past his desk into the living quarters beyond. The tastefully furnished parlor was softly lit, and the French style furniture that Kelly had inherited from the previous owner seemed inappropriate for the old cowprod.

"It's stuffy in here," Kelly said as he opened a window. "But at least there's the smell of rain on the wind."

"Mmmm," Holden murmured.

"Easy on the cushions," Kelly said as he poured some coffee. "They're made for more genteel sorts."

Holden set down his shotgun and tossed aside his hat before easing himself into a chair. He took the cup from Kelly. "I won't sleep tonight," he said after chewing a sip.

"Who can sleep these days?" Kelly answered and sat on the sofa.

"Especially at the High C."

Holden seemed very serious.

"What do you mean?"

"The monsoons bring no comfort there."

"I thought all Arizonans looked forward to the rains."

"Most do."

"But not you?"

"Not my little girl."

"Colleen?"

"Mmmm."

"She's rather old to be afraid of thunderstorms, isn't she?"

"She's the bravest girl in the world."

"Sorry. I didn't mean anything by it."

Holden sighed. "You just don't understand. But who can?"

"Then help me."

Holden hesitated, and then said, "I'll tell you—but it dies with you."

"A fair deal."

"Collie is the bravest and toughest girl I've ever known. I've seen her bloody her knuckles on the jaws of foul-mouthed boys half a foot taller than her . . . but I suppose we all have one aching spot in our souls. . . ."

"Some of us more than one."

"She's tortured by nightmares—one nightmare, actually. Over and over."

"I see. You don't have to tell me any more about it."

"I want to. I'm sure *she'd* want me to. She thinks the world of you."

Kelly smiled. "The folly of youth."

"The wisdom of youth."

"All right, share it if you think it's right."

"The first time it happened, Collie was thirteen. Kathleen was away and had asked if I'd sleep in the house while she was gone. I heard a horrible scream in the middle of the night. As if somebody was suffocating and then managed to break loose and howl for help. I ran to Collie's room and she was sitting up and hugging herself and shaking like she was freezing. This was in August and she was soaked with sweat but still shivering. I lit a lamp, and she gave me a look of terror that I'll never forget. I sat down on the edge of the bed and held her and she just rocked back and forth in my arms. I—."

"You're an old softy, cowboy."

"I asked her if she wanted to talk. The words just poured out of her. She said she dreamed she was home by herself at night during a storm and that it was so loud that she couldn't

64

hear anything but the crashing of the rain. She was sitting in the dark and looking out the window when she saw a lone horseman far off approaching the house. Even though it was night, she could see him good and clear. The downpour didn't affect either him or his horse. They weren't trotting or loping, just a steady walk. It's as if they didn't even feel the rain, though she said it looked like bullets cutting into them. They just kept coming. She said she stepped outside into the rain and that suddenly she was certain he was there to harm her. To commit some unspeakable act. She called for help, but the rain was so loud that no one in the bunkhouse could hear her. She called and called and was finally screaming as the rain tore into her and pounded in her ears and the rider slowly bore down. It was that last wail that jolted me out of bed."

A long silence followed.

Finally, Kelly said, "And she has this dream every monsoon season?"

"Hell, she has it every month or so. She hates going to bed. She lives in terror of one thing, the rider in the rain."

Kelly shook his head. "I wish I could help."

"I think only God can do that." Holden set his cup aside. "So tell me about your trip. I assume that's why I'm here. You don't look too rested."

"If it had been a real vacation, it might have been pleasant. . . ."

"But?"

"I went to Denver, to the Pinkerton office. I decided to call on a few colleagues."

"So you *did* work for Pinkerton's."

"Yes."

"No wonder you're always up so late. I heard you boys never sleep. Isn't that the motto?"

Kelly ignored that and took a sip of coffee before setting down the cup on the side table. Then he picked up the folder lying there. "I found out a few quaint details about Barbicane. I spoke to Jamie McParland about him. That conniving old strike breaker runs the Denver office. Our wealthy friend down here is in serious trouble. Financial distress of the first order. Did you know that?"

"No, but it's not a shock. He's wasted a lot of time twisting the tiger's tail. Every faro dealer in the territory knows him by his first name."

"That might explain why he's had to take out a second mortgage on his ranch. So now he's sitting on some cash. Presumably that's how he can offer to buy out Harlo Stone. And maybe Kathleen Callaghan."

"But they're not selling."

"Yet."

"Why would they?"

"Well, I can't answer for the behavior of Mrs. Callaghan, but I think Barbicane is going to make life less than cheerful for dear old Harlo. Wear him down and squeeze him out." Kelly pulled a document from the folder and handed it to Holden. "Collie got a glimpse of this yesterday."

Kelly picked up his cup and let Holden read at his leisure.

"He sounds real pious," Holden said when he had finished. "But what does a fellow in prison have to do with Barbicane?"

"He's not in prison. The conviction was thrown out a while back. Probably a well-placed bribe. Kelliride is coming here. Barbicane hired him as a range detective."

"Christ! Just another name for a back shooter."

"Sometimes."

Holden shook his head and remained quiet.

"Kelliride was working freelance for some of the Pinkerton agents, but even that hard bunch found his table manners a mite rough. So he's coming to Arizona to buff his nails on the faces of Harlo's men. And maybe open up their backs as well."

"Then, dammit, it's time to call in the Pima County sheriff."

"To do what? Stop Barbicane from protecting his stock?"

"Then what do you suggest?"

"I don't know. This is *your* play. You're the cattleman. Offhand, I'd say that Harlo has to keep his men and his beef on the right side of the fence and not let himself be provoked." Kelly shrugged. "Or he could sell his place to Barbicane."

"When are you going to show Harlo what you've dug up?"

"Harlo's problems are none of my business."

Holden looked baffled. "You traveled all the way to Denver for this and you're not going to tell him?"

"That's not why I went to Denver." He stood up and stepped over to the sideboard and got a bottle of Jameson Irish whiskey. "Here, hold out your cup." He poured out a healthy dose. "This will round the edges off that a bit."

"Not without a chisel."

Kelly sat back down and put the green file folder on his lap. "There was something about Collie's description of the stranger that stirred a memory in me. It didn't really take shape until I was lying in bed that night. Then all of a sudden the way she'd described the power of the man's presence lit a match against the darkness." He paused and took a long sip of his coffee. "For years there have been hints and whispers coming out of Sonora about a mysterious gang of *pistoleros*. Bandits who preyed upon bandits. Killers whom other killers feared." He tapped the folder with a forefinger. "I went to Denver for this."

"What is it?"

"What Collie almost saw before I stopped her — the Dark Archangel."

"Jesus," Holden said, staring at him in admiration. "You Pinkertons *are* good."

"The Pinkertons make up in efficiency for what they lack in grace. Or scruples."

Holden took the heavy folder.

"They didn't want to let that out of their hands," Kelly said. "Yet I still had a few markers to call in. But I have to get it back to them soon."

Holden hefted the folder and set it down. "I'm a slow reader, Pat. Can't you just give me the meat?"

Kelly swirled the whiskey around in his coffee and stared absently at it. "Everything I'm going to share with you is based on hearsay. McParland told me that there's not a flinder of hard evidence for any of it. All of it could be just a big story. . . ."

"But you believe it?"

"It doesn't matter what I believe."

"All right."

"I'm going to split fair with you, but you have to promise me something first. You're not to tell Collie any of this. Or Kathleen, for that matter — I've never known a woman who could keep her mouth shut to another woman, especially her own daughter."

Holden hesitated. "I understand about Collie, but Kathleen, too? She might need to know. She — ."

"No."

Holden sighed and set aside his cup. "I can't promise that." He stood and picked up his hat and shotgun. "Thanks for the refreshment."

Holden got as far as the doorway before he turned and looked around at Kelly, who was casually sipping his coffee.

"Jesus Christ," Holden said, "I'd hate to face you across a poker table." He came back and sat down again and added more Jameson to his coffee. "You have my word."

Without preliminaries, Kelly began. "About eight or nine years ago, some Arizona rustlers decided to make a good living by raiding the small Mexican *ranchos* in Sonora. They'd steal the stock, but they were smarter than the typical rustlers and didn't try to bring the cattle back across the border. They'd sell it to the rich *ganaderos* down there. Nobody is better at exploiting Mexicans than other Mexicans. And the poorer ones had no defense against the rustlers. They were just crippled calves waiting for slaughter. And who really cared if the pathetic bean eaters and their children starved to death anyway?"

"I must have still been in Texas then. I've never heard of this."

"But after one of the raids, a group of rustlers never returned to Arizona. Some of their friends rode down to look around. They found them. They'd all been shot to death and the Mexican silver was long gone."

"I'm guessing you're going to tell me that this wasn't just a fluke."

"It happened three more times, but on those raids the rustlers were spared and made to walk back to Arizona. They told their friends up here that about thirty bandits had waylaid them after they'd been paid for the Mexican stock. When the other rustlers heard this, a few of them got clever and talked to the Pinkerton Agency. Naturally, they told the Pinkertons a real tear squeezer about how they'd paid for the cattle and then been robbed. So they hired some agents. The Pinkertons dressed like saddle tramps and slipped across the border. . . ."

"And?"

"And the tale told down there was very different. The scraps the Pinkertons picked up from the peons and the smaller *rancheros* said that there were really only five bandits beating the hell out of the Arizona rustlers. Two of the bandits were Americans, one Mexican, and an Apache from the Chiricahuas. They kept a share of the silver but returned the majority of it to the small *rancheros*. They bought themselves a lot of goodwill with that. The rumor was that they were based in Magdalena. When the *Rurales* came looking for them there after a lot of screaming from the American consul, the peasants just shrugged and offered the *Rurales* a tortilla."

Holden laughed.

"So how's that so far?"

"It's a hell of a story."

"I agree. But you've missed something."

Holden smiled. "Why do you newspaper people always have to act so superior? What did I miss?"

"Two Americans plus one Mexican plus one Apache equals four. But I said there were five."

"The leader?"

"Nobody can agree on who he is or what he is. Gringo, greaser, or redskin—he's been called all three."

Holden's smile slowly faded.

"But," Kelly said, "Colleen Callaghan knows him."

"Good God, her *Arcángel*?"

"Yes."

"What did you learn?"

"It's all rumors and shaky testimony. You have to understand that."

"I don't give a damn. Tell me."

"Several of the best agents pieced it all together. It's in that folder."

"All right, let 'er buck."

"Where he's from nobody knows. Some Arizona lawmen insist he's an American called Matt Wood. A few of the old folks from Magdalena say they're certain he's a Mexican named Mateo Madero."

"Half and half maybe?"

"Could be."

"Collie told me that he said his mother had blue eyes, so that might be true."

"Supposedly he was abandoned at the door of a church. Or a convent. The story is murky. Two or three informants whispered that he's a catch-colt. Some say he was raised by the nuns. It—."

"I told you," Holden said with a smile. "He's an educated man."

"His youth is a mystery. The guess is that he ran off and lived on the streets somewhere in Sonora. . . ."

"Fell in with a bad pack—isn't that what people usually claim?"

"Most of the information on him comes from when the Arizona rustlers started preying on the Mexicans, and the bandits wiped them out. It's not known if he was just a member of the gang or the leader at the beginning, though eventually he did become their *patrón*. As I said, what *is* known is that they showed no mercy to that first unlucky bunch of American outlaws."

"Not much information there. No surprise they've never been caught."

"The peasants in Sonora are protective of the whole gang—and especially of him. But a few of the Pinkertons were shrewd enough to encourage some of the Mexicans to brag about him. And they did."

Holden laughed. "The older ones, right? I've seen that before. Once the *ancianos* get started, they can talk a burro's hind leg off."

"The small *rancheros* said that he has no fear. A few of them told the Pinkertons that they weren't sure if he was brave or if he just didn't care about his own survival."

"Why did they think that?"

"I don't know."

Holden looked concerned. "This isn't good. A man who doesn't care about death . . . the most dangerous type there is."

"Well, whether or not he's afraid of anything, one thing is certain, and that's that he's feared by others. And yet none of the *rancheros* ever saw him pull a pistol or strike a person or even raise his voice. Or use any kind of weapon, for that matter, though only a lunatic would go unarmed in Sonora. The one thing just about everyone did mention to the Pinkertons was that he was a terror at the poker table."

Holden smiled. "The hands at the Lazy S found that out."

"Oddly enough, he'd often clean out his own men and then give them back their money, minus a small amount—'For the instruction,' he'd tell them."

"Now *that's* different. In my fifty-five years I've never known anyone to do something like that. Poker is a blood sport to everybody I've ever stared at across the green."

Kelly shrugged. "Maybe this man had his own reason for not wanting to see it as a blood sport."

"What do you mean?"

"Maybe he's seen more than enough blood everywhere else."

Holden stared at him for a long time and then shook his head helplessly. "And, yet, to Collie he's the Dark Archangel."

"There are lots of other tales, but one kept coming up again and again. In Magdalena and elsewhere. The peasants said that somehow he always knew when they needed him. And he'd always appear at the right moment. Strange."

"They might all be Catholic down there, but that doesn't mean they're not superstitious. I wouldn't put any stock in that."

"Don't discount the mystical, cowboy. Or the unexplainable." He smiled. "If the Irish did that, how could we believe in leprechauns?"

"Oh, for God's sake."

"You're too practical, Rake. Too linear. *There are more things in heaven and earth, Horatio, than are dreamt of in your philosophy.*"

"What the hell does that mean?"

"A touch of the Bard." Kelly smiled again and sipped his coffee. "In a cowhand's terms, you've spent too much time doggie roping and shit kicking. Stop reacting like a startled herd in a thunderstorm. Relax. Let yourself feel and dream—like the Mexicans. Or us Celts."

"I don't have that luxury. I have two women to worry about."

"Don't we all? Time for you to put your feet up in a darkened room and lean back with some Irish coffee. Sit by the window and smell the night air. And dream. Not about what's rational, but about what's real. Believe me, the real is never truly rational."

"This man is a killer."

"Perhaps."

Holden reached for the folder and began flipping through the pages. "Aren't there any photographs of him?"

"None. Not so much as a sketch. Even the descriptions of him contradict each other. But it's certain he's the man you met. The facial wound proves it. About two years ago, he was seriously hurt. According to everyone the Pinkertons talked with, he was stabbed in the face."

"Well, he survived it easily enough."

"But he turned over the leadership of the gang to one of the others and vanished. Some believe he went east. A few even think he traveled abroad. There seems to have been some trauma that—."

"The wound, you mean."

"I don't think that's it. He didn't disappear until at least half a year after he was hurt. One of the old men in Magdalena implied to the Pinkertons that something happened to him during those six months."

"Any idea what?"

"None. But he evaporated as though he'd never been more than a fantasy. Until a few weeks ago when he stood on a hillside and spoke with a pretty and trusting young girl named Colleen Callaghan. . . . And when, I think, she looked more thoughtfully into him than anyone else ever has."

9 CLOUDBURST

La Cantina de la Luna had been misnamed. Rather than being a distant moon orbiting a larger heavenly body, the cantina comprised the social center of San Miguel. Unlike the other saloons in town, *La Luna* was a suitable eating place even for virgin spinsters and geriatric nuns. Don Luis, the proprietor, had seen to that from the outset. No one had to feel uncomfortable in his establishment.

While rough-edged entertainments, like poker and the roulette wheel and the faro table, engrossed the cowhands, these diversions had been separated from the area where families could dine in relative seclusion. What the original builder had neglected in the way of a wall Don Luis had rectified with several Chinese screens he had purchased from one of the Celestials. The lamps in the dining room had been tastefully arranged to create a mellow ambience, and colorful Oaxacan rugs hanging from the walls and covering the floor softened the texture of the room in a manner beyond the physical. A baby grand piano sat in one corner and, under skilled fingers, would delight the diners and assist their digestion. Don Luis had even cut out a family entrance in a side wall so that parents and their children could enter the dining space without having to endure the bar-side ravings of cowhands who had swilled too much coffin varnish.

It was a particular quirk of Colleen Callaghan that she liked just about everyone, but Don Luis Dámaso occupied a special niche in her shrine. Unlike most people in town, he had always spoken to her as if she were an adult even when she had been much younger. It was widely known that he was a childless widower, and they had bonded quickly. What was not so well known was that it had been Collie who had innocently bestowed on him the honorific *Don* when she was only ten, and it had stuck. No one had thought it inappropriate. Though he was simply the owner of an eating and drinking emporium, he had become a quiet eminence to whom people often turned for guidance and advice. It was believed that he was the only saloon owner in town who kept no firearm beneath the bar. His look of displeasure alone was always enough to quell the most raucous cowboy or the bitterest loser at the poker table. And although he employed saloon girls to beautify his cantina, they had to deport themselves in a manner befitting the high regard in which he held all women everywhere.

A Spaniard, Don Luis was, so the tale went, the son of a matador. Instead of following his father to the *corrida*, he had become an actor and had sailed from Barcelona as a youth looking for adventure. Supposedly he had traveled Sonora and the American Southwest as part of a touring company and had finally alighted in San Miguel. About fifty now, he was as dashing as a Spanish player was expected to be. His wavy hair was still as black as iron, and he sported one of those lean straight moustaches sharp enough to slice a lady's lip. Despite blatant temptations, the widower had acquired a certain fame for resisting the advances of several townswomen who had decided he needed their comfort. In fact, he much preferred the company of youth, whom he regaled with tales that might even have been true.

Since she had been a little girl, Collie had considered Don Luis the most enchanting man she had ever seen, but her feelings had matured. His striking looks and continental manner she seldom noticed now. More precious to her were those dark understanding eyes that brought her that uniquely Latin masculine comprehension she had sought her whole life and which she had never received from any other, until, perhaps, a few weeks ago on a hillside.

"A big evening today, yes?" Don Luis said to Collie with a smile as he folded his arms and leaned against the wall of the roofed veranda.

"*Sí,*" she answered, staring south toward the dark gray thunderclouds over Mexico. She was standing in front the large table that was being set up for the supper that Barbicane had arranged.

"Why so grim?"

"Oh, I don't know. . . ." She looked over at Don Luis and realized for the thousandth time that he could not be deceived. "It's just that I don't like the storms."

"Ah, but they bring life to the desert."

"But they destroy the peace." She turned again toward the south.

A pair of riders was hurrying north along the road from the border toward San Miguel.

Don Luis followed her gaze. "They're trying to beat the rain."

"I hope they make it."

He smiled. "It's not *víbora* venom. It's only water."

"But why would anybody ride in the rain?"

"Well, I don't think anyone wants to."

"But what if someone did want to?" She turned back to him. "Or what if he didn't care?"

"Then it would probably mean that where he was going or whom he was going to see was more important to him than his own discomfort."

She looked again toward the south.

"*¿Qué pasa, chica?*"

"I'm not sure. But I don't feel well today. Inside I mean."

"A prayer to Our Lady is always a wise choice."

"I prayed to her all night last night."

"And for what did you pray?"

"Oh . . . a helper. Somebody to stand with us. Then I asked Mr. Kelly if . . . . but I know that's not right. He doesn't know my mom very well."

"He's a good man."

"I'm worried about my mom."

"The *señora* fears nothing. Why should her daughter be afraid?"

"That's the reason. She's too stubborn to be afraid."

"So you worry for her?"

"Every day."

"But God knows that. He always provides."

"But what can he possibly give for that kind of worry?"

"*Chica. . . .*"

She looked up at him.

"That sounds like *blasfemia*. God is God. He can grant anything."

"But will he?"

"Do not doubt."

She smiled at him. "You always make me feel better."

"It's a gift," he said, returning her smile. "God's gift."

Collie sighed and glanced at the table. "What are we having for supper?"

"*Pollo*. Cattlemen weary of beef."

"Why are there so many places set?"

"Señor Barbicane's request."

"I thought it would be just the four of us."

"More than four I was told. Will Señor Holden be here?"

"He wanted to, but you know my mother. She always has to prove she can handle things herself."

Don Luis sighed and seemed to indulge himself in an unexpressed thought, as he so often appeared to do.

"Nothing makes sense to me today." Collie turned away. "My mom should be here soon. She wanted to pick up a few things at the mercantile."

"Let me go now and finish getting things ready."

He stepped away and lit the lamps around the veranda and then returned to the kitchen.

Don Luis was barely gone when Barbicane came out of the dining room onto the veranda. Four men accompanied him. All of them removed their hats when they saw her.

"Hello, Miss Colleen," Barbicane said.

"Good evening, sir." She was embarrassed that her voice sounded so washy.

Collie recognized Kelliride immediately from the photograph in the file at the *Clarion* office. In the flesh, he had a permanent half-smile on his face that made her uneasy. The other three were new to her. One was a pale, clean-shaven man with sparse sandy hair and a burn scar distorting the right side of his scalp. He was speaking to an older companion, gaunt and ravaged and who looked like he fed on carrion. Wispy brown tendrils of a moustache wilted and drooped around his mouth and looked as poorly nourished as their owner. Both men seemed to defer to the fourth man. Although not as tall as Kelliride, this one seemed equally powerful. A thickly-muscled body pushed out against his neat blue suit, and if he had tensed he looked like he might split a seam. He was carrying a black bowler that had concealed a head of bright golden hair. He turned and looked at Collie, and instantly she felt chilled by eyes that shone like blue ice.

Don Luis's kitchen helpers were starting to bring out the food, and Collie hurried past the five men and into the dining room to look for her mother.

Kathy was just coming in through the family entrance.

"Mom, I think we should get Rake," Collie said as she ran up to her.

"He's back at the ranch. Why? What's wrong?"

"Mr. Barbicane isn't alone."

Kathy peered past Collie and out onto the veranda.

Collie watched her eyes. She knew what came next. Her mother would try to fake a calmness she did not feel. Unfortunately, as she had gotten older, she had become less effective at it.

"Well, they're not exactly a sewing circle, are they?"

"Oh, mom, stop it."

The outer door opened again, and Mr. Kelly came hurrying through as though worried he might be late.

Collie actually heard herself sigh with relief, although to her it sounded more like the bleating of a lost lamb than anything human.

Kathy turned around to see what had caused it.

"Good evening, Kathleen," Kelly said, removing his hat.

Collie smiled. He looked as elegant as a duke.

"Hello, Pat," Kathy said. "I'm sorry, but we don't have—."

"A dark-haired angel told me that your gentleman caller split a spoke on a wheel and ran into a ditch, so you might need an escort this evening."

For the first time in her life, Collie felt immune to her mother's glare.

"What am I going to do with you, young woman?"

"Gratitude might be in order," Kelly said.

Kathy put an arm around Collie's shoulders and smiled. "I think you're right. It looks like we could use some moral support tonight."

Kelly extended his left arm, and Kathy hooked her right arm around it.

"I really appreciate this, Pat."

"Shall we feast?" he said with a smile, and they went on through.

Harlo had come around to the veranda from the outside, and now everyone was present.

The supper turned out to be an odd affair. The storm finally roared in from Mexico, and thunderclaps boomed an odd overture to a peace parley. Fortunately, the wind was still fairly gentle, and the diners were sitting in far enough under the tile roof to stay dry.

Collie looked to see if any cowhands on the road from the south had been caught in the rain. Although the evening was young, little light seeped through because of the cloud cover, and she found it difficult to see. She began to turn away just as a sizzling crack of pink lightning shot across the sky and lit a lone rider making his way up the road in their direction.

Seemingly indifferent to the storm, he moved at a steady pace as if there were no rain at all, and Collie felt suddenly cold as she gazed at this terrible vision brought to life from her dreams. The wind picked up, but the graceful mount remained one with its rider and was impervious to the gale engulfing them, as if this were the animal's natural element in a brutal and unnatural world.

Collie felt her mother's hand on her arm, and she turned and looked at her.

Kathy just smiled. "It's all right."

Collie looked back south, but the darkness and the driving rain now shrouded the horseman even as the thunder rolled off into the distance.

Barbicane seemed to be in a grand mood this evening and chatted enthusiastically about the splendors of Arizona, as if all those present were not already aware of them. The four men with him ate in silence. It had struck Collie as odd that he had not introduced them, but the supper had been ready and perhaps that would come later.

Harlo said nothing at all, and Kathy occasionally commented on the glories of Don Luis's marvelous kitchen.

More than anyone, though, it was Kelly whom Collie watched. He observed the four men like someone eyeing a circling pack of wolves. This was a man not to be duped by a cattleman's jawing or by a sumptuous spread. She was so glad that he had taken her up on her sledge hammer hint about coming to the supper. She would have felt even better if Rake had been there as well.

When the meal was done, a fine cognac was brought out, and Collie was surprised when her mother poured her some. After a sip, she realized she would have been just as happy without it, since it tasted to her like nothing so much as liquid timber.

"Now," Barbicane said at last after setting down his glass, "let us have peace."

"And how do you define that, Lawton?" Harlo asked.

"You're weary, old friend," Barbicane said. "Everyone knows that. You've had some bad years on the range. It's time to retire and relax."

"And how do I do that? Sell you my ranch?"

"That's a possibility. Just a part of it, naturally. Keep a nice slice for yourself. Spend some time with your boy."

"Don't worry about my boy."

"He's a fine lad."

"He takes after his mother."

It sounded to Collie as if Harlo had said that with less feeling than he would have had for a stillborn calf.

"I'll give you a reasonable price," Barbicane said, ignoring Harlo's tone. "And I asked Kathy here for her fair mind and wise judgment."

"And," Harlo said, "because her ranch sits between ours."

"That, too. All that patchwork is an encumbrance. I can smooth it out if you see reason."

"And are these your negotiators?" Harlo gestured at the men beside Barbicane.

"They're my stock detectives." Barbicane's voice had an edge now. "The days when your men can cut through my wire to steal my water are finished. These men know how to deal with criminal trespass."

"I'm sure."

"Don't prejudge. Let me introduce them. To my —."

"No," Kelly said.

Collie jumped at his voice.

"Let *me* introduce them," Kelly went on. "Kelliride is a convicted thief who was let off on a technicality. That's another name for a bribe. Ian Craksi was a scalp hunter until the Apaches torched his head and left that beauty mark. That's probably when he went for a career change. How many pelts was it that you sold to the Mexicans?"

"Countin' kids? Hard to say. Maybe forty. And every one a beauty."

"Our lean friend there," Kelly went on, "is Armand Scateen. *Seldom he smiles, and smiles in such a sort as if he mocked himself and scorned his spirit that could be moved to smile at anything.* Trains and express offices were his specialty until he found head-smashing for the Pinkertons more to his taste and bank account. Isn't that right?"

A half-smothered animalism coiled in Scateen's eyes. He nodded and said nothing.

"But these are just outriders compared to Mr. Sutorius," Kelly said. "He of the nice suits and the bowler and the glacial smile. He's the intellect here. Isn't that so, Maart?"

"I didn't think you'd remember me, Pat," Sutorius said in a surprisingly friendly tone.

"Who else cuts a swell like you?"

"No need to dress in rags."

"And who could forget a man iron-hearted enough to be fired by the most iron-hearted organization this side of the Tsar's secret police?"

"Anarchists need crushing," Sutorius said.

"And miners and ranchers?"

"Those, too. Sometimes."

"These are your stock detectives, Barbicane. Enjoy them. But be careful — they eat their young."

"It wasn't my goal to hire kittens, Mr. Kelly." He turned to Kathy. "I need to protect my rights." His voice had a pleading quality when he spoke to her.

"We all have rights, Lawton," Kathy said.

"But we don't all have patience. I'm fed up." He looked at Harlo. "Name your price."

"I'll leave the ranch to you in my will."

"A tempting thought," Sutorius said with a smile.

"That's a terrible thing to think!" Collie said.

Sutorius looked at Kathy. "Mrs. Callaghan, if a girl can't be taught respect with words, she needs to be taught with the whip."

Kathy eyes shot fire at him. "What makes you think you're man enough?" She glared at Barbicane. "Lawton, this man is trash."

"That's enough, Maart," Barbicane said.

"Who are *you*?" Sutorius suddenly asked as his gaze swung back to Collie.

She stared at him in confusion. "What? You know who I am."

His eyes seemed to drill straight through her and out the back of her skull and beyond. Then she realized he was not seeing her at all.

"Threats," said a soft voice, "are the currency of cowards, weaklings, and fools."

Collie spun around in her chair.

"Hello, Blackie," the tall man said with a smile.

Collie stared in surprise and wonder and then grinned at the stranger who was not so strange anymore.

Draped in a black oilcloth slicker dripping water onto the stone floor, he winked at her and pulled off his soaked hat. He then swept the slicker from his shoulders as if he were a continental count and hung it with his hat on a rack by the wall.

He was dressed as he had been the day she had first met him, except now a long-barreled revolver was tucked butt forward into the sash at his right hip. The stag grips seemed to glow against his dark clothing, and the conchos down the legs of his *calzoneras* caught the light of the lamps on the veranda.

"This is a private supper, sir," Barbicane said.

"I'm a private man." He turned when he heard Don Luis approach from behind. "*Una botella de Don Rodrigo, por favor.*"

Don Luis stared at the stranger for a moment and then glanced at Collie. He seemed reassured by her smile.

"En seguida," Don Luis said with a smile of his own and went back inside.

The stranger stepped toward the table, and Kelly stood up.

"Pat Kelly," he said, holding out his hand. "Señor Mateo Madero?"

"Yes," Madero said as he shook hands. "The Pinkerton man? The one who never sleeps?"

Kelly hesitated and then smiled. "I thought *I* was the one who had secret knowledge, but I'm afraid you have the advantage of me."

Madero turned away from him. "Hello, Kathleen."

"Hello, Matthew," came an unsteady reply.

Collie snapped her head around and stared at her mother in disbelief. Kathy seemed too shaken even to reach out and touch the hand that Madero had extended. Finally she took his fingers in hers but with a hesitation that Collie had never seen in her before.

"And you . . . ?" Madero said, for his gaze had already moved on.

"Maart Sutorius."

Don Luis came back with a glass and the bottle of tequila Madero had ordered.

"Colleen Callaghan is a special friend of mine," Madero said, staring at Sutorius. "Wise is the man who remembers that."

"Consider it remembered," Sutorius said.

Collie thought that Sutorius seemed unsure.

Madero stepped forward and placed a hand on Collie's shoulder. She could feel his warmth through her shirt.

The two men took each other's measure.

"May we continue?" Barbicane said, trying to regain control.

Collie looked up at Madero. As indifferent to the cattleman's words as he and his horse had been to the storm, Madero continued gazing with an eerie calm into the cold eyes of Sutorius. Finally he squeezed Collie's shoulder lightly, and that delicate and reassuring gesture spoke volumes to her. Then he turned, took the tequila from Don Luis, and left the veranda.

"Where does this little fiesta go from here?" Harlo asked Barbicane in an attempt to break the unnerving spell the stranger had cast.

"What happens now rests completely with you."

No it doesn't, Collie thought. *It now rests with a man greater than all of you.*

PART TWO

*It is as if ivory carvings and elaborate fretwork
and fair enameling should be found with worms
and ashes amongst coffins and the works of some
forgotten life or some abolished nature.*

—De Quincey

10 SWORDSMAN

Madero rubbed the soft towel over Buddy's black mane and then across his withers, and the animal's eyelids drooped in the languid pleasure for which all horses longed but which too few ever found. The glow from the lantern lit Buddy's red coat as strikingly as a soft cloth burnishing old copper. The horse was already dry, but Madero liked to finish up with the gentle kneading that this most tactile of creatures cherished as much as the first grass of spring.

The storm still pounded in the darkness, but the stable had a good roof and all inside remained dry. The sorrel and the buckskin down the barn row seemed mellow about these two visitors, and yet they remained attentive to danger, just in case.

Madero had taught himself long ago to train an ear to each person's footfalls so he could recognize an individual's steps in the dark or without turning to see.

"Thank you for this," Madero said as he heard Luis come in from the open doorway.

"*De nada.* I came to tell you that supper is done and Mrs. Callaghan and Miss Colleen would like to see you."

"Could you do a favor for me and tell them I'll be with them in a few minutes?"

"I already have."

Madero turned toward him and smiled. "*Gracias.*"

"A handsome animal."

Madero turned back to Buddy to finish the rubdown. "Women usually buy a horse for color and beauty, but men are much more practical. . . ."

"But . . . ? You're about to say more."

"But an old *vaquero* in Sonora told me when I was a boy that sometimes color matters. He said, 'Chico, when you get your own horse, make sure it's a bay. *Los caballos bayos* always have sweet souls.' Every time I've ignored that, I've regretted it."

"He does have a soft eye."

"And a kind heart."

"He's from the colonel?"

"He is." Madero delicately wiped the area around Buddy's eyes.

"The colonel is a fair man. For a horse trader."

Madero finished by gently running his fingers through the tangled black forelock that hung a third of the way down his horse's face. He repeated this several times until the hair fell straight and smooth.

"Is there a hotel or rooming house in San Miguel?"

Madero took a hoof pick from a saddlebag and began cleaning Buddy's feet.

"You're welcome here."

"Thank you. I'll bed down right here with Buddy. I always like to sleep close to my horse. And I prefer the scent of hay to a perfumed boudoir."

Luis got a flake of hay and fluffed it a bit and tossed it into a stall feeder and then put some fresh straw onto the bottom of the stall.

"Horse heaven," he said with a smile.

Madero set aside his grooming tools and led Buddy to the stall. Like all horses, Buddy waited for no formalities but immediately began to eat.

"I can do better for you than this," Luis said and picked up the lantern and led Madero across the barn to a human-sized door at the back.

Luis pressed the latch, and Madero followed him inside.

A pleasant sitting room with a maroon sofa and a pair of French chairs spread out before him. A small dining area had been set up toward the far wall. Near it sat a carved spirits cabinet with a tray and glasses on top. As in the cantina, Oaxacan rugs had been spread about for color and softness, and a few hung on the walls as well. A black stove against cool winter nights sat off in a corner.

"Someone is a scholar," Madero said, gesturing to the large bookshelf across the room.

"Those are mine. I come here for *un tiempo de reflexión*."

Madero looked at Luis and smiled. "Maybe there's some benefit to me if I linger here. Wisdom is bound to come."

Luis smiled back. "Perhaps."

"And my poor peasant dialect should certainly soften in the sea of your Catalonian cadences."

Luis nodded, as if to himself. "There's more to you than meets the eye."

"There's more to *everyone* than meets the eye."

"A bedroom through there and a bathtub through the other one," Luis said, pointing to two closed doors.

"Very nice."

"The original owner was a fastidious man." Luis set down the lantern onto a lyre table with a statue of Our Lady of Guadalupe. "This place was San Miguel's first *caballeriza*. The old fellow who had it also owned the cantina. When he passed on to his reward, his family sold me both. By that time, this stable was only for his own use. The new one had all the business. I use it now just for my own horses. These quarters were built for the stable manager long ago. I keep the rooms furnished and clean for any friends who come by."

"Thank you. I'll pay whatever you say."

"I offer them *un gratuitamente* for *el Arcángel Oscuro*."

Madero looked at Luis in surprise. "Who coined that term?" he said as he slid his Remington from the sash at his waist and laid it beside Our Lady.

"Please sit."

Madero untied the silver bandana from around his neck and tossed it aside and then dropped into a chair. The cushion felt like a cloud after all his hours in the saddle.

Luis sat on the sofa across from him. "May I ask you a question?"

"Why not?"

"Why did you ride here tonight?"

Madero studied the handsome face creased with the sort of wisdom that one discounted only at one's peril. "It was on a whim."

87

"Mmmm. But isn't a whim merely God inspiring someone in secret?"

Madero barely knew this man, but he was very rapidly beginning to like him. "Interesting thought, but God gave up trying to inspire me centuries ago."

"You were seeking the Callaghans tonight?"

"Yes."

"Why?"

Madero smiled. "As the *gringos* say, 'God only knows.'"

"You parry harmless questions like *un esgrimidor* with his blade. And yet tonight that same swordsman stared seemingly without care into the dark hearts of some very hard men."

Madero said nothing.

"Was it on behalf of the young lady?" Luis asked.

"What young lady?"

"Ah, a weak parry. . . ."

"Colleen Callaghan?"

"*Sí.*"

Madero gave him a bemused look. "It must be difficult for you here. . . ."

Luis seemed puzzled. "Owning a cantina? How can—?"

"No, being the conscience of San Miguel."

That evidently caught him off guard.

"And no questions for me about buying a horse for someone?" Madero stood up and walked toward the door.

"I was thinking of no horse," Luis said. "I was thinking of a gentle hand on a vulnerable young shoulder."

Madero turned back toward him.

"You have a manner about you, *señor,*" Luis said. "A manner that few men have—to touch the heart and shelter the soul of an innocent young girl."

"Don't fool yourself," Madero answered in a dismissive tone as he turned away and headed out. "I'm just a good actor. I've been doing it all my life."

Madero walked through the rain across the alley and through the family entrance of the cantina. The dining room was crowded with patrons as he made his way among the tables. Kathy, Colleen, and Kelly were sitting at a table at the far end. Kelly stood up as Madero approached.

"I'll leave you now," Kelly said to Kathy.

"Why?" Madero asked.

"Isn't this private?"

"It is. Sit down." It was not a request. Kelly obeyed.

Madero slid out a chair near the wall and winked at Collie as he sat. She smiled at him with the conspiratorial look that all sixteen-year-old girls have mastered.

"You were watching over them, weren't you?" Madero said to Kelly.

He hesitated and then said, "I was."

"I expected no less."

Madero turned to Kathy. She seemed to have recovered her poise.

"I can't believe it," she said, shaking her head. "All this time."

"I had to get Buddy out of that toad strangler out there," Madero said. "San Miguel seemed as good a place as any."

"My rider in the rain," Collie said softly.

Madero glanced at her, but she quickly lowered her eyes.

"You look wonderful," Madero said to Kathy.

She just stared at him for a moment and then said, "It was you who bought Colleen the horse. . . ."

"A minor gesture."

Kathy laughed and it was pleasant and relaxed. "You used to say that all the time. Long ago. Whenever you did something for someone." She turned to Collie. "Mr. Madero and I were friends many years past."

"It's been almost twenty years, hasn't it?" Madero asked.

Kathy hesitated. "More or less. Where have you been all these years? Mexico?"

Madero glanced at Kelly, but Kelly gently shook his head no.

"Is there something you're keeping from me?" she said to both of them with a smile.

"Your friend here is a man of honor," Madero said.

Don Luis came up carrying a tray with a plate of sopapillas, a pot of honey, some cups, and a big enamelware coffee pot. He filled everyone's cups with a steaming Mexican brew black as the rivers of Hell.

"Truly, Matthew, what brought you here?" Kathy said.

"I thought it was a whim, but someone told me otherwise. A barkeep can be quite the philosopher."

"Don't fool yourself. I'm just a good actor." Luis's eyes were smiling. "I've been doing it all my life."

Then he was off to the kitchen as smoothly as he had arrived.

"I was hurt a while back," Madero said. "Hurt very bad—and I thought I'd like to see you one more time. When I got here, I heard you'd recently been widowed, so it didn't seem proper for me to—."

"Recently? My husband died before Collie was born."

"So much for the reliability of my information. I should have consulted with the Pinkerton man. In any case, I'd heard you had a daughter, and I saw her on the hill, and—."

"How did you know her?" Kathy asked in surprise.

"Her green and grassy face."

Collie burst out laughing.

"Anyway, she wanted that horse so bad. So I took care of it and then figured it was sensible to go. I thought you were still in mourning. I had no idea your husband had died so long ago."

"I wish you could have met him," Kathy said, staring down at her coffee.

"I'm sure I'd have been the better man for it."

She looked up. "What did you mean that you wanted to see me one more time? Are you moving on permanently?"

"Aren't we all? Fate can be malignant."

"You've always answered questions with another question," she said with a sigh. She was clearly concerned. "Are you ill—or still suffering from your injury?"

"It's had some lasting effects."

"We have a fine doctor here."

"I need a healer of a different sort." He turned to Kelly. "So what about that dross at dinner tonight? I assume you've investigated them."

"I have files in my office, if you'd like to stop by."

"I would."

"You're staying?" Collie blurted.

"Colleen!" Kathy snapped at her.

Madero smiled. "Why not?"

Collie smiled back.

90

"Barbicane is calling his crew range detectives," Kelly said.

Madero nodded. "And I'm the King of Persia."

"Please, enough of this talk now," Kathy said. "Do you have a place to stay, Matthew?"

"Don Luis has been very kind. Where's Holden tonight?"

"Holden? You know him?"

"He annoyed me for a while in Tucson."

"He's at the ranch."

"You're not going back home in the dark in this storm, are you?"

"I'm giving us a treat. Collie and I are staying at the hotel tonight."

"Then I'll leave you to the rest of your evening." He stood up and turned to Kelly. "Do you live alone?"

"At *The Clarion*."

"Keep the door locked after sundown. And have an iron on you no matter where you are."

"I don't usually do that."

"Start."

Madero was almost at the door when he turned at the footsteps behind him.

He smiled at Collie. "Yes?"

"I wanted to thank you, sir . . . privately . . . for buying Diablo for me. I already love him so much."

"Mmmm. Good name. Could scare off a horse thief. 'Cold Corpse' might work, too."

Collie grinned.

"Let's go outside." Madero opened the door.

They stepped into the alley between the cantina and the stable and stood in the drizzle.

"So is he still a loner?"

Even in the faint light of the lamp hanging by the doorway, Madero could see she looked embarrassed.

"I don't think he ever was, sir. I just repeated what the colonel told me so you wouldn't bid on him."

"Ahhh. Has he worked out for you?"

"Oh, yes, sir. He's wonderful. How's the bay?"

"Smartest horse I've ever owned. And with a brave heart."

Collie smiled.

"Anything else?"

She held out her hand, and Madero shook it. "I'm really happy to see you again, sir." She continued to hold his hand longer than was customary.

"And I you."

She finally released him. "My mom can use a friend."

"Only your mom?"

Collie looked uncomfortable. "No, sir."

"It seems to me as if your mother has some fine ones already."

"Oh, she does. You met Rake. He's tough as God makes them."

"Well, he's a Texan."

"And Mr. Kelly is a good man and very smart. A detective, too, before."

"So I understand."

"But they're not . . . " Reflexively she glanced at the place on Madero's hip where his pistol had been earlier in the evening. "They're not you."

Madero remained silent.

"There were bad men here tonight. I'm sure of it."

"A fair judgment."

"Not Mr. Barbicane, though. I think he's just foolish. But those others . . ."

"Yes."

"My mother doesn't have many friends. I know she isn't the warmest person. . . ."

"Unlike her daughter."

Collie hesitated and then said, "My mom always says I took after my father. I never knew him, but she told me he touched people without even trying."

"I'm sure."

"But please don't judge her. She has a good soul. She needs . . . we all need. . ." She lowered her head and turned away.

"Are you going?" Madero asked.

"I'm sorry, for pestering you, sir. I won't do it again. Thank you for Diablo." She walked toward the door.

"I'll miss you."

That made her pause, and then she suddenly spun back toward Madero and grabbed his right hand. "Thank you for caring about us," she said, holding on and not letting go. "Thank you for coming back."

"And in the rain, too," he said with a smile.

With that, she startled Madero by squeezing his hand even more tightly.

"Yes," she barely managed to say. "In the rain."

Madero gently laid his other hand on top of her head. "What's wrong, Blackie?"

"Nothing," she whispered, still gripping his fingers. "Nothing in all the world."

11 THE RUN OF THE TABLE

Gunfire roared across the grasslands, and Madero twisted in his saddle to find its source. Centers of sound were always maddeningly difficult to locate anywhere in the Sonoran Desert, whether in the lowest creosote flats or here in the high grasses. Madero glanced at Buddy's ears and smiled. Horses never made a mistake. Madero rolled Buddy to the right and made a kissing sound and Buddy loped off. Unlike ill-bred ranch horses, which loped with all the fluidity of a buckboard on square wheels, the Texas Ranger bay devoured the ground with a supple canter that would have made English fox hunters gape with envy.

Soon man and mount were approaching a ridge that dropped off gradually at the north end of the Callaghan ranch.

"Ho," Madero said so faintly that only a horse that was listening would hear it.

Buddy stopped as if he had hit a wall. Madero scratched his horse's neck, and then grabbed his carbine and slid from the saddle. He looped the reins loosely around the horn, and the horse stayed as still as if he were tied to a picket pin.

Madero wiped away the sweat running down into his eyes and moved silently forward. He dropped to one knee when he reached the soft crest.

Below him, part of the High C wire had been snapped and flattened during the storm by a branch flying off a dead mesquite. Five head from the High C had wandered through the gap onto the Barbicane spread. Apparently Holden had been about to drive them back when two riders appeared from the Bar Double B and one of them fired a shot over his head.

Madero immediately recognized Kelliride by his size. He looked absurd on his small mount. The other man was the gaunt scavenger who had been sitting at the table with the rest of them at dinner. Both were holding carbines.

The three men were too far away for Madero to hear what they were saying, but the newly minted range detectives were obviously making life less than cheerful for the old cowhand from the Four Sixes. Their expressions and the tone of their jabbering clearly showed that they were enjoying it.

While the lean man was badgering Holden, Kelliride drifted around behind him. Now Holden had to keep looking back and forth to keep both men alternately in view.

Madero sighed. These cowboys, what children. Madero turned and whistled, and Buddy immediately came up. Madero slid his Winchester into the scabbard and mounted. He squeezed Buddy lightly, and horse and rider descended the grade at a right angle to the three men below.

Kelliride's horse turned its head toward the intruders and alerted its rider.

"Raise that carbine any higher, big man, and you'll be looking God in the face." Madero's voice was a gentle as a priest's. "What's the confusion?"

"Trespass," Kelliride answered with all the confidence of a crap shooter with loaded dice.

"I'm sure this fool is grievously sorry for that," Madero said and turned to Holden. "Aren't you?"

"Oh, yes," Holden said, although he seemed confused at Madero's play.

"Now," Madero said to Kelliride, "this old pod from Texas is going to head these cattle up and drive them back up the hill."

As it always did in moments of crisis, Madero's revolver on his right hip suddenly felt warm to him against his skin, as though its own dark pulse had just quickened.

"You can tell Barbicane you earned your pay," Madero said. "And all of us can live to see the moonrise."

Kelliride looked to his comrade, who nodded yes and slid his carbine into his saddle scabbard. Kelliride did likewise. Then the two men rode off.

Madero watched them until they disappeared down into a distant wash.

"Thank you," Holden said to Madero.

"Texans," Madero answered in exasperation. "It's a mystery that any of you live long enough to reproduce."

The two of them began driving the cattle back to High C land.

"When I went to meet Kathleen in town this morning, she told me about the dinner last night. She said you're old friends."

"Don't come out here alone again. Barbicane's louts are looking for excuses for trouble."

"I realize that."

"Then you should know better. I don't like having to confirm fools in their foolishness. And I hate having to bury them."

"Fair enough."

"My guess is that those shining knights are trying to push Stone more than Kathy, but you were raw meat out there. Too tempting for them just to walk away from."

They rode in silence for a while.

"Are you all right?" Holden said as Madero used his silver bandana to mop his wet face.

"A little under the weather."

"The weather is perfect."

Madero said nothing.

"Do you mind if I ask why you came back to Arizona?"

"I don't mind."

Holden waited for a bit and then laughed and shook his head. "Why do you always take me literally?"

"Texican, you're lucky I take you at all."

"So why were you up here today?"

"Does it matter now?"

"I guess not."

"Do you gamble?"

"Not very much."

"Before I roll the dice, I always like to bring my eyes down to the level of the baize. To check the lie of the table. This one doesn't run true. I don't like it."

Both men remained quiet for a while, and then Holden said, "Where are you headed now?"

"To see Kelly in San Miguel."

"Are you here to stay?"

"None of us is here to stay."

Holden's sigh was audible even above the hoofbeats. "Well, you've made Collie very happy. This morning she was rattling like a telegraph key."

The obvious sincerity in Holden's voice caused Madero to turn toward him. "You mean that, don't you?"

"Of course I mean it."

Madero turned to the front again and continued scanning the horizon. "Sad is the man who can't make at least one child happy."

"Or at least one young woman."

"Yes," Madero said, his voice trailing off. "At least one."

12 REBIRTH

A hatless blood-spattered boy of about sixteen was leading his horse to a trough when Madero and Buddy swung into the top of Angel Street. The boy seemed vaguely familiar, and Madero watched him for a bit and then followed him to the water.

"Your father must be very proud of you."

The boy gave a start and spun around and looked up at Madero. "Sir?"

"A man who takes care of his horse before he takes care of himself is a true man."

Had Madero laid the riches of the pagan East before the boy on a silken carpet he could not have looked more grateful.

"Thank you, sir."

The boy's split lower lip was as swollen as a rotten plum and was dripping blood onto his plaid shirt.

Madero pulled off his bandana. "Here."

The boy took it and pressed it gently against his mouth.

Madero knew the worst was still to come, as well-meaning buffoons would begin asking the boy, "What happened?"

Every male on earth could see what had happened.

Madero ran a forearm across his brow to sop up the sweat before it ran down and burned his eyes. "Is there a doctor in this town?"

"Yes, sir. Doc Briscoe. He's a great doctor. He fought in the war."

"What war?"

The boy looked surprised. "The War of the Rebellion."

"Which rebellion?"

"You don't know? Really?"

"My country is the land of rebellions."

"The Southern Rebellion."

"Mount up and show me where his office is."

Madero followed the boy toward the edge of San Miguel to a modest adobe house near Mater Dolorosa Church. A small shingle hung outside the house.

"In there, sir."

"Come with me," Madero said, dismounting. He had no halter and lead, and, since he tried never to tie a horse by the reins, he dropped them in front of Buddy.

"Stay," he said, giving the reins a gentle tug as they hung to the ground.

"Do you always ground tie your horse, sir?" the boy asked as he dismounted.

"Not always. Let's go inside."

When Madero stepped away, Buddy snatched the hat from his head.

Madero sighed and smiled at him. "Always the clown."

Buddy looked enormously pleased with himself with the brim between his teeth.

Madero turned to the boy. "Do you know horses can smile?"

The boy shook his head seriously. "No, sir."

"They do it with their eyes. Look at him. All right, *pícaro*, let me have that."

Buddy obliged and Madero slid the hat from his mouth and stroked his forehead. Then he turned and led the boy up to the door.

A stout, pleasant-faced woman answered his knock.

"Good afternoon," Madero said and removed his hat. "Can the doctor see my young friend here?"

"Oh, Willard, what happened? Come on in."

Madero followed the woman and the boy through the living area and into the doctor's consulting room in the back of the house.

"Mrs. Briscoe?" Madero asked.

"Yes, sir," she said, glancing at the pistol tucked into the sash at his hip. "And you?"

"Just a stranger who happened by."

The room was furnished with a leather-covered examination table and a large glass-fronted cabinet filled with all the potions and tinctures required of the modern medico.

"Is the doctor in?"

"He is," said a voice from the doorway.

Madero turned away from the cabinet of concoctions.

A tall, white-haired man had come in. For a moment he stared at Madero with a surprising intensity and then looked at Willard and shook his head. "Another street brawl?"

"Yes, sir."

"Let me have this," Mrs. Briscoe said, taking the bloody bandana from the boy. "I'll soak it before it stains." She turned and left the room.

"Doesn't look like it needs a stitch, Will," the doctor said. "Just a washing with some carbolic."

The boy winced at the mention of that and climbed onto the examination table, but when the doctor went to work the boy made no sound, although tears of pain ran down his face.

"And you are, sir?" the doctor asked without taking his attention from his cleansing of the wound.

"Mateo Madero."

"Colleen's friend?"

"I see there's no privacy in this town."

The doctor laughed. "There's no privacy in any town. Please have a seat."

The doctor finished with the boy's colorful lip and began cleaning off the blood that had caked on his chin.

"Doc, I don't have any money with me but — ."

"That's all right, Willard."

"I'll pay you for your trouble, doctor," Madero said.

"Very kind of you, sir," Briscoe answered, "but I'll do this *pro bono*. That means — ."

"I know what it means."

Briscoe looked sharply at Madero. "Yes, indeed."

Mrs. Briscoe came in with two small bowls and spoons. "I was just making some vanilla ice cream," she said with a smile that could have melted it. She handed a bowl to the boy and to Madero.

"This should soothe that lip a little," she said.

"Yes, ma'am!"

Madero smiled at the boy as he ate. "Willard is it?"

"Yes, sir. . . . My mom used to call me Buck. But when she died, my father went back to calling me Willard. I hate it."

"I didn't know that," Mrs. Briscoe said. "I'm sorry."

He looked down at his bowl and went back to eating in silence.

"Last name?" Madero asked.

"Stone, sir."

"Harlo's son?"

"Yes, sir. Do you know my father?"

"Passingly. Buck Stone—I like it. How did you get that?"

"When I was little, my mom gave me a buckskin shirt that I never wanted to take off. So she called me Buck."

"Then Buck it should stay," Madero said as he finished his ice cream.

The boy smiled at him, and something whispered to Madero that those smiles were rare.

"The Leek brothers call me Bleeder or Willie because they know I hate those names. They were doing it today."

"And hence the lower lip," Doc Briscoe said.

"Yes, sir. They're bigger than me, but I don't care. And some stranger was goading them on."

"Who, Wil—Buck?" Mrs. Briscoe asked.

"I don't know, ma'am. He had an ugly scar on the side of his head. When he heard one of them say my last name, he told them he'd pay them to give me a good thrashing."

Mrs. Briscoe looked at her husband. "Why on earth would anyone do that?"

"Because of who Buck's father is," Madero said. "And because the man with the scar is a twisted savage."

"We need a sheriff in this town," Doc Briscoe said. "I'm going to talk with some of the ranchers."

Madero set down his bowl and stood up. He felt a shiver coming on.

"Please relax a spell," the doctor said.

The boy finished his ice cream and handed Mrs. Briscoe the empty bowl.

She looked at both men and then said, "Come with me, Buck. We'll see if the bandana is done soaking."

The boy stood up and followed her out of the room.

"It was kind of you to bring him here." Doc Briscoe sat in a wicker chair across from Madero.

"A small gesture."

"That's the kind that matters most. Anyone will pull someone out of the way of a stampeding herd. But a battered and lonely boy. . . . That's something special."

Madero said nothing.

Briscoe folded his arms and crossed his legs. "How long have you had malaria?"

Madero smiled. "You not only look the part, you *are* the part. A little over ten years."

"You should go home now and rest before the shakes knock you out of the saddle."

"Unfortunately, doctor, I don't have that luxury. People are depending on me."

Briscoe studied him closely. "Well, I trust it's for something important."

"It's what people have always depended on me for," Madero said as he stood and tensed his body against the shivering.

"And what is that?"

"Everything."

Mrs. Briscoe and Buck came back in, and the boy was smiling despite the pain it must have caused him. He handed Madero the bandana.

"It's damp but it's clean."

"I see that," Madero said. "But I think you should keep it. A memento of the day that Buck was reborn."

The boy grinned. "Thank you!"

Madero reached for his hat.

"Thank you for bringing Will in today," Mrs. Briscoe said.

Madero put on his hat and winked at her.

Mrs. Briscoe might have had silver hair tied into a proper bun, but now she blushed warmly enough to melt snow on the Huachucas, had there been any.

"I'm privileged to know you, sir," Doc Briscoe said as he stood up.

Madero ignored that and stared out the window toward the back of the church. "I've never seen a doctor's office so close to a graveyard. Must be a great timesaver for you."

Mrs. Briscoe pressed a hand to her lips to hide a smile, but the doctor laughed with gusto.

13 BY THE BARREL

"Not exactly the disciples of Christ, are they?" Kelly said.

"No." Madero set down the last of the folders on the sofa cushion beside him in the living quarters behind *The Clarion*. "Now tell me about Sutorius."

"Is that helping?" Kelly asked, gesturing to the blanket around Madero's shoulders.

"Not much. It doesn't matter. Later tonight I'll be burning up."

"Do you mind if I ask where you're staying?"

"The old stable manager's quarters at Don Luis's barn."

"If you can't afford something better, I can—."

"There *is* nothing better. It's well-furnished and comfortable. Large enough for me and small enough to be *muy acogedor*. As relaxed as a monk's cell. Perfect."

Kelly smiled. "Odd, but I don't think of you as a monk."

"Think a little harder."

"But a barn?"

"I've always preferred the company of horses to the company of men."

"But if you're not feeling—."

"Sutorius."

"Well, the Pinkertons let him go. He'd been used by them in putting down some of the strikes and labor riots around the country. But there were too many tainted juries and suborned witnesses. Not that the Pinkertons are sensitive about those sorts of things, but even they can't cover up everything. There's a story that Sutorius believed that one of his labor informants was holding out on him. Sutorius was famous for paying well, but he was ruthless if his spies didn't deliver. So he roped this one and dragged him. Shredded him like a cabbage. So the story goes. After that, Pinkerton thought he was too much of a liability."

"So they cut him loose."

"Exactly. He's an absolute fanatic about people he considers diseases infecting society. To him they're all anarchists that have to be cut out. Like a cancer."

"Any weaknesses?"

"Only his own fanaticism—if you can consider that a weakness. He has a heart of ice."

"So what are you going to do about it?"

Kelly looked puzzled. "Do about what?"

"Don't you realize what's happening here?"

"Maybe I should have you tell me," Kelly answered without attempting to conceal his annoyance.

"Today that Texican was almost goaded into trying something stupid. Later an innocent boy was beaten. If you—."

"What boy?"

"Stone's son. Craksi prodded a couple of boys into going beyond a schoolhouse taunting. It's clear that Sutorius is planning to put pepper in the grain every day until people do something foolish and he can legally strike them down. Permanently."

"I don't believe Barbicane is that kind of a man."

"The men he hired are. The tail is wagging the dog here. Never think otherwise."

"What about Craksi and Harlo's boy?"

"He'll answer for what he did."

Kelly turned away and said nothing.

"And then there's Kathy," Madero said. "Are you the gentleman in her life?"

"That's a personal question."

"Then give me a personal answer. I don't have time for nonsense."

"I'm not certain. Before yesterday I'd have said no." He turned back to Madero. "But the expression in her eyes when I walked into the cantina touched me in a way I never expected."

"I know," Madero said quietly.

"You know from experience, don't you?"

"We were very young. An old *vaquero* saw us walking together once, and later he laughed and sighed and said to me,

'*Los hombres de piel trigueña siempre tienen debilidad por las pelirrojas.*' It means that dark men always have a weakness for redheads."

Kelly smiled. "Who can blame them?"

"And throw in the fair skin and freckles *y estamos perdidos* – and we're just lost."

"And it was obvious when she looked at the dark man last night that she feels the reverse version of that."

"But that was long ago. Don't concern yourself with it now."

"All right. You asked me what I was going to do. . ."

"And?"

"I don't know yet."

Madero shook his head. "God save us from reasonable men."

"What does that mean?"

"Are you just going to wait for Sutorius to act?"

"What else can I do?"

"Do you know why people like Sutorius can cow most of the human race? It's because of people like you who like to congratulate themselves that they're fair. Who are always trying to be reasonable and sensible."

"That's a fault?"

"The most pathetic one since Eve listened to the snake instead of stepping on its head. If someone punched you in the face what would you do?"

"What do you think I'd do? I'd punch him back."

"Exactly."

"What would you do?"

"I'd strike him *before* he struck me. And if I failed and he hit me first, I'd make certain that by the time I was done with him he could never bring himself to look in a mirror again."

"Not exactly a balanced response."

"I'm not interested in that."

"Do you think that's fair?"

"It's final."

"I don't like extremes. I think Aristotle was wiser than both of us when he counseled moderation in all things."

Madero's laugh was as harsh as bones in a meat grinder. "It's because he was never in a gun battle."

That seemed to bring Kelly up short.

"Beware the moderate man," Madero said. "The most malleable of dupes. The moderate are never truly sure, so they spend their lives searching for excuses to betray."

"That's a frightening thought."

"Yes."

"Well, what do you expect from me here?"

Madero said nothing. He knew that Kelly's own question would eat at him only if allowed the corrosive effect of silence.

"Well?" Kelly said finally.

"You're asking Madero of Sonora to be your conscience?"

Kelly laughed softly. "I guess it sounds crazy, doesn't it?"

"Do you have a file on me?"

"I do."

"Is the person in that file the man you want to be the *ángel de la guarda* of your soul?"

"Possibly. At least the guardian of those I care about."

"Then take my advice."

"And do what?"

"Use the power in your hands."

"What kind of power?"

"Isn't there a saying about someone who buys ink by the barrel?"

Kelly laughed. "I've been reminded of that lately."

"Hit them every morning with a banner headline before they even have a foot in the stirrup. Don't wait. Hit them hard. The problem with good people is that they always wait for the bad people to act first. That's insane. Never let them take the offensive. *You* act—make them *react*."

"You make it sound easy."

"Is anything worth doing easy? And always keep a sidearm *a mano*."

"All right. I'll consider it."

"And in return for my sage advice you can do a favor for me. Instruct a boy in how to box. I've heard you have skill there."

"Some. But I suspect you could teach him how to defend himself better than I."

"The things I could teach him no young boy should know."

Kelly got up from his chair and went to a sideboard and came back with two glasses and a bottle of Jameson.

"This is better than blankets," Kelly said and poured Madero three fingers of the golden elixir.

"Thank you."

"Madero, why are you here?" Kelly asked as he sat back down in his chair.

"Everyone has to be somewhere."

Both men sipped their whiskey and remained silent for a while.

"This might surprise you," Kelly said, "but for an Irishman I'm not a very good drinker. Yet for some reason tonight I'd like to get full as a tick."

"I understand. It's hard being a watchdog over the vulnerable."

"The voice of experience?"

Madero studied Kelly's eyes and liked what he saw. "You've read my file."

"But is it accurate?"

"Now how could I know that?"

"Would you like to read it?"

"What for?"

"To look for errors. To correct it."

"Why would that matter to me?"

"It would to most men."

Madero smiled. "Do I have to tell you . . . ?"

"That you're not most men?"

Madero raised his glass to Kelly and then took a sip.

"I've read it seven times," Kelly said.

"What on earth for?"

"I'm a writer. I thought—."

"You're not a writer. You're a journalist."

"You know, for a man whose first language isn't English, you're pretty damn smooth."

"I've always lived in two worlds," Madero said seriously.

"The man in that file would make a grand subject for a book."

Madero decided to remain quiet rather than to tell Kelly that the thought appalled him.

"I'd be willing to change your name. . . ."

"Why would I care?"

"Well, I thought that maybe—."

"I'm immune to fame," Madero said, staring off into a past only he could see. "And indifferent to infamy."

14 OUT OF THE DARKNESS

Collie had heard her mother crying in the night. It seemed like she had wept on and off for a week. After a night of fitful sleep, Collie finally got up just after dawn and was surprised to see Ernesto cooking breakfast for the crew.

"Neto, have you seen mom?"

"She's out with the horses." His smile was always as refreshing as a sunrise.

Collie found her mother in the corral and wielding a manure fork as if it were as powerful and mystical as Excalibur.

"Mom, it's only horse hockey."

Kathy jumped at the sound of Collie's voice. "I needed the exercise," she said and went back to her task.

Collie walked into the corral and pulled the fork from her mother and took her by the hand into the barn. She led her to an empty stall, and Collie sat on the fresh straw.

"Please tell me why you were crying."

Kathy sighed and sat Indian style on a pile of straw across from her daughter. Collie knew that by any standard of beauty her mother was near the top of the list. This morning she looked like a haggard washer woman twenty years older than she was.

"I'm sorry. I didn't think you could hear me."

"Mom, people at the Benson railhead could hear you."

Kathy looked down. "Everything just came rushing back last night."

"Mr. Madero?"

"Yes."

"You were sweethearts, weren't you?"

"Yes, before I met your father."

Collie took her mother's hands in hers. "What does it matter now? That was so long ago."

"It matters."

"Why?"

"Because of how I ended it."

"*You* ended it? Why?"

Kathy just shook her head and said nothing.

"Mom . . ."

"Because . . . oh, I can't say it."

Collie remained quiet.

"Because . . . because I was afraid of what people would say."

"About what?"

"About a Mexican." She pulled her hands from Collie's and covered her face. "God in Heaven, I disgust myself. How could I ever have felt such a thing? A girl from the Irish slums of New York? Who was I to look down on anyone or care what anyone thought?"

"But you weren't much older than I back then. The both of you weren't much more than children yourselves."

"No, that doesn't excuse it."

"But it explains it. Was he a bandit even then?"

"You know?"

"Oh, mom . . ."

Kathy leaned forward and cried against Collie's breast with an eerie softness that Collie found unsettling. She pressed her lips to the top of her mother's head. "Can I say something, mom?"

Kathy pulled back and looked up at her daughter. "You're the greatest thing that ever happened to me, Collie." She struggled to clear her throat. "Do you know that?'

Collie smiled. "Can I say something?"

Kathy kissed her on the cheek. "Tell me."

"Don't call him Matthew. No matter who his blue-eyed mother was."

Kathy smiled at her daughter through her tears. "Keira, you're so much wiser than I was at your age."

"It's because I have a wise mom."

Kathy rested her head on Collie's breast. "God must have forgiven me, because He gave me you. And yet there's still so much to forgive."

"Anyone alive around here?!" came a shout from outside.

"It sounds like Harlo," Kathy said in surprise and stood up.

They both went outside. Harlo was on his horse near the corral.

"Come in for breakfast," Kathy said and walked up to the house.

Ernesto's chorizo and eggs this morning were incendiary. As the three of them sat around the table, Harlo laughed at the enthusiasm with which Collie indulged.

"That a freckled Irish girl can devour this stuff is a miracle of nature," Harlo said. He looked at Kathy. "Thank you for inviting me."

"You caught me at a weak moment," she said, smiling.

"I couldn't sleep last night, and I've been out riding since before dawn."

"Must be catching," Kathy said.

Harlo gave her a puzzled look.

"Is something wrong?" she asked.

"I don't know. I just have an odd feeling this morning. Yesterday Willard was in a fight with the Leek boys and got a cut lip. He said that Craksi goaded those two worms. Afterward, this Mexican Madero saw Will and—."

"Stop," Kathy said. "He's not 'this Mexican.' His name is Mateo Madero and he's an old friend of mine."

Startled, Harlo hesitated and then said, "I'm sorry. He took Will to see the doc and was willing to pay for it as well. Then he took him to the merc and bought him a beautiful buckskin shirt. The kind his mother used to buy him. How do you figure that?"

After a brief silence, Collie said, "Mr. Stone, why does something nice have to be figured?"

"What did Willard say?" Kathy asked.

"He said he told Madero that his mother used to call him Buck because of the shirt he'd had—which is true. And so Madero took him to get another. And when he got home, he insisted I call him Buck again. No more Willard."

"And?" Kathy said.

"My first reaction was to consider slapping his face, but . . ." He glanced quickly at Collie with a look of embarrassment and then turned back to Kathy. "Before I could give him the back of my hand, the oddest thing flashed across my mind. I thought that if I struck him he might tell Madero . . . and just the idea of that . . . well, it scared me."

"Why on earth would it do that?" Kathy asked.

"Because *he* scares me — and there aren't many who do."

"Colleen!" Kathy snapped at her daughter, who had not been able to suppress a smile at Harlo's remark.

"That's all right," Harlo said. "I wouldn't admit this in front of just anyone. Anyway, now I have to go deal with Craksi."

"Harlo, Will doesn't need to be an orphan," Kathy said.

"Well, I can't just let this sit, can I?"

No one spoke for a long time. Then finally Collie said, "Mr. Stone, will you thank Will for bidding on Diablo for me? I'm . . . I'm sorry I misjudged him."

Harlo smiled. "I'll do that."

"How's Will now?" Kathy asked.

"He's Buck Stone for good." Harlo laughed. "I don't want to face the kind of glare Madero gave Sutorius."

Silly adults, Collie said to herself, recalling the warmth of Madero's hand on her shoulder. *You just don't understand.*

15 BATTLEFIELDS

Bert, the massively mustachioed barman who usually worked evenings at *La Luna*, had mentioned to Madero that Luis had once been an actor, and it showed.

Madero usually entered the cantina from the side door near the stable, but tonight he walked through the main entrance. The old actor certainly had mastered stage design. The massive back bar dominated, as it did in almost every saloon and cantina in the West. This dazzler glittered with three large mirrors framed by mahogany arches worthy of a Romanesque cathedral. An imposing brass statue of Bacchus lorded over the counter before the center glass, and all three mirrors were fronted by triple-tiered racks sporting an impressive selection of excellent spirits. Padded barstools added a measure of comfort not encountered everywhere, and they were widely separated so that patrons who chose to stand could do so with ample space on either side.

The manner in which everything else had been arranged also betrayed a theatrical touch never seen in the shabby saloons scattered along the border. When a patron entered here, his eye had the tendency to glide in a wide arc from left to right, as though drawn inward and around by the complementary colors of a great painting. Nearest the door against the smooth stucco wall to the left, the craps table, with its clatter and crowds, immediately sucked a visitor's attention into the action. Beyond that, the slightly less raucous world of the roulette wheel and its striking green baize layout pulled the patron's eye, and his money, farther in. After he had squinted past the countless lamps reflected in the trio of mirrors behind the bar, his gaze swept around toward the right to the faro table, usually fairly sedate, as was the semicircular blackjack table beside it. Closer to the main entrance and just past the opening in the Chinese screens sat the house poker player, back always to the partition to thwart gawkers and peeks.

A half-moon arrangement of tables for casual eating or a hand of cards was arrayed in the center of the cantina with the concave end fronting the bar. The tips of this graceful curve reached no closer than about fifteen feet of the bar rail. If a punch landed on the jaw of a roostered cowhand, the rowdy drunk naturally needed some place to fall.

Two arched openings flanked the bar. The one on the left led to a room unused except for storing a jumble of tables and chairs, but the arch to the right opened onto a modest reading room providing not simply a collection of not-too-stale periodicals but also more serious fare. Just outside the archway sprawled a five-foot-long glass cigar humidor tended by a smiling blonde-haired girl of about eighteen, should someone choose to enjoy the delights of the leaf while savoring Cervantes in the original. And the soft tobacco haze and aroma that filled the cantina was gently comforting to cowhands whose rare pleasures often included a quiet smoke in the bunkhouse or around a fire on the trail.

Madero approached the bar, and Bert already had a bottle of *El Tesoro de Rodrigo* ready for him.

"*Gracias*," Madero said as Bert poured.

Madero turned his gaze toward the gamblers as he sipped his tequila. With seeming indifference, he watched the players at the gaming tables like someone just enjoying the show. After about fifteen minutes of this nonchalant observation, he called down the bar to Bert. "Don Luis?"

Bert pointed and Madero turned around as Luis came up behind him.

Madero nodded. "This rum hole isn't half-bad."

"Praise indeed," Luis said, raising an eyebrow. "Are you all right? You look worn out."

"I was a cinder last night, but the fires are banked for now." He nodded toward the Chinese screens. "I especially like the way the music from the piano in the dining room softens the yelps of these cowpunchers."

"Need I tell you that this is not an accident?"

Madero smiled. "You need not." He pointed toward the room through the archway to the left of the bar. "Have you ever thought of making that into a billiard room instead of just a storage bin? It would add something special to the place."

"So I suppose you've been to the Congress in Tucson."

"Everyone has been to the Congress in Tucson."

"Another person recently made the same suggestion you did. A friend of yours." He smiled. "Señor Kelliride."

"Ah, now there's a name of *distinción*."

"He told Bert that he's a master with the pool cue."

"I'll have to verify that sometime."

"In fact, there's a table waiting for me at Campbell and Hatch's in Tombstone. It's an older one they want to sell. They're holding it for me until I save up enough money."

"And I thought you lived on velvet. Looks to me like the takings here are good."

"They are, but I haven't paid off *La Luna* yet."

"Who owns the mortgage?"

"Señor Barbicane."

"Oh, that's perfect," Madero said, laughing. "How much do you still owe on it?"

"Isn't that a personal question?"

"Life is short."

"A little less than two thousand."

Madero sipped his tequila for a bit and then turned to the room behind him and gestured with his glass. "Are all these dealers under contract to you for a percentage?"

"*Sí.*"

"Who do you have to keep an eye on the gamblers?"

"Keep an eye on?"

"*Vigilar.*"

"No one but me."

"And do you know enough about this sort of thing to do that?"

Luis grinned almost boyishly. "No. Why?"

"There's a cheat at the poker table."

"Who?" Luis asked in surprise as he turned around.

"The lean one in the gray suit."

Luis studied a once-handsome gambler with a neat gray beard. In his slightly worn clothes, he seemed as if his best days were past. "Are you certain?"

Madero gave Luis a look that no man ever wanted to see.

"I'm sorry," Luis said. "I just don't want to risk accusing falsely."

"He's called Peeker Tweed. He travels the circuit. I saw him thrown out of the Bird Cage in Tombstone about five years ago. He can't walk down Allen Street now without being recognized. So he slides into the smaller saloons and cantinas where nobody is likely to know him. Then he sucks their blood like a kissing bug."

"Does he know you?"

"Yes."

"And does he always cheat?"

"Nobody *always* cheats."

Luis watched the man carefully. "Then how do you know he's cheating now?"

"What caught my eye first is his pile of chips. Lucky night for him. Then I realized who he was, so I watched him for a while. When the deal rotates to him, he always plays stud. Nothing necessarily odd in that, but it bears watching when a player always chooses the same game." Madero sipped his tequila. "He gets the next deal, so pay attention."

When the hand was finished, Tweed took the deck and called five card stud.

Luis turned to Madero.

"Don't look at me. Watch the table."

Play commenced, and the house dealer, a young sandy-haired man immediately to the left of Tweed, tossed in a chip. One of the other four gamblers dropped, but the other three saw his bet.

Three of the four players stayed to the last card, but Tweed dropped and the house man won a modest pot.

"Did he cheat that time?" Luis asked.

"Like the professional that he is, but sometimes the cards just aren't there, so he dropped."

"What didn't I notice?"

"Did you see how often he checked his hole card? Do you think his memory is that bad?"

"I didn't see that at all."

"You saw it, but you didn't comprehend it. And you wouldn't—unless you'd spent too much of your youth in gambling hells."

Luis looked back toward the table.

"We'll wait until he gets the deal again," Madero said. "Pay attention and learn why they call him Peeker Tweed."

The house dealer won two of the next three hands, and then the deal came back to Tweed. He called five card stud again and dealt five hole cards. Everyone checked his own, and then he dealt five cards face up.

The house man to Tweed's left placed a sizable bet, and the other three players paid to stay. The man in gray seemed indecisive.

"Watch his left hand," Madero said. "See how sloppy he's holding the deck. Amateur card players do that all the time. But he's no amateur."

With his hand wrapped casually around the bottom of the deck, he let his wrist rotate carelessly so that now the top of the deck was facing down toward the table.

"Now he'll check his hole card again. I guess he forgot what it was. Watch the thumb of his left hand."

In a move undetectable to anyone not looking for it, he pressed his thumb against the deck and the top card slid a fraction of an inch to the side until the corner pressed against his forefinger wrapped around the pack. The tip of the card curled against his finger and bellied infinitesimally, flashing the index to him for an instant.

"Now he knows what the next card is and whether or not it'll improve that player's hand. Checking his hole card gave him the excuse to look down."

Tweed shook his head and dropped out.

Madero smiled, because the next card paired the king the house dealer already had showing.

"He didn't want to go up against a pair of kings right at the beginning. He knows that more players lose money at stud in chasing big pairs than anything else."

Luis looked as concerned as a man seeing his barn burn down.

"This kind of thing happens all the time. The cheat sat himself to the right of your dealer because he figured your man would probably be the best player at the table. The man to beat. His cards were the ones that would matter most. Because the cheat is to his right, your man's cards were the ones he'd get to peek at while he acted as if he was deciding to stay or drop."

"It sounds so simple."

"Only in theory. Not so easy to pull off. But your dealer is really too young to be a house man."

"His name is Terry. He wanted the job so bad that I gave him a chance."

"He hasn't seen enough. And this would never have worked years ago, but when they put indexes on cards back in the seventies, they did all the cheats a favor."

Luis took a long deep breath. "I've never had this problem before."

"Yes you have. You just haven't noticed it."

Luis had taken only a single step forward before Madero grabbed his elbow.

"No."

"Why not?" Luis asked.

"He's heeled. Count on it. He's known to have killed two men. One with a knife, the other with a derringer blast to the face. There's another story that he was caught cheating in Bisbee once and took a saloon girl hostage to get out of the place. I don't know if that's true. Supposedly she was never seen again."

Luis studied Tweed closely.

"You're unarmed, aren't you?" Madero asked.

"Yes." He glanced at Madero's hip. "But so are you."

"I can afford it."

"But this is my cantina." Luis turned and strode across the room to the poker table.

Like all seasoned card players, the gambler sensed Luis behind him long before he got there. He turned in his chair.

As Luis spoke softly to Tweed, he bent down toward him, putting himself in a foolishly vulnerable position. When he was finished speaking, he straightened and stepped back, giving the man the opportunity to stand and leave.

Tweed stood slowly and with a surprising grace. He had obviously done this many times before. He began talking to Luis and gesturing with his left hand as his right slid ever so innocently into his coat pocket.

Madero flipped his hat up and let it fall down his back by its string. He then took a casual step away from the bar. With two fingers, he brushed the bottle of *El Tesoro* over the edge, and it shattered against the brass bar rail and startled everyone.

For an instant, Tweed's attention was diverted and he glanced past Luis's shoulder in Madero's direction and then again at Luis. Suddenly his eyes shot back toward Madero.

The man's confident expression faded like ocotillo leaves in the June sun. He studied Madero closely, as if to be sure.

"Another time, perhaps," Madero could just barely hear him say to Luis.

Then he turned and took his hat and left the cantina without looking back. His winnings were still on the table.

"I'll get that," Bert said when Madero bent down to pick up the shards of glass. The barman's grin was as wide as a faro table while he swept up the pieces of the broken bottle.

"I'll get you another," Bert said as he took away the slivers and chunks and allowed the sawdust to absorb the soul of the agave.

Madero turned away from the room toward the bar, and Bert came back with another bottle and also handed him a fine Tuscan cheroot that he got from the girl at the humidor.

Madero struck a match from the ceramic holder and lit up an exceptional smoke. "Is she your daughter?"

"Who? Sally?"

"Is that her name?"

"Yes, but she's not my daughter." He reached for a bar rag.

"Niece?"

"No."

"But you wish she was."

Bert looked sharply at Madero. "Why do you say that?"

Madero smiled. "It's all over your face like a coat of paint. Though I'm sure it runs deeper."

"All of Sally's family are dead. She had no way to earn a living . . . honorably. So Don Luis gave her a job here." Bert gazed down the bar at her and this time made no attempt to conceal his fatherly affection. "She's a fine girl. And because of Don Luis she's the best paid cigar seller in Arizona. I look in on her when she needs anything. She doesn't have anyone else to watch over her."

"You're a good man, Bert."

The barman shrugged, but Madero could see the caring in the old bachelor's eyes.

"*Bien*, that was interesting," Luis said as he returned to the bar. "I've never had a man run from the sight of me before."

"We all have talents that would startle the world — if only we choose to use them."

Bert was about to say something, but Madero frowned at him and the barman quickly went to rearranging some bottles on the racks in front of the mirrors.

"He did threaten, though, to come back for his winnings."

"Then he will. I'd have handled it differently."

"How?"

"I'd have asked the other players how much they thought they'd lost to him and I'd have taken their word for it. Then I'd have divided up Tweed's money accordingly and given him what was left and shown him the door."

"That's all?"

"Of course that's not all. I'd have told him that if his face ever showed in my doorway again, I'd slap him down like a dog in the street."

Luis sighed and shook his head. "Such is not my manner."

"I'm not talking about manner. I'm talking about survival."

After a pause, Luis said, "Mateo, I have a proposition to make. . . ."

"Words never spoken without the threat of doom lurking in the shadows."

"*¡Por Dios!* You have such a strange mind."

"If you only knew."

Luis laughed. "Well, if I knew, I suppose I wouldn't ask."

"Astonish me."

"May I hire you to 'keep an eye on' the gambling here?"

"No, you may not, but I'll do it in return for the cozy quarters you've given me." He held up his cheroot. "And for free choice of these fine Italian cigars."

"Thank you," Luis said with a smile.

Madero saw Luis's gaze slip past him and his expression change. Madero turned around.

Sutorius and Craksi had just come in and were crossing the gambling floor toward the entrance to the dining room. No weapon was obvious on Sutorius, but Craksi was wearing a shoulder holster holding a Schofield revolver.

Madero smiled and gestured with his cheroot. "Now there's a pair to draw to."

"I've thought of making my patrons check their firearms at the bar. Perhaps I should start now."

"Why?"

"In Tombstone, firearms aren't allowed within town limits unless they're checked."

"When you go to pick up the billiard table, make a side trip to Boot Hill and ask the innocent dead who were shot down unarmed how it helped *them*."

Luis looked exasperated. "Do you have an answer for everything?"

"Everything that matters."

Madero relaxed against the wall in the shadows outside *La Luna* and smoked as he gazed down Angel Street. A short and violent thunderstorm in the late afternoon had cooled the day, and now a pleasant moist breeze blew through town.

Even on a Saturday night, San Miguel seemed at ease. The saloons were no noisier than they needed to be, and no drunken cowhands were looking for trouble.

San Miguel was a family community of ranchers and merchants, unlike the silver fiefdoms and gold-glutted boomtowns that had erupted across the West over the previous twenty years. In those already legendary haunts, pleasures of the most suspect sort could be sampled with no more effort than reaching out and taking. And what sometimes began as a single audacious sip of a hidden thrill often led to more captivating sins and, occasionally, to unpardonable crimes.

Yet the fleshpots of the silver kings could endure only until the veins played out. Those mining bonanzas were the West's meteors, flaming and dying even before one's eye could follow them to the horizon.

Here, in San Miguel, one found real permanence. Madero could see that this was intended to be a place with roots, where people fully expected their children's children to grow and thrive and carry on the family name. And even if one had no kin, here one could eat well, play sensibly, worship quietly, and live with dignity. And, perhaps, die with it.

Yet evil men were now abroad in the land and, as with all communities with good intentions, San Miguel suffered from the vulnerability of its own virtue. Like people everywhere, its citizens nurtured the reassuring fantasy that tomorrow would inevitably be as placid as today. Who on earth could envision the prospect of an adult happily goading two boys into giving another boy a bloody beating? Lulled by a toxic tranquility, the decent rarely made allowance for the debauched, the lethal, and the depraved. Good people comprehended the bad no better than the sane ever truly understood the mad.

Madero had no doubt that Mater Dolorosa Church was filled on Sundays. Yet he also knew that, without a lawman, the *Miguelanos* required more now than simply the blessings of their *padre*. They needed a man not dulled by peace but one who had been so scarred in conflict that he had nothing left to lose. One who, as in the half-remembered poem the sisters had taught him, had reeled under the pain of adamantine chains and penal fire and was now appallingly capable of enduring anything. And, most crucially of all, capable of doing what no one else dared even to imagine.

Madero took a soft draw on his cheroot and stared serenely off into the night.

16 A DARKER HAND

After-church cocoa was turning out to be a bit different this Sunday afternoon. Collie sat with Kathy on the sofa in the living quarters of *The Clarion*, and Collie held her cup in one hand and the newspaper between the two of them in the other hand so they could read together.

GUARDIAN ANGELS IN SAN MIGUEL?

DETECTIVES CAUSE CONCERN

MIGUELANOS PUZZLED

It has come to the attention of this journal that one of our most esteemed citizens has brought four range detectives to our quiet community. The last time we checked, the range was still there, and so we are left to wonder what precisely these armed minions are planning on detecting. There has been no evidence of rustling, as far as we are aware, and the formidable Apache Manolete still resides, if perhaps a bit restively, at the agency in San Carlos. Consequently, we view this incursion of outsiders in the same manner that a cattleman regards any invading organism, namely, with wariness, annoyance, and distaste.

"Brief," Kelly said, "but I think it makes the point. It went out today. Special Sunday edition. A San Miguel first."

Collie looked at her mother but said nothing.

"Maybe a bit too pointed, don't you think, Pat?" Kathy asked.

"Cutting with a dull knife is usually even more painful. I think it's best to slice to the heart of the matter at the outset."

"Maybe you should moderate it a little. If you — why are you smiling?"

"A friend of mine — at least I think he's a friend — says that moderation is one of the world's great follies."

"Well, it's easy for him to say."

"I think not, actually. He seems to choose his words very carefully."

"Good for him."

"Mom, Mr. Kelly is talking about Mr. Madero."

Kathy turned to her in surprise. "How do you know that?"

"I just do."

"Wise daughter you have, Mrs. Callaghan," Kelly said with a smile.

"In any case, it's you I'm worried about," Kathy said.

"Thank you, but I'm more concerned about you and Collie."

The door of the outer office opened, and Kathy jumped.

For some strange reason, footsteps on the wood floor of the print room this morning sounded to Collie like hammer blows.

She quickly got up and went to the doorway before Kelly could reach it.

"Colleen!" Kathy said.

But Collie was feeling invulnerable these days.

"Good morning, Miss Colleen."

"Hi, doctor," she said cheerily.

Doctor Briscoe stepped up to the doorway. "Good morning, Pat."

"Come on in, Doc. Cocoa or coffee?"

"Coffee, thanks." He removed his gray bowler. "Hello, Mrs. Callaghan."

Collie smiled as she watched her mother try to appear relaxed.

"Good morning, doctor."

Kelly pointed to a chair and handed Briscoe a cup of coffee.

"Are you feeling all right?" the doctor asked Kathy.

"Yes, thank you."

Collie figured that if her mother were any stiffer, she would surely crack.

Briscoe took a sip of coffee. "Pat, you know more than anyone about what happens in this town, so I've come to ask you something. Are you acquainted with a man named Ian Craksi?"

"Only slightly."

"Is he a local cowhand?"

Kelly pointed to the newspaper and Collie handed it to Briscoe.

"He's one of those debutantes," Kelly said.

Collie watched Briscoe read the piece with the earnestness she could imagine in a scholar pondering a weighty text.

"I see," Briscoe said, setting the paper down. "Are you aware of what happened to the Stone boy?"

"Yes, we all are."

"Evidently Craksi was involved."

"So I gather."

"Well, this morning Craksi is convalescing in my consulting room. He came to my office late last night. Staggered more likely. Amazingly, his pistol was still in its scabbard." Briscoe set the cup down and had a look like his stomach had suddenly soured. "You know I served in the war, don't you?"

"Yes," Kelly said.

"A doctor is always shocked when he sees his first casualties, but soon it all becomes commonplace. He realizes very fast that this is simply what one has to expect from the random horror of industrialized killing." He paused and then said, "Last night I saw something far worse. In a moral sense, I mean. I'd never seen anything like it before—and, God knows, I thought I'd seen everything."

Kelly stood up. "Let me warm that," he said and took Briscoe's coffee cup.

He went to the sideboard and added a shot of Jameson and returned it to the doctor.

Briscoe sipped and savored it for a moment. "Craksi had been beaten. He said he couldn't see his attacker in the dark, but it's obvious that Harlo tracked Craksi down and took his revenge. It wasn't nearly as bad as the shredding I saw come off the battlefield, and yet I couldn't sleep afterward. He has no broken bones as far as I can tell, and nothing was touched but his face. But this wasn't a brawl. It was a scientific hammering.

Every blow just screamed two purposes, to cause the most pain and the greatest disfigurement. Which means the maximum amount of humiliation. Last night Craksi looked terrible. This morning he's indescribable."

After a long silence, Kelly said, "I witnessed many ugly things in my days as a detective. Sometimes people get carried away."

"No, that's not the case here. This was no blind fury. Not rage, but wrath. A frightful and unstoppable reckoning."

"Good Lord," Kathy said. "Is he mutilated?"

"The wounds might heal, but the helplessness and horror of it Craksi carries to his grave."

Collie had always felt that Kelly displayed a lightness of touch, no matter what the circumstances, that was very attractive. Now, though, she studied a face that was more pensive and serious than she had ever seen it before.

"Do you think Craksi's three friends would hunt down Harlo?" Briscoe asked.

"They'll probably just write it off as Craksi being a fool. They won't be willing to bleed for it."

"I don't understand this," Briscoe said, shaking his head. "I've never thought Lawton was the kind of person to hire men like that."

"He probably isn't, but he's a naïf in these matters. Now he's let slip the dogs of war. There's no pulling them back. And the result . . . *foul deeds that smell above the earth . . . with carrion men.*"

Collie watched Kelly. He always adopted a different tone when he quoted Shakespeare, and she knew he did so only when he was most deeply moved.

A century seemed to pass, and then Briscoe finally said, "I'm still worried about revenge against Harlo, Pat. Especially with those three — ."

"Why do you keep talking about Harlo?" Kelly's voice was oddly harsh. "Craksi's bloody toweling has nothing to do with Harlo."

Collie felt the hair on her arms stand up.

"What?" Briscoe asked in surprise. "Then who?"

Kelly went to the sideboard and added whiskey to his coffee and walked to the doorway and stared out across the office toward Angel Street. "A far darker hand than that."

17 PROVIDENCE

Madero sat astride Buddy and gazed across the grasslands with their new burst of green. The magical monsoons had waved their wand over the land and the Sonoran Desert's second spring surged to life.

Madero looked with pleasure at the stunning rebirth, and yet a perceptive bystander might have noticed something else in his expression. As he so often had in the past, Madero reflected on such splendor with a fierce resignation. Long ago, he had accepted the reality that, to a man without a wife or children or even any known relatives, one of the most desolate moments of life was a beautiful Sunday afternoon.

But, then, there was always Buddy. Madero reached down and scratched him on the side of the neck. Buddy's ears cocked backward for a moment at Madero's touch, and then he sighed and relaxed, for all was now right with his world.

According to Colonel Buxton, Buddy had been severely injured in a freak accident as a colt. His left mandible had been broken and he had no future but a bullet. Yet a compassionate veterinarian had said no, the animal could be spared. And so he was saved by a man of skill whom Madero thanked every day of his life. Buddy still sported a notch toward the back of his jaw where the break had been, and, if one reached underneath, scar tissue could be felt where the veterinarian had sewn him back to life.

The colonel had said that Buddy was later bought by a Texas Ranger who rode him for several years before the ranger was shot out of the saddle during an ambush. The ranger had been scouting ahead, and, when the other rangers found him, Buddy was still standing over the dead lawman like a sentinel.

Somewhere along the line, the colonel had picked up Buddy as surplus. Now the bay's more than half-ton of muscle and spirit rested beneath Madero in the greatest serenity a horse can know.

Madero was always amused by people who said they wished that horses could be like dogs. So lighthearted and loyal. What those people failed to see was that dogs could afford the risk of their devotion. After all, they were predators that had nothing to fear except bigger predators. Horses had everything to fear. And yet a horse allowed a man to climb on his back, the predator's perch where the horse could barely reach with a bite and never reach with a kick, and permit the man to direct him anywhere, even through fire and storm to the ends of the earth. A dog's allegiance was heartwarming and fun, but a horse's faith was miraculous.

However, such trust was not always given as Buddy had given to the lonely man astride him now. A horse might tolerate countless owners and yet turn an indifferent eye on all but one or two. How a true bond was forged even the finest horsemen were at a loss to say. Yet somewhere in the mists of prehistory a primeval spark had flashed and, despite eons of travail, had never died and was now reserved for only a fortunate few.

During fruitless wandering, Madero had experienced the crush of cities and their contempt for the independent man. Always that had made him ache for life back in the saddle. To him there was no doubt whatsoever that the man on horseback was the last truly sovereign soul on earth.

Madero leaned forward and rubbed Buddy between the ears. He smiled at the thought that the intellectual toil of the Mediaeval scholastics had not really been necessary. Even during his moments of greatest despair, Madero knew that the horse was the single irrefutable proof for the existence of God.

The July afternoon furnace was now roaring at full blast, so Madero laid a rein against Buddy's neck and they turned about and headed back to San Miguel.

At the stable, Madero unsaddled him and tied him near the pump and trough. After giving him a drink and a bath and a rubdown, Madero hitched him next to the stable to dry in the shade. Only then did he tend to himself.

It impressed Madero that *La Luna* was the only saloon in San Miguel that closed on Sundays. The dining room remained opened for any wayfarers needing a meal, but Luis was very particular about observing the Lord's Day with regard to drinking and gambling.

Madero entered the cantina from the street. The doors had been opened to air the place out, but only a few of the lamps were lit.

Bert was behind the bar straightening and organizing things, as he always seemed to be. Luis had told Madero that he was grateful to have Bert. The barman was one of those unmarried middle-aged men wed to his job and who performed it with missionary zeal. Even on his day off, as Sunday always was, he would be here, for he truly had no other place to be. Nor, evidently, did he desire one.

Madero walked around the room to look things over, including inspecting the craps table for any wear marks or irregularities and checking for any wobble in the roulette wheel. All was well. He then took a seat in the shadows. To him there was something soothing about an empty cantina. The subdued lighting imparted to *La Luna* the aura of a quiet sanctuary, befitting the soft arcs of its ecclesial style. The chairs were neatly upended onto the tables and the old sawdust had been swept away and the floor buffed. Polished brass gleamed under the few lit lamps, and the mirrors now reflected only Bert. For Madero, luxuriating in the ambience of a silent cantina on a Sunday evening was as restful as slipping into a darkened church on a Wednesday afternoon.

Voices from the reading room caught his attention, and he turned and peered through the half-light. Luis was sitting in the rear opposite a woman, whose back was to Madero. A small trunk lay on the floor beside her, and a carpet bag and a hat rested atop the trunk.

Luis's words were inaudible, but his tone was clear, as was the look on his face. It was the regretful expression of a potential employer who had to say no. Madero knew that Luis already had more saloon girls than he needed, since he was always the softest of soft touches. Yet there had to be a limit. Madero saw the woman avert her gaze to the hands in her lap for a moment and her upper body rise and fall in a silent sigh.

Madero signaled to Luis. He caught Madero's wave and squinted across the cantina.

Madero nodded yes.

For a moment, Luis stared at him and then turned back to the woman with a smile as genuine as the man himself. He spoke to her softly, and she reached out and grabbed both of his hands.

"Thank you, *señor*, thank you," she said loudly enough even for Madero and Bert to hear.

Luis smiled back, and Madero could see him offering to help her with the trunk. She shook her head no, and Luis bid her good evening and returned to his office behind the reading room.

She put on her hat and picked up the trunk with the carpet bag atop it and headed out through the empty cantina.

"Hello, Kaney," Madero said from the shadows.

She spun toward him with a sharp intake of breath and almost dropped the trunk.

Madero stood up.

She just gaped at him for a moment and then smiled a smile that could have melted marble.

"Set that on the floor before you drop it on your toes," Madero said.

She put down the chest and took a hesitant step forward.

"My God . . ." she whispered.

"Rather less than that."

She grabbed his right hand and squeezed it until it hurt. "It's so good to see you."

Madero removed the other chairs from atop the table.

"Relax and tell me how you happen to be here brightening my evening."

But she still just stood there staring at him.

He reached out and took the hat from her head and set it onto the table. "Kaney . . ." He pointed to a chair.

She sat down as delicately as if she thought the chair would break.

"I just can't believe it," she said with that smile that wiped a decade from her face.

"Now explain to me my good fortune," Madero said.

She rested her hand on her chin the way she had when she had first seen him. Now she seemed just to take pleasure in his gaze. "I'll never forget that night. Never. The night I misjudged you."

"Did you? I barely remember."

"Do you know that you're the only man who ever bought me dinner who didn't expect me to supply desert?"

"Well, I figured that what you'd provide would be far too rich of a diet for this poor *campesino rústico*."

"You're such a rogue!" she said, laughing.

"What happened?"

"I was fired from the Congress. I—."

"You don't need to tell me."

"No, it's all right. I struck one of the customers."

"I'm sure he deserved something even harsher."

"I'm used to men saying off-color things. . . ." She lowered her gaze to the table. "But when he touched me . . . where no one has ever touched me except my husband—well, I waled into him and cut his face with my ring like it was a piece of rotten fruit."

Madero laughed. "I wish I'd seen that!"

"Some cowhands told me later that the man was an outlaw and a mankiller. I didn't know that when I hit him."

"I doubt it would've mattered to you if you had."

"After I cut him, he threatened to hit me, but a few of the cowboys told him they'd shoot him down right there if he touched me. They told me later that his name was Cord Wilson. Tall, like you. And he was yellow looking. Like he had a diseased liver. Just horrible. Anyway, when I was fired I decided to leave Tucson. I wanted something more peaceful."

"Well, sitting at a table with me is hardly that."

She rested her chin again on her hand again. "I think you paint yourself far darker than you are."

"How did you get here?"

"In a wagon with a family traveling south. And Señor Dámaso was kind enough to hire me."

"He's a very perceptive man."

"This is such a nice place. And he even offered to give me an advance on my salary, but I can't do that."

"There's a boarding house at the end of Angel Street. Can you afford that?"

"For about a week maybe. I'll manage."

"How are you fixed?"

"Not too well. But I get by. I've always depended on Divine Providence."

Madero smiled. "You sound like Don Luis."

"I knew I liked him!"

"Have you eaten?"

"Not since this morning."

"Bert! Two steaks medium rare, *por favor.*"

"On the fire," Bert answered cheerfully and went off to the kitchen.

"Thank you," she said.

"Employees eat free."

"Do you work here?" she asked in surprise.

"In a manner of speaking."

"See? I told you — Providence."

"Well, let's eat, and then we can discuss the finer points of that."

Madero set down the trunk in the middle of his sitting room and tossed his hat onto a chair and lit some lamps.

"What a cheerful place!" Kaney said as she laid her carpet bag atop the chest.

"You can stay here until you get established. I know you won't accept any silver from me, so this will save you a rooming house bill for a while."

"But it looks like someone is already living here," she said, glancing around.

"*I* live here." Madero pointed. "There's the bedroom and the bathroom next to it."

"I don't understand. Only one bedroom?"

"How many do you need?"

She smiled. "The sofa looks comfortable enough."

"You can sleep in the bed." He took her hat. "Have a seat."

Madero saw her glance at his revolver next to Our Lady on the lyre table before she eased herself onto the sofa.

Madero sat in a chair across from her.

"Now, sir, do you really believe I'm going to evict you from your bedroom?"

"I'll sleep with Buddy. He's very mellow."

"Who's he?"

"My friend in the stable."

"Your horse? No, no, that's just silly. At least use the sofa."

"I don't want to compromise your reputation. I mean that seriously."

"I understand, Mateo, but that doesn't concern me."

"It should. What does a woman have without it?"

"I agree, but my reputation is between me and God."

Madero folded his arms and smiled at her. "There's more to you than meets the eye."

"There's more to *everyone* than meets the eye."

"All right, I'll sleep on the sofa and you can use the bedroom."

She hesitated and then said, "Why do I feel that I've just been manipulated?"

"Please don't slap me."

She tried to suppress a laugh but failed.

"I'm not brave enough to bear the shame of the Mark of Kane."

She laughed even harder now and shook her head. "You're one of a kind."

"The human race is grateful for that. I'll tell Luis about the arrangement. He's a godly man. And he also likes to know what's happening around him."

"Do you think he'll mind?"

"He has a very high opinion of womankind, but he'll be fine when I reassure him of my commitment to your honor."

Kaney smiled, but there was a tinge of seriousness to it as well. "You know, don't you, that you don't have to reassure *me* of that? I trust you. I'll always trust you."

Madero smiled but said nothing.

She smiled back.

"Why don't you get settled? Have a bath and get comfortable." He stood up.

"Mateo . . . why are you being so generous to me?"

"Should I be ungenerous?"

She just sighed.

"Believe me, it's a small gesture." He reached for his hat. "I have to go out for a bit." He stepped over to the table and slipped his pistol into the sash at his waist. "Lock the door while you're in the bath. I'll be back soon."

Angel Street had long since gone to sleep, and Madero cherished the stillness. Lightning bolts lit the heavens to the south, but the storm was too far off for thunder to be heard. Madero had always felt that the flash of lightning in a silent black sky was one of nature's most underappreciated gifts.

Madero made a point of always walking down the middle of a street after sunset. Although it did make him an obvious target for a longarm, it also helped him avoid the bludgeons of cowards lurking in backstreets and shadows.

The Clarion office was still lit, but Madero was glad to see the shades were down. He knocked gently.

"Yes?"

Kelly's muffled voice came from back in the living quarters.

"Madero."

Quick footsteps sounded across the hardwood and then the door was unlocked.

Kelly seemed genuinely happy to see him.

"A nice surprise," Kelly said. "Come on in."

Madero was pleased to see a Colt sticking out of Kelly's waistband.

They went to the living area, and Kelly took Madero's hat.

"Make yourself at ease and tell me what flavor of the bachelor's friend you'd like this quiet evening. Believe it or not, I was having some cocoa."

"What kind of Irishman are you? You're starting to kill my faith in the Celts."

"A glass of Jameson?"

"But then Blackie did tell me that you make the best cocoa in Arizona," Madero said and sat in one of the chairs. "I'll have that."

"Probably the *only* cocoa in Arizona." He went and poured some for his guest.

"Thank you," Madero said, taking the cup. "Any blowback yet from your editorial?"

"Oh, yes, quite a nice flash of powder. Barbicane stopped by with Sutorius." Kelly smiled. "Dear Lawton objected in the most frightful language."

"Even though you never mentioned him?"

"San Miguel is small enough that everyone who read it knew whom I meant."

"Any threats?"

"Only the one implied by Maart's presence. But the Happy Dutchman never said a word."

Madero smiled. "I told you that you had power."

"Remind me not to dispute you again."

"You won't need reminding." Madero looked over at the desk covered with papers. In the lamplight lay a green file. "I need a favor. May I borrow that?" He gestured with his cup.

Kelly looked toward his desk. "What?"

"The file."

"Ah ha! I knew it! You can't resist reading it."

"Don't be ridiculous."

"Then why do you want it?"

"Why not let the detective doze for a while?"

Kelly went to his desk and got the folder. "I was working on my book tonight."

"What book?"

"*Montero of Sonora, el Arcángel Oscuro.* I've changed your name."

"Oh, for God's sake."

"If you ask me not to do it, I won't finish it."

"Who am I to forbid your follies?"

They both drank in silence for a time.

"May I ask you a question?" Kelly said after a while.

"Can I stop you?"

"There's a story in that file that's . . . well, it's unsettling. . . ."

"What did you expect to find? Tales of Mediaeval knights?"

"There's a report that you killed an unarmed man."

"Only one?"

"Are there more?"

"Which one are you talking about?"

"It was over a horse."

"Ah, that one. It's true."

"Was he unarmed?"

"He had a quirt in his hand, but that's not much."

"Can you tell me about it?"

"Doesn't the file tell you?"

"I'd rather hear your version."

"My version?" Madero made no attempt to conceal his sarcasm. "Do you think it differs from the truth?"

"I didn't say that."

"It wasn't far from here. He was a freight agent abusing an exhausted horse. Beating it with a quirt. So I hit him."

"That's all?"

"That's all."

"With just your fist?"

"Just?" Madero said with a harsh laugh.

"And he died?"

"At my feet. Like a dropped bird that flew into a pane of glass." Madero sipped his cocoa.

"I assume it was an accident. You certainly didn't expect to kill him with a punch."

"Of course I did. If I hit a man, it's to kill him. There have been exceptions to that now and then, but not often."

"What do you mean? I've never heard of such a thing."

"Then you haven't heard enough."

"But what if it's a lesser situation?"

"I'm not sure I understand that."

"What if it's not a matter of life and death? An insult or something."

"Then I walk away."

"Even if it makes you look like you're afraid?"

"Why would I care about that sort of nonsense?"

"Yet the horse was different?"

140

"Certainly."

"But since when is striking a horse a capital crime?"

"It is by *my* code. Anyone who beats a horse should be killed. Struck down without mercy and left for the vultures to pick clean."

Kelly turned away.

"Am I upsetting your love for gilded romance?"

Kelly shook his head no, but his manner said yes.

After a short silence, Madero said, "I hope I'm not using up too much of your night. I have a lodger who's freshening up after a long journey. We all need privacy sometimes."

"That's fine. Is he one of the *pistoleros* mentioned in the file?"

"He?"

Kelly looked surprised. "I'm sorry."

"It's a fair mistake. She's just a friend."

"No she's not. No one is 'just' anyone to Madero. I've learned that."

"Maybe so."

"But I'd never think anything improper of you with regard to a lady."

Madero said nothing.

"And I'll make sure Collie understands that," Kelly said.

"You're a sharp one, Pinkerton man. Thank you."

Madero finished his drink and then took the folder and got his hat. "By the way, have you ever heard of an outlaw called Cord Wilson?"

Kelly thought for a bit. "The name sounds familiar, but I can't place it at the moment. Why?"

"Just a stray thought. He was a brief acquaintance of a friend of mine."

Madero had reached the doorway when Kelly called after him.

Madero turned.

Kelly hesitated and then said softly, "Craksi. . . ." He spread his arms in a silent question.

"He's still alive. If I'd have beefed him, people would have accused Harlo of murder, and that wouldn't have been fair."

"So you —."

"Let's say that he's gotten a few months off his time in Purgatory — by being able to offer up his earthly sufferings for his sins."

"And, as usual with *el Arcángel*, no trace of official jurisprudence. . . ."

"There's the law," Madero said, putting on his hat. "And then there's justice."

18 AN ABOLISHED NATURE

After visiting Kelly, Madero took his time walking back and stopped to give Buddy some attention before unlocking the door to his rooms.

"It's Madero," he said as he went in.

Kaney was just coming out of the bedroom. She was wearing a light blue dressing gown over a white nightdress and had on a pair of maroon velvet slippers. Her thick hair was still damp and hung past her shoulders.

"I polish up well, don't you think?" she said with a smile.

"You'd make a man squint at the light. And then maybe think darker thoughts, too."

She narrowed her eyes playfully. "Well, I'm just lucky that you're the altar boy I know you to be."

Madero looked away and went to the small table and laid down his pistol and the folder.

"What's wrong?" Kaney said as she came up and placed a hand on his shoulder.

"I really was an altar boy once." He turned to her. "Would you believe that?"

She stared as deeply into him as Collie had that day on the hillside. "Yes, I would."

He reached out and touched her upper arm gently. "Is there any spirit that you like—other than fake rye?"

"I have very elevated tastes, *señor*."

Madero smiled as he tossed his hat onto a rack by the door. "If you did, you certainly wouldn't be here."

"You're incorrigible, do you know that? Do you think Señor Dámaso might have some brandy?"

Madero went over to the spirits cabinet and smiled as he pulled out a bottle. "The centaur himself."

He set two tulip-shaped glasses upright on the tray and poured some of the Remy Martin for both of them.

"Do you know cognac, too?" Kaney asked. "Is there anything you don't know?"

"I've been abroad. Let's relax."

Kaney went to the sofa and sat down sideways and pulled her legs up beneath her.

Madero handed her the glass and sat with her.

"A toast," Kaney said, raising her glass. "To Providence."

They both sipped their drinks.

"I have a question," she said.

"Only one?"

"Well, I have a thousand, but let's start with this one. . . ."

"Go ahead."

"Señor Dámaso wasn't going to hire me—in fact, he turned me down outright, though I don't think he wanted to. Then I noticed that something behind me seemed to get his attention. When he looked back at me, I was hired. How do you account for that?"

"Providence."

She reached out and laid a hand on his. "That's what I'd call it, too. So now, tell me why you're so serious tonight."

Madero took another sip of cognac. "I have to explain some things to you. Things about me and about what's happening here. Your safety is involved and you have a right to know."

"Very well," she said with a smile. "I'm just mellow enough to accept anything. Like Buddy is."

"But tell me about Kaney first. You owe me something for the cognac."

"Perhaps I do." She paused and then said, "My husband and I came out here from Pennsylvania eight years ago. For a life away from the crowds and chaos of the city. For something fresh and new. He planned to work on a ranch for a while and put money away. With that and the savings we brought with us we hoped eventually to get a small place of our own. But he died from a fever a few months after we got here. I was thirty-three years old and I had no skills, and I went through our savings very fast. But I was still pretty then, so there was always some saloon owner willing to hire me to look pretty and smile at lonely men."

She turned away, and Madero stared at her perfect profile.

"What the men don't know, though," she said, "is that those women are even lonelier than the men are." She turned back to him. "Incidentally, my full name is—."

"No, don't tell me. You're Kaney, the woman in the blue dress who rested her chin on her hand and gazed at me from across a room."

Madero was startled to see tears fill her eyes. She turned quickly away.

"What's wrong?"

She shook her head sharply from side to side. For an instant she seemed almost childlike.

"I'm sorry, but when I think . . ." She hesitated and took another sip of cognac. "When I think where I was a few hours ago. Tired and dirty. No job and no home. And now . . ." She looked back at him. "I'll never forget this, Mateo. No matter what the future turns out to be. If I die tomorrow, I want you to know tonight that this moment . . . this moment right now is one of the most amazing moments of my life."

Madero smiled.

"And please," she said, laughing through her tears, "don't say that what you've done is a small gesture."

"I promise." He noticed her hands shaking. "What's wrong?"

She pressed one hand over the other until they steadied. "I'm sorry. My hands always tremble when I'm really happy. I've had that since I was a little girl. Crazy, isn't it?"

"I find it endearing," he said with a soft smile.

"Anyway, what do you want to tell me?"

Without preliminaries, Madero began with his meeting with Collie on the hillside and then described everything that had happened in the struggle of the Callaghans and the Stones with Barbicane. Kaney was a remarkably attentive listener in a way that was not simply reassuring but, also, oddly attractive. She had a way of just barely tilting her head and frowning in a focused fashion that flattered the speaker and reminded Madero of a schoolteacher engrossed in a student's recitation. Had she truly been a teacher, Madero was certain that every boy in the classroom would have been breathless.

When Madero had finished, she remained quiet for about a minute.

"I drank that too fast," she said, handing Madero her empty glass. "But who can blame me? What a story."

"I wanted you to realize that I'm not on Barbicane's Christmas list, so staying with me has its risks."

"Oh, you foolish man. As if that would matter to me."

"I was obligated to tell you in any case."

"I know, and I'm very grateful."

Madero got up and poured her some more cognac.

"I don't think that's a good idea. Another glass of that and I'm liable to doze off."

"No you won't."

Madero picked up the green folder and handed it to her along with the cognac.

"I want you to read this."

Kaney swung around and put her feet on the floor and the file onto her lap.

"It's fairly long," Madero said, "so I'll leave you alone while you make your way through it."

"No, please. Don't go. I don't want to be alone anymore tonight."

Madero sat on the sofa but all the way at the end, as though distancing himself from her because of what she was about to learn. She gave him a curious look and then opened the folder.

She picked up the top sheet and began reading it with that uniquely attentive frown. She sipped the cognac while she read. When she had finished the initial page, she set it down and looked at Madero.

"This is from the Pinkerton office?"

"It is."

"Is it true?"

"I can't say. I've never read it."

"Any of it?"

"None."

"Then why did you give it to me?"

"The Pinkertons can be sloppy sometimes, but they're not fools. Some of it must be true. You have a right to know at least a few of the things that people claim about the man beside you. Kelly wants to make a book out of it."

"Who's he?"

"An old Pinkerton hand. He owns the newspaper here now. He's a good man still trying to find his way."

She glanced down at the page. "I see." Then she again looked deeply into his eyes. After what seemed like a week, she pointed to the file and said, "I do have one question about all this. . . ."

"Feel free to ask it."

"Why on earth would I care?"

She closed the stuffed folder and placed it at the opposite end of the sofa where it could not lie between them.

"You're not any of those things. Not Mateo Madero or Matt Wood or anyone else that these strangers think you are. You're the fiercely striking man who smiled at a lonely older woman across the room and bought her dinner and escorted her to her door. If that doesn't ransom the remission of sins, then God is not merciful." She smiled. "But I know he is."

Being caught unaware was a rare experience for Madero and could be a death sentence in the life he had led. Stunned by Kaney's reply, he stood up and walked to the window. He pushed the curtains aside and gazed out as thunder rolled up from the south.

"Sounds like we'll be getting that storm after all."

He heard the clink of Kaney's glass as she set it down. "Those southern storms are always the most frightening," she said, "but great good can come out of Mexico. I know."

Madero continued staring into the darkness in silence.

"May I ask you another question?"

"I'd have thought you learned more than enough for one night," he answered without turning around.

"I learned everything but what I want to know the most."

Surprised again, Madero turned and looked at her. "For someone drinking a bandit's cognac and stealing his bed, you can be *muy impertinente*."

"No, no—being flippant isn't going to put me off this time."

"All right. What didn't I tell you?"

She patted the cushion next to her.

Madero went over and sat down beside her as the rain began to fall.

"You can tell me why you came back."

"Back?"

"The second time."

"Why not?"

"No, no, please don't answer the question with a question. You said you rode back here in a storm. That's strange, to say the least. And then you distracted me from that fact with all the other things you told me."

"Did I?"

"Oh, for God's sake!" she snapped, and apparently startled herself as much as Madero.

"Kaney, I've told you more in one evening than I've told anyone else in a lifetime. And I don't even know the reason. . . ."

"Then why can't you stop answering me with questions and tell me the rest?"

"Because if I do, I have to tell you things you'd rather not know. And once you know them, you can't un-know them."

"I'm willing to take the risk."

"That doesn't mean that *I* am."

She frowned. "I don't understand."

Madero took a long breath and let it out slowly. "Many years ago, one of my *pistoleros* said that the most baffling thing about me was that I didn't care what other people thought. About me, about life. About anything. . . ."

"And?"

"And tonight I do care. And I'll be damned if I know why."

"You care what *I* think?" she said in surprise.

"Mystifying though that might be," he answered with a sad smile.

"But don't you trust me to keep these things in my heart?"

"Kaney, Kaney, Kaney," he said, shaking his head, "of course I do. But I don't think you *want* them in your heart. Once in, they can never be expelled."

She gazed at him with the most compassionate look he had ever seen in his life.

"All right, then," she said softly. "I understand." She laid her head back on the cushion. "Let's just sit here and listen to the rain."

"Please look at me."

She turned her head toward him.

"Kaney, I have a sickness. I was convinced it wasn't curable. But then something happened on the side of a hill that gave me hope. That's why I returned."

She sat up.

"If you want to leave here when I'm done telling you, I'll give you money for a room at the boarding house. *¿De acuerdo?*"

"Agreed."

Madero stared straight ahead. "About two and a half years ago, this happened." He pointed to the scar on his cheek. "We were relieving some Arizona rustlers of their tainted silver when one of them produced a throwing knife from somewhere and hurled it into my face. One of my *pistoleros* shot him to pieces before I even slipped from the saddle. I stopped him from killing any of the others before I passed out. My men took me back to Magdalena as fast as they could. I had someone there to nurse me to health. . . ."

Kaney smiled. "I'm sure she's wonderful."

"A couple of my teeth were knocked out and my palate was cracked. The pain was indescribable. But we always had plenty of laudanum around for gunshot wounds. That's what got me through. That and my wife's love and care."

"Your wife? Did . . . I mean . . ."

"It seemed like it took a century for the pain to go away, but I had the laudanum. I drank it as if it was as virtuous as tequila." He turned toward her. "It's not."

He paused, and they both sat in silence for a while.

"What I didn't realize was that there was a noose tightening around my heart. I didn't notice it first, but Aracela did. After a while the opium starts to numb your feelings along with your body. I was taking it every day several times a day. Within a few months the poppy was beginning to strangle my soul. Normal emotions—good emotions—just get duller and duller. You can still love someone, but only in the way you love a distant memory."

"But what about Aracela? Couldn't you still love her?"

"It was horrible for her. Before you know it, the people you care about are just companions. It's as if you're seeing them

149

through a sort of emotional . . . I can't think of the word . . . *neblina*."

"A haze?"

"Yes. You still care about them, in a way. . . . But all you're really ruminating about is your next sip."

"But you don't take it anymore, do you? I haven't seen you do that."

"No, I threw it off. That's another hideous story. At that time, though, Aracela was certain I couldn't stop it, that there was no way I had the strength to do it on my own. So she gave up. She took all the laudanum."

"But couldn't you just get more?"

"No." He turned away from Kaney. "She *took* all the laudanum. And she went to sleep. She's still sleeping."

For the first time in two years, Madero felt the most terrifying emptiness a man can feel. The thought of looking at Kaney now was unbearable.

She reached up and turned his face toward her as tears welled in her eyes. "I'm sorry."

"It's murder, Kaney," he said as matter-of-factly as if he were discussing the weather. "As surely as if I'd stabbed her in the heart. Which I did."

"But that's not your fault. How could it be? She must not have been well herself — inside I mean. In her heart."

"Well, that could be true. She was always *muy volátil*, and my way of life was driving her mad. And she loved me more than I could ever have deserved. Can you imagine loving someone like that?"

"Yes," Kaney said softly.

"But when she died, I could barely even mourn. Opium is the damnedest thing. It doesn't dull just pain, it dulls everything. Even love. My soul was numb."

"What did you do then?"

"I gave up the bankrupt life I was living. Why is it that it always takes a death to make us understand life?"

Kaney said nothing.

"Then I traveled abroad. Spain, Italy. Across the Mediterranean, where I might feel at home. Have you ever tried running away from yourself? Trust me, you can't run fast enough. Even on horseback."

They sat in silence for a while, and then Kaney said, "But what does all this have to do with your coming back to Arizona? The second time I mean."

"Because of what happened the first time." Madero got up and poured himself more cognac and sat back down. "I'd gotten malaria years before, and the attacks were getting so bad that I was afraid one of them might kill me. So I decided to see Kathy one more time. We'd meant a great deal to each other long ago. . . ."

"I'm sure she was happy to see you."

"I don't believe so, although she did a fair job of trying to fake it. She was certainly surprised. And I'd heard that she had a daughter, and someone had described her to me. So when I saw the girl on the hillside, I walked over to see her. Just a happenstance, no?"

Kaney remained quiet.

"But when she looked into my eyes and spoke to me, it felt odd. And very pleasant. There was something familiar about her. If I believed in reincarnation, I'd have thought I'd known her in some previous life. And for the first time in two years, I sensed something pleasant inside myself. Can you imagine feeling nothing—and I mean goddammed *nothing*—for two years?"

Kaney shook her head no.

"I didn't know what had happened. I still don't. Collie has this kind of half-humorous way about her, sort of . . . *irónico*. . . . It just touched a part of me that I'd thought had been smothered into oblivion. And those blue eyes and freckles but with the black hair—I'd never known anyone who looked like that."

"Black Irish."

"Exactly. I'd never heard that term before. She looked like some special new creation that God had dashed off as an experiment. Or just for his personal delight."

Kaney smiled.

"And what I realized after talking with her was that there might still be a live ember inside me. And somehow—without her even knowing it—she'd breathed on it and made it glow."

"So you came back to see her again?"

"That wasn't the plan. I went to visit my *pistoleros* in Magdalena, but one night down there I had a terrible dream. Collie was lost and I was looking for her all over Mexico. Then

Arizona and Italy and Spain. But it was hopeless. I woke up shaking." He sipped his cognac. "You know how intense feelings are when you dream them. So I felt I had to come back to see if she was all right. Of course, I didn't have any reason to believe she wasn't. It was completely irrational, but that was the miracle of it. Only a man with real emotions can be irrational. Somehow, on that hillside, she'd brought the dead to life."

They sat quietly and listened to the rain for a long time.

"You should sleep now," Madero said at last. "You've had a brutal day."

"One of the most special days of my life. Thank you for sharing so much."

"I need a favor from you now. I have nightmares. Often. When I do, just stay in your room. Please don't come out. No matter what you hear. Promise me that."

She hesitated.

"Promise me."

"I promise." She reached out and touched the deep scar that sliced through his cheek. Then she smiled gently, as if in acceptance of all his imperfections. "Good night, my friend."

19 SPARKS

Collie had just finished cleaning one of the corrals out back when she heard two riders coming. Like a symphony conductor with a cherished musical score committed to memory, she knew the rhythm of every one of her own horses, and these gaits were different. She walked around front and saw Barbicane and another rider dismounting. Her mother had just come out.

The appearance of Barbicane's companion startled Collie. It took several moments for her to realize it was Craksi. His face resembled nothing so much as a purple cabbage that had caught some disease during growth and now sported lumps and twists and knobs. Worse, it looked like the vegetable had begun to go to rot, with the purple starting to yellow and even appearing greenish in irregular ugly swaths.

"What is it?" Kathy said to Lawton without a trace of warmth as she dried her hands on her apron.

He removed his hat. "Kathy, this business is getting out of hand. If you have any influence with your friends, it's time to ask them to be rational. Your friend Kelly is now slandering me in print. Are you aware of that?"

"By name?"

"By implication."

"No one lives by implication. We live in the real world."

"A man's reputation is everything. You know that."

"Then a man should devote more attention to its care."

"What does that mean?"

"You know exactly what I mean."

He scowled. "It's time to be sensible."

"Like you?"

Collie saw Barbicane's fingers tighten around his hat brim.

"Don't you agree I was reasonable with everyone at dinner?"

Kathy said nothing.

"Well? Can you honestly say I was not?"

"Can anyone be said to be reasonable with a creature like this at his side? Especially one who's too uncouth to remove his hat in the presence of ladies."

"Mr. Craksi may be excused, I think. He was brutally attacked without cause."

"What is that to me?"

"For heaven's sake, Kathy, do you think the beating is a coincidence?"

"I suspect it's a reckoning."

Craksi took a half step toward Kathy.

Collie quickly walked across the yard and stood in front of her mother.

Kathy placed her hands on Collie's shoulders and slid her to the side. Then she gazed calmly at Craksi. "There's a Mexican saying that a horse with a tail made out of hay should never stand too close to the fire."

"Your friends are escalating this beyond anything I wanted," Barbicane said. "If you strike a vesta in a powder magazine, you have to accept what comes."

"Do I, Lawton?"

Collie smiled to herself and turned to her mother. Kathy's blue eyes were as cold as an Irish rain.

Barbicane looked like he was about to burst. He turned to his horse and mounted, and Craksi did likewise.

"By the way," Lawton said, "that greaser friend of yours is—."

"If you use that word in my presence again, so help me God I'll hit you myself."

Lawton gathered his reins. "He's keeping house with a saloon girl at *La Luna*. Enough to turn a man's stomach. Or a lady's."

He pivoted his mount and rode off with Craksi right behind him.

Kathy slid her arms around Collie from behind.

Collie stared at Barbicane as he faded into the distance. "That's not true, mom, is it? He's lying."

Kathy hugged her and sighed. "I don't know."

"But he wouldn't dishonor a woman, would he?"

"Dishonor? No, he'd never do that. I'm certain of it. But . . . I don't know."

"I don't understand," Collie said, turning to look at her.

"A woman might . . . you know what I mean."

"Seduce him?"

"That's not a proper word for a young lady."

"But that's what you mean, isn't it?"

"Yes," she said in a near whisper.

"He's a very attractive man, mom. We shouldn't blame a woman who'd be tempted like that."

Kathy squeezed her even more tightly.

"Mom . . ."

"Mmm?"

"I've tried to be a better person since I've known him."

Kathy spun her around to face her. "Better? You're the best daughter anyone could hope for."

"I haven't always been the most ladylike. . . ."

Kathy smiled. "You mean my profane angel?"

"You know about that?!"

"Of course I know."

"That embarrasses me now."

"It's not important."

"I used to think that being tough meant talking like that. But Mr. Madero showed me it's not."

Kathy smiled again but said nothing.

"I've never heard him even raise his voice, but look at him. Those were tough men at that table, and he gelded them all with just a stare."

Kathy burst out laughing. "You have a way of putting things like no other girl in the world."

"I wish . . . I wish he were my brother. Then he would always be here."

"Keira, I think he'll always be here for you."

"Really? Honest?"

"Yes."

"How can you be sure?"

Collie was startled by the sudden look of anxiety on her mother's face.

Yet Kathy smiled through her unease and leaned forward and kissed Collie on the forehead. Then she turned and went back up into the house alone.

Collie quickly cleaned herself up and filled her canteen. Then she tacked up Diablo and slid her Winchester into the saddle scabbard and rode off toward San Miguel.

Several miles from the High C property, Collie heard riders. In the distance, she could make out the Leek brothers coming from the east. That struck her as odd since the only things out that way were the remains of the old mining town of Esperanza. Now the Leek boys seemed to be headed toward San Miguel.

For reasons she could not explain even to herself, she was glad she had brought her carbine.

20 A WORLD OF RUIN

"My name is Kristen Kane, doctor. Thank you for seeing me."

Dr. Briscoe closed the front door behind her and pointed to his consulting room.

"My wife will be with us in a moment if we need to —."

"I'm sorry, doctor. I wasn't clear. I'm not ill. I just came here for some medical information. I'll pay you for your time."

"I never charge for information. Let's go into the parlor."

After seeing that they were not in the consulting room, Mrs. Briscoe retreated to the kitchen and returned in a short time with a tray and tea service.

Dr. Briscoe smiled. "Mrs. Briscoe believes that hot tea is the perfect potion for a scorching summer day." He spread his arms helplessly. "It's a mystery modern science cannot explain."

Kaney removed her hat and sat on a hard maroon sofa as Mrs. Briscoe placed the tray on a table beside her.

"Sugar and milk?" Mrs. Briscoe asked.

"Just sugar, please."

Mrs. Briscoe mixed some in and handed Kaney the cup. "I'll leave you now."

"No," Kaney said. "Please stay."

Mrs. Briscoe sat beside her husband on a wicker settee.

"How may we help you, young lady?" the doctor asked.

"Señor Dámaso told me that you served in the war, doctor."

"Yes."

"May I ask if you ever treated wounded men with laudanum?"

"Far too often."

"I have a friend who was addicted to it at one time and —?"

"At one time?"

The skepticism in his voice was as heavy as human pain.

"He was able to give it up."

"That's very rare."

"But it's possible, isn't it?"

"It is."

"But it haunts him. He believes . . ." She stopped and gazed down at the cup in her hands.

"What is it, miss?" Mrs. Briscoe said.

Kaney looked up at her. "He believes it's destroyed his soul."

"Oh, no fear of that," Mrs. Briscoe said in a kindly tone. "Only Satan can do such a thing." She turned to her husband.

"Did he say that to you?" the doctor asked.

"Yes. Maybe not in those words, but that's what he meant."

"And what would you like me to do?" Dr. Briscoe asked.

"More than anything in the world I'd like you to tell me it's not true."

The doctor sighed as only a weary doctor can. "I cannot tell you that."

"Oh, Clarence," Mrs. Briscoe said.

"I don't know the man, Martha. Who can say?"

"But what did he mean?" Kaney asked. "He tried to explain it, but he might as well have been speaking Portuguese. I pretended I understood, but I'm not really sure what he was describing." She looked at Mrs. Briscoe. "How could I be sure?"

"Clarence, please," Mrs. Briscoe said.

"I have to be honest," he said to his wife and then looked at Kaney. "Isn't that so?"

"Yes."

"There's much torment that drips from the cut of the poppy. One of the first things that happens to a person is the loss of self-esteem that comes from being a slave to the juice of a plant. I've known many advanced opium habituates, and they've all said this, even though it's a fully accepted part of the pharmacopeia."

"But he doesn't take it anymore," Kaney said.

"Guilt can outlive even a century plant. Every habituate I've ever known said he felt as if he'd committed some abomination before the throne of God—that he was a hopeless pariah guilty of some secret shame."

"But if it's a medicine, that doesn't make sense."

"No, it doesn't. But the feeling is real nonetheless."

"Is there anything else?"

"Oh, my dear, there's much else."

"Then please tell me, doctor."

"Well, after long opium use, a man finds his sanity might still be intact but his intellectual faculties are diffuse. They're a beaten army. Scattered and dazed. Or, perhaps more accurately, his mind is like a big hotel filled with occupants whose room numbers have been rubbed off and whose furniture has been rearranged."

"But does that have to be?" Mrs. Briscoe asked.

"With opium nothing *has* to be. That's the terrible mystery of it. Even a man's ability to think abstractly can begin to deteriorate. And besides the intellectual fragmentation, he can find himself crushed by a sort of leaden apathy. He's flattened by an insurmountable indolence."

For a long time everyone sat in silence, until finally the doctor said, "And there are the nightmares."

"He did mention those."

"Not all habituates get them, but those who do curse their mothers for having brought them into the world. Opium seems to have a profound effect on the dreaming faculty—at least for people who already have vivid dreams."

"He told me not to come into the same room when he's having a nightmare. Last night was just horrible."

No one spoke for several long minutes. Finally Kaney said, "I just lay in bed in the dark listening. I couldn't . . ." She shook her head.

"Are you living with him?"

"Clarence!" Mrs. Briscoe said.

"I'm boarding with him."

"In the beginning, opium reveries and dreams can be luscious, but once they become fouled—and they always do—they're the most ghastly experiences on earth. Sometimes they're just simple things like ordinary nightmares. In some people, though, they're horrifying."

"How?" Kaney asked. "You can tell me."

"I have a whole shelf full of personal testimonies from habituates in my files. There are three, though, that stand out. They were my patients during the war and for years after. All three men were highly intelligent and imaginative types. One wrote poetry, and two were musicians. They suffered endlessly from nightmares of shattered worlds and universal cataclysms. Cosmic upheavals. They said that at other times their souls seemed to split in two, with the good and the evil halves battling each other for primacy. And all if it happening right in front of them. Like something from the Book of Revelation but without the balm of faith."

"But my friend doesn't use opium anymore."

"People can still experience these terrors even when they've stopped taking the drug. It differs among individuals."

Kaney hesitated and then said, "I'm afraid to ask if there's more. . . ."

"Well, I can tell you that the variations are endless. One thing, though, is feeling cold in the dream. That's common. Another. . ."

Suddenly even the calm clinician seemed reluctant to continue."

"Please go on, doctor."

"Sometimes . . . sometimes there's a desperate searching for something of importance. Or someone. The horror of it is that the dreamer can't always remember whom he's looking for. He wanders in a hopeless quest for a phantom just out of his reach. The habituates I've known who dreamt this told me that this was the greatest anguish of all."

After a brief silence, Mrs. Briscoe stood up and poured Kaney some more tea.

"But what you're describing isn't a man's soul, doctor. That can't be what he meant."

Kaney saw Dr. Briscoe glance at his wife.

"Go on, Clarence."

He looked at Kaney. "Miss Kane, the affections are damaged, too. Sometimes completely destroyed. There's an emotional deadening."

"In what way?"

"The habituate grows more and more distant even from those he loves. More apathetic and inward turning. He becomes obsessed with his gloomy inner self. It's not that he doesn't want

160

to care — he does. But his finer sensibilities are overwhelmed by a massive emotional torpor from which he can't escape."

Tears filled her eyes but she fought them back. "Please continue, doctor."

"An opium habituate of many years phrased it best when he said to me that his powers of affection were buried alive, crying without hope beneath the debris of dead tissue."

The tears rolled out now, and Kaney lowered her eyes and let the tears fall into her lap.

Mrs. Briscoe came over and sat beside her and wrapped an arm around her shoulders.

"I'm sorry," Kaney whispered.

"Do you care for this man, hon?"

Kaney looked up at her. "I barely know him."

Mrs. Briscoe brushed the tears from her cheeks. "Yes," she said gently.

"Last night after the sounds I heard, I couldn't bear it any longer. I cracked the door open and peered out into the other room. One lamp was lit, and my friend was sitting on the edge of the sofa. He was awake now and bent over with his arms resting on his legs and he was staring at the floor. Never in my life have I seen anyone who looked so lonely. So lost."

Mrs. Briscoe squeezed her tenderly. "Just always remember, hon, that Morpheus can never be even half as strong as a woman's heart."

"But I feel so weak. Today I could see that he knew that I'd heard him last night. I was about to say something this morning, but he held up a hand to stop me. Then he said, 'My sleep is my Hell. Accept it. I do.'" She peered through her tears at Mrs. Briscoe. "How on earth can I do that?"

21 QUESTIONS

Don Luis was standing next to a wagon in Angel Street in front of *La Luna* when Collie rode up. A large bulky object was strapped down inside the wagon under a gray tarp.

"I don't understand," Luis said to the hauler as he glanced down a sheet of paper in his hand.

"Like it says, paid for and ready for delivery, and here it is."

Collie had the feeling that she probably was not welcome in these discussions, and so she turned Diablo around and rode to the back of the cantina. She let him drink at the trough and then loosened his cinch and hitched him to the rail in the shade.

She took her Winchester and went into the dining room by the side door. In a far corner, the Leek boys were settling into a meal more lavish than the leftover scraps they usually scrounged from cowhands by riding the chucklines. As far as Collie knew, they never had any jobs other than day work, and they seemed to like it that way. Collie considered Ned, who was about sixteen, to be as clever as an anvil, but his lean older brother Eli was sharper. Yet he soured her stomach every time because he always gazed at her as if her clothes were made of window glass.

She passed through the opening in the Chinese screens and entered the cantina.

Only a few idlers nursing their beers lounged about in the middle of the day. All the dealers at the empty gaming tables looked as if they were about to doze off. Collie spotted her friend Sally arranging some boxes in the humidor.

"Hi, Collie," Sally said in her usual cheerful tone. Then she frowned. "What's wrong?"

"Just passing some time."

"You're not a good liar," Sally said.

"Have any new girls been hired lately?"

"Just one. An older woman. But very attractive. And she's really nice, too. Last night she gave me half of her tips."

"Why did she do that?"

"She told Don Luis that it would be a good idea to bring free drinks and *tapas* to the gaming tables. To keep the players happy and to stop people from milling around the cantina all the time. It worked. I helped her a little bit, and when the night was over she handed me all her tips and told me to take them into the back and split them in half."

"Did you?"

"I told her I didn't want to. That I didn't deserve that much. She smiled and said that if each of us got only what we deserved we'd all be in serious trouble."

"I've never heard of anything like that."

"Nobody has."

"Do you know her name?"

"Kaney."

Collie spun around at the voice.

"You must be Colleen Callaghan," said the tall woman wearing a dark brown satin dress.

"Hello, miss."

"Do you want to see me?"

Collie felt as if her face were on fire. "I was just curious. I heard . . ."

Kaney pointed to the reading room beyond the cigar counter.

"I feel as if I already know you," Kaney said with a smile as they went into the room. She pointed to a comfortable chair deep among the books.

Collie took off her hat and leaned her carbine against the chair and sat down. "I don't understand."

"Mr. Madero has spoken of you."

"We're friends. He bought me a wonderful horse."

"Yes, I know. And now you'd like to know if I'm his friend as well." Kaney raised an eyebrow. "Or, perhaps, if I'm a bit more than that."

Collie's entire body felt as if it were flushing as the woman's blue-eyed gaze pinned her to the chair.

"No, miss," Collie finally managed to say. "It's not that I'm jealous. Honest. It's just that he's been like an older brother to me. . . ."

"Well, that may be, but I think you came here for more than a casual chat."

Collie remained silent.

"Maybe to see how the cat jumps. To make sure that some temptress isn't taking advantage of him."

Collie moistened her lips but still could think of nothing sensible to say.

"Colleen, I can tell you that I'm not interested in becoming someone's left-handed wife. Mr. Madero's or anyone else's."

"No, I never thought — ."

"And I'm long past my temptress days, as you can see."

"Oh, no, miss. That's not true."

Kaney smiled and rested her chin on her right hand. "So I have a few good years left?" Then she winked at her.

"Oh, miss," Collie said, laughing. "That's not what I meant."

Suddenly the woman's smile vanished. She tilted her head slightly and stared at Collie like someone struggling to read a book with faded printing.

"Miss?"

"Please call me Kaney."

Yet Collie was still unsettled by that focused gaze.

"How old are you, Collie?"

"Sixteen."

Kaney slipped a few fingers around the silver locket hanging onto her breast and just gazed at Collie in silence. "Do you think we can be friends?" she finally asked. "I don't have many here."

"I'd like that," Collie said with a smile.

Again Kaney seemed to look deeply into her, and then she turned away and placed a gentle hand onto Collie's on the arm of the chair. Her puzzling expression was one that Collie could not decipher.

"Miss? Are you all right?"

"It's a trying world we live in," Kaney said, staring at Collie's fingers beneath her own. She rubbed her hand softly over Collie's and the touch of the young girl's skin seemed to soothe her.

"Don't be blue," Collie said. "It's a good world. Honest."

"Ah, if you only knew. . . . But I guess you will soon enough." Kaney slowly stood. "I'm happy I've met you."

Yet her melancholy smile seemed to be saying much more than that.

"I have to go now, Collie. Will I see you soon?"

"I promise!"

"Thank you. And God bless you."

With that surprising farewell, she turned and left with a rustle of satin and the snap of hard heels against the floor.

22 HANGFIRE

"Ho," Madero whispered to Buddy, and the horse stopped as softly as if he were trotting on cotton. In the distance, Collie and Buck were bending over a large animal lying in the grass. Their horses grazed nearby.

Madero squeezed Buddy gently and they walked over. They were only about twenty feet away before Collie and Buck heard them and turned.

"It's my bull," Buck said to Madero. "They shot him."

Madero scanned the horizon, but no riders were visible. He dismounted and dropped Buddy's reins to the ground.

"Let's take a look," Madero said. As he passed Collie, he touched her tenderly on the shoulder.

The young bull was freshly dead, but coyotes had already begun picking at it.

Madero pushed back his hat and bent down and examined the hole in the animal's forehead. "A .44 or a .45, but that doesn't tell us anything." He turned to Collie. "Did you hear the shot?"

"From far off," Buck said. "But we didn't see anybody when we got here."

"Mateo, Buck raised—I mean Mr. Madero, Buck—."

"Mateo is fine."

She seemed startled and touchingly grateful for that little favor.

"Buck raised him from a calf."

"He was a fine bull, Mr. Madero. Docile for a good breeder. I never had any problems with him. He . . ." His voice wobbled a bit. "He was a good boy."

"What are you two doing out here alone?"

Collie blushed. "Just riding."

He looked at Buck.

"Absolutely, sir. Just riding."

Madero smiled at both of them. "All right. Next time, arm yourself. Like Colleen."

"My father won't let me own weapons."

"Why not?"

"Because he thinks I'm a weakling and a fool."

Madero turned toward Collie. "But Blackie doesn't, do you?"

Collie smiled and shook her head no.

"Then that's what matters, doesn't it, Buck?"

This time he was the one who reddened. "Yes, sir. That's all that matters."

"A weakling doesn't ride out here unarmed when there are stock detectives on the prowl," Madero said. "And with only his own body between them and the young lady he cares about. A boy doesn't do it either. Only a brave man does."

Buck seemed overwhelmed by what Madero had said.

"When I get the time, I'll teach you to shoot. We'll—."

"Truly?!"

"Why not? Now mount up."

When the three of them moved off, Collie and Buck rode on either side of Madero, so he dropped back and let them ride beside each other and then he took a position on the offside of Collie.

After about twenty minutes, they reached the Lazy S ranch house. A woman was out front watering some shriveling globe mallow.

"Is my father about, Maribel?"

"In the back, Señor Willard," she said, smiling.

"Please stay for a cool drink, Mr. Madero," Buck said and dismounted.

Madero and Collie did likewise and followed him around to the veranda.

Harlo and Maart Sutorius were sheltering from the sun in the shade of the latillas. Two drinking cups and a small stack of silver coins stood on the table between them.

Harlo and Sutorius rose when the three approached.

"This is a surprise," Harlo said.

"For whom?" Madero asked, looking at Sutorius.

"Mr. Sutorius came here to pay for my dead bull. He —."

"*Your* bull? Dad, you know —."

"Quiet!" Harlo looked back at Madero. "It seems Mr. Scateen took a wing shot at a bobcat and hit my animal instead. Or so Scateen claims. I can't dispute that."

"Mr. Barbicane insists on paying twice what the animal was worth," Sutorius said.

"And what was it worth to this young man?" Madero asked.

Sutorius said nothing.

"Are you going to accept those thirty pieces of silver?" Madero asked Harlo.

"Do I have a choice? It's more than fair."

"Another moderate man," Madero said and made no attempt to hide his contempt and his despair.

Sutorius's inability to conceal the look of triumph in his eyes told Madero that the Dutchman had spent little time at the poker table. To his detriment, he failed to realize that the game had just barely begun.

"Would you like me to ride home with you?" Madero said to Collie.

She nodded. "Bye, Buck. See you soon?"

"Yes, please." He smiled at her.

"By the way," Madero said to Sutorius after Collie had left the veranda, "it's time you learned the difference between a Pinkerton and a *pistolero*."

Then he turned and walked away.

"What is it then?" Harlo asked quickly before Madero was gone.

Madero looked back around. "Unlike Scateen, *ningún pistolero* has ever shot anyone — by accident."

"It was deliberate, wasn't it?" Collie asked Madero as they rode back toward the High C.

"As deliberate as the sunset. But Barbicane didn't order it. That's why he paid double the value for the bull. He's probably telling himself that it really was an accident."

"Who then? Mr. Sutorius?"

"Probably. Barbicane has no idea what he's unleashed."

After they rode on quietly for about another mile, Collie broke the silence. "I've met Miss Kaney."

"Yes, I know," he answered as he scanned the horizon. "She talked about you all evening."

"Why would she do that?"

"I assume you impressed her."

"How? That doesn't make sense."

"It did to her."

"She seems very nice."

Madero pointed to the creek in the distance. "Let's give the boys a drink."

Harlo's cattle moved off the bank as the riders approached. Madero and Collie dismounted and led their horses to the stream.

"The monsoons are being good to Harlo this year," Madero said and looped his reins around the horn. "We'll rest the boys a bit."

Madero tossed his hat aside and sat against the trunk of a cottonwood. Collie sat across from him in the shade.

"Thunderheads are moving in," Madero said, gazing toward the southern sky, "but we have some time."

Collie pushed her hat off and let it fall down her back by the string.

"Blackie, I'd like you to do a favor for me. When you want to see Buck away from the prying eyes of your mother, do it in town. Don't ride out here alone. Will you do that for me?"

She smiled. "I'd do anything for" — she suddenly seemed to catch herself — "Yes, I'll do that."

"I'm sure you could part a ground squirrel's hair with that Winchester, but we don't want to ride that road, do we?"

"No, sir. . . . Mateo."

Madero smiled.

"Can you tell me why Miss Kaney — ?"

"No," Madero said. "I don't know her well enough to tell you why she thinks what she thinks. So you'll have to ask her

170

yourself. All I can tell you is that after we talked about you, she was very subdued."

"I think she thought I was watching over you."

Madero's eyes smiled. "Were you?"

Collie nodded and looked down into her lap.

"She probably thought that you were checking to make sure she wasn't a heartless Siren singing her seductive song."

Collie blushed and turned away toward Diablo grazing nearby.

"Why so *pensativo*?"

"Just wondering," Collie said.

"That's the best part of youth. You haven't lost your wonder."

She looked back at him in surprise. "Do adults lose that?"

"Oh, yes. Far too soon."

"But not you. I can't imagine that." She laughed and then seemed startled by her own giggle. "You wonder about everything."

"Diablo is looking well."

"He's wonderful. Now I just want to learn to be as good a horseman as you. I've watched you."

"I rode very young, but I didn't learn to be a horseman until later."

"Did you work on a ranch?"

"Oh, no, it wasn't *vaqueros* who taught me. Many of them are great horseman, but if you really want to learn how to be one with your animal, you learn from a cavalryman."

"The Mexican cavalry?"

Madero smiled. "No, he was an American. He'd taken an arrow in the hip and couldn't ride without pain. So he quit the army and took a job with Castello's Circus and Menagerie. I saw them in Denver."

"I've never seen a circus. My mom says they're cruel to the animals."

"They can be. Especially in the old days. And once in a while, somebody with a twisted mind will get a job with a circus. *Un sádico* who likes to hurt animals to make himself feel bigger. But as soon as he's found out, he's thrown out. Sometimes after getting his face kicked in."

"But don't they have to beat wild animals to get them to behave?"

"No, it's the opposite. You can beat a horse or a dog and get away with it sometimes, but not a wild animal. I've seen more cruelty in corrals and horse barns than I ever saw in a circus."

"Then how do you train a wild animal?"

"You have to be the *jefe*, but if you really hurt him, he'll wait his chance and kill you sooner or later. The cruel trainers usually end up maimed or dead. And a beaten wild animal won't learn well, either. So the kind trainers know it's not only cruel, it's useless. And besides, most circus people love their animals. The good trainers reward the animals with food during training that the public doesn't see. Especially the Germans and Italians. They're the best. All the flash and swagger they act out is just for *el espectáculo*."

"Did you work for the circus?"

"For twenty-five cents a day and found. I wanted to be around the animals." He smiled to himself. "I've always liked being near animals. Much more than people."

"Me, too. Sometimes."

"That's why I ran away when I was young. The sisters were kind to me and gave me a good education, but I prefer animals. Beasts as God made them. They all have honest souls. Unlike men."

"But my mom says you always got along with people really well. Even when you were young."

"Well, if I do it's just a fluke of nature." He smiled. "Like freckles and black hair."

She grinned back at him.

"Anyway, the horse soldier took a liking to me. Taught me most of what I know about horses."

"But how was he different than the *vaqueros*?"

"He had to be because in the circus he worked horses from the ground in a ring and without leads. Even a horse that's a real man-eater can sometimes be ridden. But on the ground, you're at an animal's mercy. He taught me to read a horse's soul."

"Were there other animals, too?"

"Oh, yes. They had lions."

"Stop it!"

"I'm not joking."

"Holy Mary, real ones?!"

Madero laughed. "I don't mean stuffed ones."

"Did you work with them, too?"

"I cleaned out their cages. And they had a cheetah, too. That's a spotted cat from Africa."

"Like a jaguar?"

"Thinner and sleeker. And he was tame. He'd wear a collar and leash and sit on the coach with his handler during parades."

"I'd love to see that!"

"And they had an elephant. But somebody as green as I was wasn't allowed to work with a bull, either."

"Why not? Do the males have big tusks?"

"It was a female, but circus people call all elephants bulls."

"How long were you there?"

"About a month. We left Denver and traveled by wagon all over Colorado. Central City, Georgetown, Golden, Boulder. The cavalryman said he'd hire me permanently. Next we'd be going to Wyoming and then by rail to Utah. But I went off the grounds to see a friend one night, and the next morning when I got back they were gone. They'd pulled up stakes overnight and headed north to the railroad station at Cheyenne."

"Why didn't he tell you in advance?"

"He probably didn't know. Circuses are very strange, and the people in them are even stranger. The owner must have decided for some reason to leave that night. They were gone by dawn. So eventually I went back to Sonora."

"You didn't follow them?"

"No." Madero turned away and stared off into the past. "I don't think there was any other time in his life when your friend was happier than that month in Colorado."

They were both quiet for a long time.

"If you ever have a moment like that, Blackie, savor it. Those special times just race by. They're so intense that they seem eternal. But permanence is just a fantasy. You blink and it all vanishes . . . like a shimmering mirage at sundown."

"I'm sorry, Mateo."

"Don't be."

"You should have followed them."

"I guess so." He looked back at Collie with a smile. "But, then, if I'd done that, I'd never have met you. And that would be very bad, don't you think?"

She smiled back. "Yes."

They were quiet for a while, and then Collie said, "I'll bet it hurt your feelings, didn't it? I mean them abandoning you like that."

Madero gazed out toward the horses. "Tell me about Buck and his father."

"It's never been good. I asked my mom about it a long time ago, and she said that when Buck was born his mother became the best mother in the world but forgot how to be a wife."

"I see."

Collie seemed hesitant. "Do you know what I mean?"

"I think so."

She looked away.

"So old Harlo resented Buck since he was a baby."

"That's what my mom says. I think it's true. He's never had any time for Buck. Sometimes I think he called him Willard instead of Buck just to make him feel small."

"He seems like a sensitive boy."

"I never realized that until recently. But he is. And he really wants to impress his father."

"And you as well."

She nodded.

"Well, that's a good thing. A man is never greater than when he's reflected in the eyes of a loving woman."

"I didn't say love!"

Madero smiled.

"I've never seen a six-shooter like that," Collie said, suddenly changing the subject.

"It's a .44 Remington."

"Is it rare?"

"Well, they're not very common. The Colt is the workhorse out here, but the Remington has always fit my hand better."

Madero slipped it from his sash. His long fingers slid across it with an ominous comprehension. Pointing the muzzle toward the ground far off to the side, he pulled back the hammer to half-cock, flipped open the loading gate, and ejected the five cartridges one at a time into his right palm. He kept the pistol at half-cock when he handed it to Collie.

"It's a heavy one," she said as her wrist bent under the weight of it.

The stag grips had been carved and fitted by a master craftsman, and twin interlocking "M's" had been inlaid in German silver in the metal below the hammer on the backstrap.

"This is one of a pair," Madero said. "They were given to me by a quiet little man named Harry Dunn. He was taking a vacation through Arizona. I met him at the Congress in Tucson. I'd just gotten over a malaria attack. I needed a change so I showed him around a bit. I took him up to San Carlos and introduced him to some Apaches I know. He was thrilled."

Collie grinned.

"Well, little Harry went back to his home in Ilion in New York and I forgot about him. A few months later a package came to the Congress for me. Twin Remingtons. Seven-and-a-half-inch barrels, gorgeous stag grip plates, one pistol inlaid with my initials. Some claim that the Remington isn't as rugged as the Colt, but it's always been my *amigo en la adversidad* — and the '75 is the most beautiful revolver ever made. I don't care much about material things, but I treasure these. And I'll never forget quiet little Harry Dunn."

Collie handed it back to him. "My mom says that a tool of death should never be made beautiful."

"It's not a tool of death," Madero said and reloaded it and slid it back into his sash. "It's the hand of life."

Collie's freckled face crinkled in almost childlike bafflement.

"It's the guardian of the hearth," Madero said. "In a land where the people are brutalized—in my land—this is more valuable than gold. Where the farmers are stripped of their dignity by stronger men because they have no sting, this"—he tapped the butt—"restores the sting."

"But most poor farmers can't afford weapons, can they?"

"No, they can't. But those who can buy them have a chance to avoid being crushed. Degraded into the human wreckage that would cause the Pope to despair of God."

After a long silence, Collie said, "Why no holsters?"

"They just get in my way. Too much rigging. The sash is much more comfortable, and the pistol snuggles in there like a bird in its nest."

"Why do you carry it backwards? That looks awkward."

"That's the old cavalry draw. I was taught to shoot by a young cavalry lieutenant from Fort Lowell named McGregor. That reverse position goes back to the percussion days when a gun sometimes went off accidentally. If it did, the ball would go into the ground behind you instead of into your foot."

"But it looks like pulling it out would be slow."

"It is."

"But don't you want to be fast?"

Madero smiled. "I'd rather be accurate."

"Can't someone be both?"

"Rarely."

"Where's the other one, Mateo? Don't you ever carry that one, too?"

"Too much weight. And the men who strut around with two pistols usually can't shoot with both hands anyway. It takes an enormous amount of practice to become skilled with a sidearm. The two-handed *pistolero* is very rare."

Collie seemed disappointed.

"Carrying two pistols is really just to have a reserve. It's another thing that goes back to the days before cartridges. If a spent cap fell into the lockwork, the gun would jam. And there were lots of misfires, too, because the powder had sucked in moisture. The hammer falls, the cap pops, but nothing else happens. So having two guns gave you some comfort, even if you could shoot with only one hand."

Collie looked even more disillusioned.

"And there was one thing that was worse than all the others. It was when a charge had a delayed ignition. The hammer falls but nothing happens. You think it's a misfire. Thirty seconds later it goes off and puts a ball through your own body or cuts down a friend. That's called a hangfire. There's nothing more dangerous on earth."

Madero stared in silence out across the grassland.

After he had said nothing for a long time, Collie leaned forward. "Mateo? What is it?"

He looked back at her. "That's exactly what Barbicane has done by bringing in these killers he calls detectives. He doesn't realize it, but he's squeezed the trigger and the hammer has already fallen. Now the charge is sizzling, but there's no way to predict the moment of ignition."

As Collie turned away, Madero thought he saw the hint of a smile.

"Would you like to explain the humor that I'm missing?"

When she looked back at him, she made no attempt to conceal her smile.

"Well?" he said.

"No matter what you say, how could I ever be afraid? *You're* here."

Madero leaned his head back against the tree and folded his arms. "How do you know *I'm* not afraid?"

"How do I know the sun won't rise in the west?"

Madero had to bite his lip to stop from laughing. "But what if I'm just acting?"

"Oh, yes. And what if I'm not Black Irish?"

Her sudden grin startled Madero and flashed its warmth straight to the center of his soul. Now he realized how truly helpless he was before this child-woman. And he knew beyond doubt that it was the most wonderful helplessness a man can know.

23 BOLAS

ZOOLOGY ON THE RANGE

STRANGE BEAST SIGHTED

INVESTIGATION TO CONTINUE

This journal has been apprised of a curious claim. We have been informed that a stock detective recently mistook a hulking two-thousand-pound ruminant for a swift thirty-pound carnivore and, evidently in fear for his life, dispatched it accordingly. We remain skeptical that anyone with functioning gray matter can make such an error, but, in the interests of the public weal, we shall investigate this matter further. If the claim be proved correct, we shall consider sponsoring a seminar, at this journal's expense, on the subtle and delicate nuances distinguishing the appearances of an ever elusive feline and a now sadly defunct bovine.

Madero smiled and set down the sheet on the *La Luna* bar. "You're a poet."

"Adequate?" Kelly asked.

"It's perfect. Their goal is to intimidate and infuriate. Sarcasm is the perfect counterpunch." He turned to Bert. "Some Jameson for the bard here."

"It appeared this morning," Kelly said. "Collie gave me the details."

"Expect another social call from Barbicane."

"Or someone sterner."

"Possibly. Keep Sam Colt at hand."

Bert set a glass of Irish before Kelly.

"I like that," Kelly said, gesturing toward the new billiard emporium that had been set up in what had been the storage room to the left of the bar. "Kelliride is in there now running the table."

"Maybe I'll challenge him someday."

"I didn't realize Luis was so flush. It's a nice table."

"Divine Providence," Madero said.

"I think not."

Both Kelly and Madero turned at Luis's voice.

"A hauler from Campbell and Hatch came here today," Luis said as he approached with an exasperated look. "He told me the table and delivery had been paid for."

"God works in mysterious ways," Madero said.

"There was someone's signature on the bill of sale. It was not Jesus of Nazareth."

Kelly burst out laughing.

"I insist on paying you in full," Luis said.

"You already have," Madero answered. "In ways you'll never understand."

"But how can I accept such a gift?"

"I don't think you have a choice," Kelly said with a smile.

"If a *bagatela* like that unnerves you," Madero said, "you'd better pour yourself some *El Tesoro*." He turned to Bert and nodded.

The barman reached under the bar and produced a tan envelope.

"What is this?" Luis said as he opened it.

Madero remained quiet.

Luis scanned the long paper and then stared at Madero in disbelief.

"Well?" Kelly asked.

"It's the title to *La Luna*," Luis said. He looked back at Madero. "I don't understand. What . . . ?"

"A small gesture."

"You're a madman."

"We can't have you in the grip of Barbicane any longer, can we? Not as long as I hang my hat here. It's simple tactics. Nothing more."

"But I don't know when I can pay you back."

"Do I have to repeat myself?"

"Then half of this is yours. It's settled."

"Don't be silly. Madero of Sonora abhors responsibility. Ask Kelly."

"True," Kelly said, nodding with mock seriousness. "Very true."

"Then how do I settle this and still sleep at night?"

"Give me a twenty percent share," Madero said. "And free run of Sally's humidor."

Something had caught Luis's attention, and Madero turned and followed his gaze.

Peeker Tweed had come through the main door and was walking toward them straight up the center of the cantina.

"Gentlemen," Tweed said when he reached the bar.

"Sir," Luis answered, clearly stunned.

"I'm broke and I'm desperate," Tweed said without preliminaries. "Can I swamp out the place or clean some stables? You name the wage."

For once, the wise Spaniard was speechless.

"Come outside," Madero said before Luis could answer.

They walked together through the cantina and out the front door. Madero pointed to a spot near the edge of the boardwalk away from the street lamp.

"You're one of a kind," Madero said with a smile as both men sat on the planking.

"My enduring charm."

"Real *bolas de acero*—you certainly have them, coming up here like this."

"If my *bolas* were a more precious metal than steel, I'd lop them off and hock them."

"Hock?"

"*Empeñar.*"

Madero laughed.

"Can you help me?"

"Not with what you want. Luis can't afford to have you seen anywhere near here. It would kill his business."

"I figured as much, but I had to ask."

"Are you really down to the blanket?"

"I'm down to a few Mexican silver coins. I'm no good anymore, Madero. My hands are stiffening up. I'm forty-four years old. They're not going to get any better."

"Let me see what you have."

Tweed pulled three eight *reales* pieces from a vest pocket.

"Do you remember where you got these?"

"Some young fool full of blusteration and ignorance. I believe his name was Leek. Or something like that. He was half drunk and crowed that he had a stash of Mexican blood money, whatever the hell that means. He's been bragging at every bit house in town."

"Let me have them."

Tweed hesitated, and then, in a remarkable act of trust, he handed them to him.

"Madero . . . I never killed any girl in Bisbee. She was a runaway. I never harmed her."

"Did I say you did?"

"Everyone thinks I did."

"Why would you care what I think?"

"I have no idea . . . but I do."

"And the two men you bedded down?"

"They were trying to kill me."

"Were you roping them in?"

"Of course I was. Gulling fools is my business. But I wasn't killing them. That was their play — and they threw a seven."

Madero stood up. "Stay here."

Madero went into the cantina. He brushed by Luis and Kelly and took three double eagles from the drawer and dropped in the Mexican silver. Luis just stared at him as he turned and went back outside.

"Fair trade," Madero said, handing him the gold coins.

Tweed hesitated. "Are you insane?"

"Possibly. Call it a loan. Now get out of here and rattle your hocks up to Tucson. Buy some new clothes, change your name, maybe shave off the beard. You can get a contract as a house dealer up there in five minutes."

Tweed looked down at the money in his hands and then back at Madero.

"Work up a faro game. It'll be easier on your hands. And play it straight."

The old card mechanic bumped the coins up and down in his palm. "Why are you doing this?"

"Why not?"

"That's not an answer."

"Let's say that I know what it's like to lose everything."

"But it's my own fault—aren't you going to jab me with that?"

"Naturally it's your own fault. So?"

Tweed shook his head in bafflement. "I've known many unusual people, but you're off the ranch."

Madero remained quiet.

"I'm good for this," Tweed said and slid the money into a vest pocket. "Truly."

"I believe you."

Tweed smiled. "So tell me, is it accurate that you're a terror at the poker table?"

"I've won a few hands."

"Fairly won? Or do you know how to work the magic, too?"

Madero laughed. "I can do card tricks. And I can spot cheating, but I've never had the time to learn the skills you have. I was busy acquiring other ones."

"I understand. You know, Madero, a man at the card table hears most of what happens in a town. I know what's going on here, more or less."

"And?"

"And Sutorius I don't know, but I'm familiar with the other three. Kelliride is the worst. I saw him in Santa Fe. He always has to be the biggest toad in the puddle. He's sick in the head, with that twisted smile he always has. Pain is his pleasure. He'd hurt anyone. Even that girl."

"Kaney can take care of herself."

"Not her. The young girl I've seen gazing at you as if she was experiencing the Beatific Vision."

"Thank you for telling me. I'll take care of him."

Tweed stood up. "Now I should go before I ruin your reputation."

"Or I ruin yours."

Tweed smiled again. "Madero, you're a man of honor in any language." He held out his hand.

Madero stood and shook it. "What's your real name?"

"Jack Tarn."

"*Vaya con Dios.*"

Without another word, the man once known as Peeker Tweed turned and walked off into the darkness.

Madero heard someone behind him, and he looked and saw Luis watching from the shadows.

"I think I might have just saved a man's life," Madero said.

"Oh, no," Luis answered. "I think you might have just saved a man's soul.

24 EL TESORO

When Madero walked into his sitting room after talking with Tarn, Kaney set down the book she was reading and got up from the sofa.

"No need to stand," Madero said, taking off his hat. "That's the sort of thing that makes a single man nervous."

"Oh, Lord," she said with a smile. "That rooming house is looking better and better."

"You have a certain sly humor about you that reminds me of Blackie."

Her smile faded.

"What's wrong?"

She shrugged. "Oh, I've been thinking about her. She worries about you terribly."

"Young girls worry about everything terribly."

Madero went to the lyre table and set down his revolver next to a stack of coins.

"That's the point," Kaney said. "I think to her you *are* everything. If anything happened to you . . ."

"It wouldn't even make the front page of *The Clarion*."

"Please don't say that."

She turned away and slumped down onto the sofa.

"What's the matter?"

"Don't pay any attention. It's just that time of the month."

"Ah."

Madero untied his waist sash and set it onto the table beside the coins stacked next to Our Lady.

"Are these your tips?"

"Pay and tips."

Madero picked up one of the coins and sat down beside Kaney.

"This one?" Madero asked.

"Part of my pay from Don Luis. I asked for it because it's a pretty coin."

"Do you know what it is?"

"It's Mexican, isn't it?"

"It is. The Territory outlawed Mexican currency a long time ago. Odd that Luis still takes it at the cantina."

"I believe it came from the Leek boys. Luis feels sorry for them I think. They don't usually have much money."

"This is an old piece," Madero said, turning it over. "You've heard of *el tesoro de los piratas*? Pirate treasure and 'pieces of eight'? That's what this is. An eight *reales* piece."

"Is it rare?"

"One this nice from eighteen forty-three certainly is." He handed it to her. "Look at the details on the eagle's feathers. After over forty years. Strange."

"Do you think they stole it?"

"I doubt it. It's too old."

"Maybe it's buccaneer's treasure," Kaney said, smiling.

"Well, when we find a Spanish galleon in the Sonoran Desert, that'll make sense. If you get any more, will you let me know?"

"Is it important?"

"I don't know, but oddities bear watching. In all aspects of life."

"Here." She handed it to him. "A little gift for putting up with me."

"Really now, my dear, I think it'll take more than this."

"You're such a rogue!"

Madero smiled and just gazed at her.

"Why are you staring?"

"Do you know why I admire you so much?"

Kaney grinned. "No, tell me. I love flattery."

"You're one of the most honest people I've ever crossed trails with. In a world hip deep in liars, you tell the truth no matter what it costs you."

Kaney looked suddenly serious but said nothing.

"No response?" Madero asked.

"What can a woman say to something as wonderful as that?"

"She can apologize for telling me a lie."

Kaney's face reddened in an instant.

"I don't know if it's true that it's that time of the month," Madero said, "but that's not what's bothering you. Truthful people are poor liars."

She turned away. "I'm sorry. . . . It's . . . ."

"No, I'm not asking you to reveal anything. If you don't want to, *está bien*. You can conceal everything, but just don't pretend. Is that fair?"

"Yes."

A long silence followed.

"It's Collie," Kaney finally said, looking directly at him. "She cares for you so much. You can see the love swimming in her eyes."

Madero said nothing.

"Don't you agree?"

"It's a terrible responsibility to be loved. I don't encourage it."

"You're talking like it's a burden to you."

"Collie? How could she be a burden?"

"No, not Collie — being cared about."

"A millstone around my neck. Too many expectations to live up to."

Kaney looked sad and turned away. "I'm learning a lot about you tonight."

"Being near Madero isn't as carefree as you thought, is it? Not all dashing pirates and sabers?"

"No," she said softly.

"But how is this connected to Colleen?"

Kaney shook her head no.

"All right, I won't ask any more. But you know I'd never let anyone hurt her."

"Of course I know that."

"Then why are you so worried?"

"It's not a person that's going to hurt her — it's the *world*. This rotten, selfish world. And there's nothing anyone can do about it."

Before Madero could say anything else, Kaney got up from the sofa and went to her room and quickly closed the door.

A permanent RESERVED sign had been placed in the middle of a table in the far upper corner of *La Luna* near the reading room. Every night around midnight, after most of the crowd had left and the smoky haze had thinned, Madero sat there with his back to the wall and spoke to each of the house men about any problems or concerns they had from the day's play at the tables.

After the dealers had spoken with Madero and he had thanked them and tipped them from his own pocket, Luis came over with a glass and sat down. Madero poured him some *El Tesoro* and slid a coin across the table toward him.

"Have you gotten many of these?" Madero asked.

"A few from the Leeks. Some from Barbicane's hands, too, I think."

"Do you know where they came from?"

"No idea at all."

"Let me know if you get any again."

Madero poured himself more tequila.

"Is everything all right?" Luis asked.

"How could everything ever be all right?" Madero said and sipped his drink.

"You really have to be on guard against so much *optimismo.*"

Madero could not help smiling but it quickly faded. "Thus spoke the Conscience of San Miguel."

Luis smiled back. "We all have our calling."

"I hurt Kaney tonight." Madero pulled out a cheroot but then thought better of it and returned to his tequila.

After a long pause, Luis said, "I'm sure it was an accident."

"My whole life has been an accident. What does that matter?"

Luis remained quiet.

"It might surprise you that I could be the object of admiration, but—."

"It doesn't surprise me."

"One of the things that people have always envied me for . . . and hated me for it, too . . . the fact that I'm indifferent to the opinions of others."

"That's a rare gift. Too many of us suffer under the recriminations of the world."

"During my youth I was misjudged by so many people so often that I learned to ignore the attitudes of others. If I hadn't, I'd have lost my mind."

"There's nothing callous in that kind of indifference."

"In the beginning, you put it on like a suit of armor. Over time, though, it stops being something you wear. It becomes welded to you. As permanent as your eye color."

"I understand.

"No, my friend, you don't."

"Can you explain it then?"

"Probably not. To me, the judgments of people are like raindrops hitting a hot rock and evaporating instantly. Of no significance at all."

Luis said nothing.

"So you can get thoughtless in your speech. Hurtful sometimes, too."

Luis nodded but still remained quiet.

"I like this stuff too much," Madero said, corking the bottle.

"In the right amounts, it soothes the soul."

"Tonight I told Kaney that someone caring about me is too much of a burden for me. An obligation I don't want. Is that outrageous?"

"To some. Probably to most. Certainly to her."

"It's a simple truth that seems ordinary to me. Barely even worth mentioning. Yet I might as well have kicked her in the face."

"But it wasn't intentional."

"She's bleeding all the same."

"Wounds heal."

"Not all of them."

Madero popped the cork again and poured himself some more tequila. "This is my favorite time of the day," he said, gazing around the quiet cantina. "The first few hours after midnight. Then there's peace."

"When there are few people about?"

Madero held up his glass.

Luis sighed and stared down into his drink. "That's very sad. And you're mistaken as well."

"Preferences can't be mistaken. They can be unwise, but not mistaken."

"A midnight conversation with you could drive a man *loco*."

"You wouldn't be the first."

Luis shook his head. "Why don't you get some sleep? I'll close up tonight."

"Sleep is the last thing I want."

"All right, then chew on this for a while. A stranger comes across a girl who has fallen in love with a horse she can't afford, and so he buys it for her and rides off without even waiting for a thank you. He sees a tired and lonely woman without a home or money and he gets her a job and a place to live—and perhaps something more, although he won't admit it. He finds good people struggling against a greedy and reckless cattleman, and he places his unprotected heart between those people and four hard cases without souls. Indifferent? Yes, indeed, the *Santo Patrón* of indifference—that's what I'd call him."

Madero could not help laughing.

"Pardon me now," Luis said, standing up. "I have a cantina to get ready for bed."

Only a single lamp burned in the sitting room when Madero returned after midnight. Light was fanning out from under the bedroom door into the dimly lit parlor. He hung up his hat and went over and tapped on the panel.

"Come in."

"Are you decent?"

"As decent as I'll ever be."

Madero was happy to hear a smile in her voice.

Kaney was wearing the white nightdress and sitting in bed against a propped up pillow. A book lay open on the sheet beside her, but Madero doubted she had been doing much reading.

"May I join you?"

She patted the bed next to her hip.

Madero sat as gently as if the mattress were made of tissue paper.

"Long night?" Madero said.

"A bit long."

"I don't believe I've ever apologized to a woman in bed before."

She almost smiled and was obviously struggling to remain stern. "I'm sure."

"Do you have any preference?"

"I don't understand."

"What kind of apology would you like?"

"I'm not asking for an apology about anything."

"I know that. But I'm offering."

"Then just say what's on your mind."

"I already did that and it didn't do anyone any good."

"Then just speak the truth."

"What I said earlier tonight *was* the truth."

"All of it?"

"No one ever speaks all of the truth."

"But why are you apologizing?"

"Because a careless man hurt someone he didn't mean to hurt."

"She's tough enough to take it."

"That doesn't lessen his guilt."

"Then maybe he should forget about guilt for once and simply say what he feels. Not what he thinks. What he feels."

"And give up the habit of a lifetime? That's foolish."

She hesitated and then said, "Can't he risk it for just five minutes in the darkness at midnight?"

"Maybe he's not as brave as some people think."

"Oh, yes he is."

"Well, he could say that he's fairly sure his life is coming to an end. And that he's completely indifferent to that. But because of it, the possibility of any woman getting *muy sentimental* over

191

him is a burden he doesn't want her to inflict on herself. Or on him. Add to that—no, don't say anything—add to it a sixteen-year-old girl who haunts his dreams and his nightmares. And who happens to think he's some kind of damned archangel."

"Is that the whole truth?" Kaney asked, her voice cracking.

"Or he could come up with a ridiculous story about a young widow who rested her chin on her hand and gazed at him from across a saloon and how there hasn't been a day since then that he hasn't thought about her. How when she simply cocks her head and stares at him, it drives him mad. And how a man who hasn't prayed in twenty years prays every night for the strength to treat her with honor."

Even in the half-darkness, tears glittered in Kaney's eyes.

"He could make up a story like that," Madero said, "but what woman on earth would be foolish enough to believe it?"

"Only a madwoman," Kaney answered, the tears now sliding down her face.

"Have you ever known one of those?"

"Just one."

Madero stood up. "I'll be right back."

He went into the sitting room and got the bottle of cognac and two glasses and then went in and sat back on the edge of the bed.

"Here," he said, pouring her some of the cognac.

"Thank you." She took a small sip.

"Better?"

She nodded. "There's something I have to ask you, but I'm not sure how."

"Take another dose of the Frenchman's friend and give it a try."

She took a longer sip and coughed a little. "Mateo, why do you think you're going to die? You look like you're made of iron."

"My body can't take this hammering forever. The malaria attacks seem to be getting more intense. And my sleep, if you can call it that, is no help. It doesn't matter how strong the wall is—eventually the artillery shells are going to batter it down."

"I can't believe that."

"Even worse is the fact that it seems to be affecting the speed of my reactions. I feel like my reflexes are slowing down. That sort of thing can kill me in an instant."

"I could never believe that either."

"Belief is a wonderful thing. Never let it go."

"You know, I think that when you agree with me, it's a bigger frustration than when you don't."

"Frustration?" he said with a smile. "Imagine a man sitting on a bed in the dark next to a beautiful woman in a nightdress. . . ."

Kaney's laugh seemed to startle her as much as it did Madero. "You *are* such a rogue!"

"It's my *vocación*."

"If you want to talk about frustration . . . well . . ."

"Well what?"

"Imagine a quiet girl from Pennsylvania sitting in bed in the dark with a scar-faced Mexican bandit who throws off more heat than burning mesquite. *That's* frustration."

Madero smiled.

Neither of them spoke for a long time until Kaney broke the silence. "Be serious with me. Just once. How can you say you're indifferent to dying? That's a terrible thing to say."

"I say it because it's true. But I don't know why it's true."

"But is it? You're not just trying to be shocking?"

"Oh, hell," he said, smiling, "I don't have to *try* to be shocking."

"But how can you not care about your own life?"

"I've never cared."

"That's not an answer."

"I don't have an answer. But I do know that the fantasies people tell themselves about the importance of their own lives are just that—fantasies."

"Good Lord, how can you believe such a thing?"

"You believe it, too. You've just never stared it in the face."

"That's ridiculous."

Madero said nothing.

"Sometimes, *señor*, you have a look of superiority that's very annoying."

"I've cultivated it."

She sighed. "All right, prove to me that you're not being ridiculous."

"I don't have to. You can do it yourself. Do you know the names of your great-grandparents?"

She hesitated for a moment. "Yes."

"Do you know anything about them?"

"A little."

"And their parents? Do you even know their names?"

"What does that matter?"

"You've answered my question."

"What you've asked doesn't prove anything."

"It proves everything. Someday, and sooner than you think, you won't even be a memory to your own descendants."

Kaney looked horrified. "How can you think something so terrible?"

"It's the price of being a fallen archangel."

She seemed lost for words.

"And as for me, well, I've never told myself any of those tales."

"But—."

"I've never valued my own life very highly. Why should I? I've never had any reason to."

"But why does there have to be a reason to?"

"Everything needs a reason."

"No, no, you're wrong. There doesn't have to be a reason for cherishing our lives. Even if we're forgotten in a few years. Life is a treasure."

"Treasure—*un tesoro*. I'm sorry, but my life is not a treasure. It never has been. Had I never lived, the world would have lost nothing."

"My God, that's a dreadful thing to say."

"Why?"

"Isn't it obvious?"

"Not to me."

"Believing something like that is the most horrible mistake a person can ever make."

"My whole life has been a mistake."

Kaney shook her head but seemed not to know what to say.

"Don't feel sorry for me. I certainly don't feel sorry for myself."

"But we do have to care about ourselves, don't we? Even if just to survive?"

"Now *you're* mistaken. Some people endure by accident. Conceived in folly and surviving by fate."

"Stop it! Don't say that."

"It's true, Mark of Kane."

"But it doesn't make sense."

"It makes far more sense than you dare imagine."

"All right, dare my imagination. Explain what you mean."

"You won't like the answer."

"I haven't liked any so far. You might as well make it a perfect night."

"All right, consider this. I've lost count of the men who've tried to kill me over the years. Arizona rustlers, crooked gamblers, Mexican *Rurales*—and yet I'm still alive and they're not. Why?"

Kaney looked suddenly fearful.

"I told you that you wouldn't like the answer."

"Tell me anyway."

"Because the most important thing to those men was their own lives."

She frowned in confusion. "Shouldn't it be?"

"It doesn't matter whether or not it should be. It's what made them vulnerable. They cared about living."

"That's what made them weak?"

"Not weak but unsure. Unsteady. Even though they wanted to kill me, they were tense, shaky. Worrying about their own survival. So there was no hope for them. . . ."

For about a minute, Kaney just stared at him. Finally she said, "Please go on."

"With me it was different. I wasn't nervous—I never am, because I don't care about my own life. And I certainly cared nothing about their beautiful weapons or their well-honed skills. None of that changes the inner man."

"So then what?"

"So while they struggled and fumbled with tension and fear, I struck them all down." He sipped his cognac and stared toward a dark corner of the room as though he were peering off to the edge of the world "As easily as if they were tin cans on a rail fence."

A few moments of quiet followed, and then Kaney said, "Because you didn't care about living. . . ."

"Now you've learned two truths that very few people know. The first is that the most effective *guardián* of your life is absolute indifference to it." He took another sip of his drink. "And the second is that no hand is more lethal than the hand of a man already dead."

The silence now seemed to last a month. At last Kaney said, "The thought of your hating yourself like that is just unbearable to me."

"Ah, but that's not what I said. A man with a wasted life behind him . . . no, I don't hate myself. I'm indifferent to myself."

"But what about the people who care about you?"

"Most of them died long ago."

"But there are some here now."

"I try to keep the list as short as possible. People reckless enough to put themselves in that ledger—there's nothing I can do for them."

"What about Collie?"

"The hero worshipping will pass. She's young—the young have the shortest memories."

"You don't believe that. You know she'll never forget you. And when you talk about her . . . no flippant remarks can hide how you feel."

Madero was quiet.

"Do you know what bothers me the most?" Kaney asked.

""*No me puedo imaginar.* . . I'm sorry, I start slipping when I'm tired . . . I can't imagine."

"The way you talk about yourself as if you're speaking about another person. It's so distant."

"Sometimes Mexicans can be very fatalistic. Like poor people everywhere."

"Yes, but how—."

"We have a proverb that expresses it well. In Sonora we say . . . I have to think about it for a second because I've never thought about it in English. . . . " He paused for a moment. "We say that for a person who's born fortunate, even the roosters lay eggs, but for someone who's born to ruin, *ni las gallinas*—not even the hens do."

They both sat quietly for a long time.

"And you, Mateo?" Kaney finally said.

"I was born to ruin long ago. But that's all right. Now that you're settled and secure, I have only one thing left to do, and that's to make sure that an idealistic young girl lives long and happily enough to have some chicks of her own." He stood up and placed a gentle hand on top of Kaney's head like a priest's blessing. "Even if I have to go down in a hail of gunfire doing it."

PART THREE

Under that corrosion arises a hatred, blind and vague, and incomprehensible even to one's self, as of some unknown snake-like enemy, in some unknown hostile world, brooding with secret power over the fountains of one's own vitality.

— De Quincey

25 OUT OF THE SHADOWS

"Mrs. Callaghan?" Kaney said as she rode Luis's buckskin up to the corral where Kathy stood watching her approach.

"Yes. Good morning."

"I'm sorry for coming here unannounced, but I wanted to see you right away." Kaney dismounted and led her horse into the shade. "I'm Kristin Kane."

"Rake," Kathy said and the foreman came out of the barn. "Please water Miss Kane's horse."

Rake tipped his hat to Kaney. "Done," he answered and led the horse away.

"Please come inside, miss."

"Mrs., please," Kaney said, and she followed Kathy into the parlor.

"Make yourself comfortable."

Kaney removed her hat and sat on the chair to the right of the sofa, while Kathy got a tray with a pitcher of water and two glasses and set them onto the table. She poured Kaney a glassful and handed it to her.

"Thank you," Kaney said as she looked around.

"If you're wondering if Collie is here, she's in town," Kathy said as she sat in the chair opposite.

"Yes, I know. That's why I came today."

Kathy gave her a puzzled look. "You're Mateo's friend, aren't you?"

"I'm his boarder." Kaney took a sip of water and turned toward the door when Holden came in.

"I unsaddled your mare, miss, and gave her some hay."

"You're Mr. Madero's friend," Kaney said.

"One never knows with that *hombre* if one is his friend or not."

"You are. Trust me. Join us."

He turned to Kathy.

"Please, Rake. Have a seat."

He sat on the sofa between them and dropped his hat onto the cushion.

"You're as lovely as I knew you'd be," Kaney said to Kathy. "Collie is too beautiful not to have a beautiful mother."

"Thank you."

"May I show you something?" Kaney set down her glass. She removed the silver locket and chain from around her neck and got up and handed it to Kathy.

"It's very nice," Kathy said, turning it over in her hand.

"Please open it."

Kathy slid a thumbnail between the halves and they popped apart.

"That's a miniature of my late husband," Kaney said. "I never remove it except to bathe."

"He was a handsome gentleman," Kathy said and closed the locket and handed it back to her.

"He's with me always," Kaney answered, returning to her chair and slipping the chain back around her neck. "Even if I should remarry, he'll still be with me."

"I understand."

"Do you?"

"Yes, I'm a widow as well."

"I know that. And yet in this very attractive and inviting room, there's no picture of your husband. Explain that to me, one widow to another."

Kathy suddenly looked alarmed. "I have a wedding picture of us together, but I've misplaced it."

"Have you?"

"What's this about?" Holden said to Kaney.

She never took her eyes off Kathy. "Tell him."

Kathy stood up. "It's time you left, Mrs. Kane."

"Haven't you ever seen Collie smile, ramrod?" Kaney said to Holden. "Look at that young girl's eyes. Not the color, the expression. For God's sake, watch her laugh and then tell me you've never seen that before."

Kathy was shaking in what looked like a mixture of anger and fear.

"How many widows, Mrs. Callaghan, have lost their own wedding picture?"

Kathy seemed incapable of speaking.

"Is it that you don't dare display it because your husband was a fair-haired Irishman — and everyone knows you can't cross two sorrels and get a black filly?"

"Missy. . . ?" Holden said.

"Are you so cold, madam, that you care nothing for a lonely man sick in body and soul and grasping at one last chance for redemption?" Kaney stood up and walked over to Kathy. "And what about your daughter? Doesn't she have the right to know that half of her generous heart comes from a man who's generous to everyone, except himself?"

"Why should I have to answer to some painted wag-tail?" Kathy shouted. "Get out!"

Kaney slapped her across the face with such force that Kathy rocked backward and fell into the chair.

"Stay where you are, cowboy!" Kaney snapped as Holden jumped up. She glared at Kathy. "If you were more of a woman and I were less of one, I'd beat you into the ground. But what good would it do now?"

Kathy straightened up in the chair.

"Mateo says he hasn't seen you in about twenty years. But his memory isn't what it once was because of the opium, isn't that right?"

"Opium?"

"It's been closer to seventeen, hasn't it?"

"Yes," she whispered.

"And now he's willing to lay down his life for a girl he thinks is just a stranger, and you'd let him do that? Go to his grave and never know? How on earth could you dare?"

Kathy hunched over and hid her face in her hands. "Please go."

Kaney took a deep breath and dropped to her knees in front of Kathy and reached out and touched the backs of her fingers.

A primordial howl of anguish burst from Kathy's throat. She slumped forward and buried her face in the hollow of Kaney's shoulder and moaned like a dying animal.

203

Kaney wrapped her arms around her and pulled her close, rocking her while she wept as the guilt and torments of a lifetime burned their way out of her heart. When the gasping sobs came, Kaney knew the purging was almost done.

"Nothing is unfixable," Kaney whispered as she lifted Kathy's head and gently held her wet cheeks between her palms. "And nothing is unforgivable except despair."

Kathy gazed at her through ragged eyes.

Kaney smiled and leaned forward and smoothed away the tears. "All will be well."

Kathy took Kaney's hands and held them between her own. "Are you in love with him?"

"I love him far more than I've ever loved myself. But I don't think he knows it."

Kathy smiled through her tears. "Oh, yes he does. He knows everything."

"Except his own worth."

"Yes, but he's never known that."

"Then . . . then do you think that perhaps some strawberry blonde could show him? Show him that at one special moment in his life he created something . . . created *someone* truly wondrous?"

Kathy looked afraid. "She would . . . if she had the courage."

"Oh, she has it. Courage is never lost. Mislaid sometimes, but it's always there in the shadows."

Kathy squeezed Kaney's hands. "Thank you for saying that."

Kaney grinned. "It's a small gesture."

Kathy just stared at her for a moment, and then they both laughed together.

26 IGNITION

Madero wrapped a many-colored Oaxacan blanket around himself and sank into his sofa. "This is useless, but I pretend," he said, shivering as he pulled it tight.

Kelly handed him a cognac.

"You're *muy generoso* with my spirits," Madero said as he took the glass.

"It's an Irish thing." He sat down with his own drink in the chair across from Madero. "Time for you to relax for a while. You look sick as hell."

"Time is what I don't have." Madero savored some of the cognac. "The attacks are getting more frequent. Who knows what will happen? Now tell me what you know about the Leek brothers."

"That's an odd question. . . ."

"Try answering it."

"What I know is mostly from Collie. They're orphans. They usually do day labor on the spreads around here. Ride the chucklines when they can't afford food. They've been accused of petty theft but nothing serious."

"Where do they live?"

"Here and there. Collie said they've been seen in a ghost town east of here. Sometimes they sleep in line shacks. I don't think they have a real home."

"Well, the starving Leek boys have been passing forty year old Mexican silver."

"Is that important?"

"It's certainly odd." Madero waited until a massive shiver had rippled through him. "Have you ever heard of the Glanton gang?"

"Scalphunters, weren't they?"

"Long ago." He took another sip. "They were wiped out by some Quechans about thirty-five years back. The gang's loot was never found. It was supposedly buried near Yuma."

"And . . . ? You think the Leek boys found it?"

"Not in Yuma."

"You can be mysterious when you want to be. What does this have to do with anything?"

"*No tengo ni idea,*" Madero said with a sigh. "But I learned something from riding on the other side of the law. When strange things happen together, it's dangerous not to pay attention. Even if they seem unrelated. Ignoring them is the shortest route to an ambush or a rope."

"Right now I'm baffled, my friend," Kelly said, shaking his head. "What strange things are you talking about?"

"I mentioned this to Holden, but I don't think he understood what I meant. I told him that I didn't like the lie of the table. It doesn't run true. Four expensive and ruthless men are hired by Barbicane to haze a few ranchers just so they'll sell out at a fair lay? Why? He doesn't need the land. Just to annoy Harlo? No. It's too weak."

"Well, I don't see how the Leeks could have anything to do with Barbicane. Do you?"

"*Amigo,* even I can't see everything. I'm not God." Madero smiled. "Just a fallen angel. But I do know that there are bumps in the baize here. The dice aren't rolling true."

The door swung open and Collie burst into the sitting room. Her face glistened with sweat and fear.

Madero stood up, the blanket still around his shoulders. "What is it, Blackie?"

"Buck, Mateo! He's been shot!"

Kelly sprang from his chair.

"Is he dead?" Madero asked calmly.

"No." She tried to get saliva into her mouth. "I mean I don't know. He was alive when I left. When I left the ranch."

"No," Kelly said, reading Madero's thoughts. "You'll shiver right out of the saddle. I'll handle this."

Madero glanced at Kelly and then looked back at Collie. The maturing young woman was gone. She gazed at him helplessly, a little girl lost at sea and slipping beneath the waves.

"Courage," Madero said, reaching out and touching her cheek, and she stopped shaking as if suddenly cured of a spell. Then Madero whipped the blanket from his body. "Let's ride."

The sun was low when the three of them reached the Harlo hacienda. Dr. Briscoe's buggy was hitched in front of the main building.

Collie hurried through the big mesquite door and Madero and Kelly followed.

In the enormous *sala*, Kathy sat on a sofa across from Harlo and Briscoe.

"He's sleeping," Briscoe said to Collie before she could ask anything. "It's the laudanum. He'll probably be awake in a little while. You can go sit with him if you'd like."

Collie disappeared down a hallway.

Madero glanced at Harlo. He was hunched in the chair like a crippled beggar.

"Fill me in," Madero said to Briscoe.

"He took a forty-four below the left shoulder. Went straight on through and looks like it missed the bone. I cleaned it and treated it with carbolic and left it open to drain. A pretty straightforward wound from what I can see. But I can't see everything."

"And?" Madero asked.

"That's it," Briscoe said.

Madero and Kelly looked at each other in equal bewilderment.

"Then why the grim looks?" Kelly asked.

Briscoe hesitated and then said, "The boy believes he's going to die. He says he wants to."

"Why?" Madero asked.

Briscoe looked away.

"Answer me."

"He says he's a failure."

"And who gave him that idea?" Madero asked, glaring at Harlo.

The old rancher kept his head lowered.

"Answer me, fat man."

Harlo looked up. He had aged a decade in a day. Now he just shook his head and turned away.

"Did Sutorius come by and tell you it was an accident and offer thirty pieces of silver to pay the doctor?"

"Mateo, please," Kathy said.

"Please what? Feel sorry for this fool?"

Madero dropped to one knee and looked Harlo in the eye. "Do you know why he wants to die? Because you never gave him a reason to believe his life was worth a damn. Now the only thing he can do to prove himself to you is to give you all he has."

"What's the prognosis?" Kelly asked Briscoe.

"He's going to die."

"From a shoulder wound?" Madero asked, spinning around.

"I've seen this before," Briscoe said. "In the war. Boys with minor injuries who believe they're going to die. Or who give up and just *want* to die. And they die."

"This is insane," Kelly said.

"What did you tell him?" Madero asked Briscoe.

"I told him it was a small wound that could heal perfectly in a month. That there was no reason to think it was too serious as long as it didn't fester. I underplayed it a little, but it's pretty much true."

"Oh, for God's sake," Madero said in disgust. "Stick with medicine, doctor. You don't know a damn thing about men."

Madero straightened up and went down the dark hallway where Collie had gone.

The bedroom door was ajar and he pushed it open.

Buck was awake and Collie was sitting in the pale lamplight beside the bed and holding his hand.

"*Hola compadre,*" Madero said and tossed his hat aside.

"Mateo," the boy whispered.

"Speak up."

"Hello," he said more firmly.

Madero sat on the edge of the mattress. "What's this all about?"

"I was rounding up some strays on the Barbicane spread and — ?"

"Weren't you told not to do that?"

"Mateo . . ." Collie said.

"Don't interrupt," Madero snapped.

"You're right. I was told not to."

"Then what?"

"The next thing I knew I was on the ground. And then I heard the shot. I think I did anyway."

"Did you see the shooter?"

"No."

"Mr. Barbicane came by," Collie said. "He was very upset. He told us that Kelliride and Scateen saw what they thought were rustlers in the half-light and Kelliride took a shot at them."

"How honest of him. Did Barbicane offer to pay the doctor bill?"

"How did you know that?" Collie said in surprise. "He did."

"So what did the doctor tell you?" Madero asked, looking back at Buck.

"He said it's a minor wound."

"He lied."

"It's not?" Collie almost shouted.

Madero ignored her. "Briscoe said wounds like that always get infected. He saw hundreds in the war. You have a couple of days. Maybe three." He turned to Collie. "Did anyone go to get Father Gallo?"

The boy's eyes filled with tears.

"Of course, it's usually young people who die from these things," Madero said. "Grizzled veterans almost always pull through. And my *pistoleros* — hell, they shake off these sorts of wounds like flea bites. But you're not one of my *pistoleros*."

Buck pushed himself higher, and Collie propped the pillow behind him so he could sit up.

"But I was going to be, wasn't I? You were going to teach me how to shoot. Remember?"

"Certainly I remember."

"It's my left shoulder, and I'm right-handed. It won't affect my shooting even if it doesn't heal right. Don't you think that's true?"

Madero slid the Remington from his sash and unloaded it and handed it to Buck. "Let me see."

The boy extended the pistol in his right hand.

Madero nodded. "Steadier than I thought. But that could be the laudanum."

"No, no, I've always been steady."

"Could be. You might even be a natural." He took the pistol back and reloaded it and returned it to his hip. "I have a .45 Colt on hold for you at the mercantile."

For a while Buck just stared at him. "I don't have that much money," he finally said. "And my father won't—."

"It's a gift, but the crabby *gruñón* behind the counter claimed he'd hold it only for a month. So the clock is ticking."

Collie slid her hand beside the bunched covers and pressed Madero's fingers.

"I can be better long before that. The bullet went all the way through. Doc Briscoe said it's a clean wound. And he's a great doctor."

"I've seen worse *médicos* I suppose," Madero said.

"Collie, could you get me some milk? And please tell Doc no more laudanum. It bothers my stomach."

Collie smiled and leaned forward and kissed Buck on the forehead. He flushed as red as a cactus fruit. Then she ran to get the milk.

"I'll see you soon," Madero said, standing up. "I have something to attend to tonight."

Buck smiled. "*Vaya con Dios,*" he said with a comical accent.

Madero nodded and picked up his hat and left the room.

Collie was waiting in the hallway.

Madero smiled at her.

She was gazing up at the Beatific Vision again. Then she reached out and took both of his hands. She held on for about a week.

"Blackie," Madero said, finally releasing her fingers, "I need a favor. First thing tomorrow, go to the merc and see if they have a .45 Colt. If not, let me know and we'll make sure we send somebody up to Tucson to get one."

Now the tears slid down her cheeks. "Thank you," she whispered.

Harlo's heavy footsteps sounded at the end of the hallway.

"Tend to your son," Madero said as the rancher came up through the darkness.

Then Madero led Collie into the living room.

"Get the milk, Blackie," Madero said, and she went off to the kitchen.

"What's your diagnosis?" Briscoe's tone showed that he was still stung by Madero's remarks.

"He didn't need laudanum," Madero answered, putting on his hat. "He needed Madero."

He headed toward the door.

"I'll go with you," Kelly said.

"No, Pat. Kathy and Collie need you to escort them home."

"What about you? Can you make it on your own? You look weak as a wet bird."

Kathy got up from the sofa and came over and laid a hand on Madero's arm. "Please don't do this."

"It'll be all right," he said with a gentle smile. "You've never lost that look of worry, have you?"

"Oh, Mateo, don't kill him. They'll hang you."

"Give my apologies to Collie for not saying goodbye."

The crowd at *La Luna* was as subdued as penitents lined up for Confession. Madero walked through the groups of quiet gamblers and up to the bar.

Bert came over immediately with a bottle of *El Tesoro*.

"Not tonight," Madero said. "Have you — ."

"Are you all right, Mateo?" Bert asked as he saw him shiver.

"Well enough. Have you seen Kelliride this evening?"

"He's in the billiard room. Cheery as an elf. I hate that smile."

"Is he heeled?"

"Didn't look like it."

"Anyone else?"

"I think Scateen is in the dining room."

"Why so quiet in here?"

"They all know what happened. Some of them said somebody should go up to Tucson for the Pima sheriff."

"Why? It was dark and the boy was trespassing. Rounding up cattle on somebody else's land." Madero slid his pistol from the sash at his waist. "So they don't hang me," he said, handing it to Bert.

"Did the boy die?"

"He's one of my *pistoleros*," Madero answered as if that were explanation enough.

Then he pushed himself away from the bar and walked toward the half-open door of the billiard room. He stopped at the entrance and looked through the doorway. Along the wall to the left below the cue rack, a cowhand on a bench sat waiting for his turn to play.

Madero placed his fingertips on the door panel. A half-dozen captain's chairs were scattered about the room and were filled by men waiting for their chance at a game. He pushed the door open completely and the billiard table came into view. Bending over the edge nearest the door was the wide back of the man he had come to see.

Kelliride's playing partner, an old drover, glanced at Madero from the other side of the table, but Kelliride was too engrossed in his own play to notice.

Madero selected an appropriate cue stick and approached the table.

"May I have the next game?" he said to Kelliride as pleasantly as if the two of them were old friends.

Kelliride straightened and turned around.

With the force of a Mediaeval axman, Madero crashed the stick with a two-hand blow fully into the center of Kelliride's face. The straight-grained maple shattered cartilage and Kelliride slammed backward against the table, banging his head on the edge as he went down.

The other men scattered to the edges of the room.

Kelliride reached up to the table to steady himself and tried to focus. His nose had been erased, replaced by a pulpy smear pouring blood. His front teeth gleamed like jagged white splinters behind the burst lips. He blinked several times at the dark figure standing before him.

"Did you think it would be easy?" Madero said.

With a roar of rage, Kelliride sprang to his feet and charged. His big head bored into Madero's stomach, and Madero grunted in pain and went down.

Kelliride spun around and seized the long bench as if it were as light as a broomstick.

Madero struggled to one knee just as the end of the bench smashed into his chest. Winded, he collapsed beneath it.

Kelliride paused to cough the blood out of his throat.

Drained of strength by disease, Madero pushed himself to his feet by colossal force of will. He now gazed through a gray haze at the unbowed figure of Kelliride. Again the big man charged.

Madero's blow at the bloody face was like a fist slammed into a locomotive. Kelliride's huge hands encircled Madero's throat. Madero fell backward and the small of his back hit the overturned bench, and he twisted in agony beneath the power and weight of the man above him. He locked his hands around Kelliride's throat, but he had little power in his fading fingers.

Farther and farther his spine arched as Kelliride battled to break his back. Madero jerked his right leg out from beneath him and slid his foot to the rear. He pulled his right hand off Kelliride's throat and fumbled at his trouser leg.

Kelliride dropped his weight hard onto Madero's chest.

Madero yelled in pain as his spine bent horribly at the edge of cracking. His fingers tore at his trouser edge like an eagle's talons, and at last they closed on the handle of the dagger in his boot. He whipped it from its sheath and plunged it into Kelliride's chest.

The killer wailed like a stricken boar. Madero wrenched the blade loose and drove it home with terrific speed. Again and again the blows fell. Each strike seemed to goad Kelliride further toward madness. Hot blood shot onto Madero's face and covered the slashing hand. At last Kelliride jerked away, the bloody handle of the knife slipping from Madero's grasp.

Kelliride staggered backward, the dagger still in his chest.

Madero pushed himself to his feet and tried to wipe Kelliride's blood from his eyes.

With a ghoulish howl of pain, Kelliride yanked the knife out of his chest.

A final image of Collie astride Diablo flashed across Madero's mind as Kelliride charged in for the kill.

The explosion startled everyone, and Kelliride's left shoulder twitched like the flick of a horse's muscle. Blood seeped from a glancing wound as he spun toward his left at this new tormentor.

The second blast hit him full in the chest. He fell back against the billiard table and fumbled for a grip.

Kaney strode into the room, a nickel-plated pistol extended straight out in her right hand. Her furious blue eyes glittered like sapphires flashed with lightning. She cocked and fired again and then again, and the twin blasts ripped through bone in Kelliride's massive chest.

Oh his knees, Kelliride confronted her with a contorted snarl of loathing torn from an Oriental mask.

Kaney advanced on the kneeling man and fired straight through his hideous mouth. Even the bullet must have felt profaned, for it did not linger but fled through the back of his head, stealing the contents with it.

Without taking her eyes off the corpse, Kaney stretched out her other arm to Madero.

He ignored her hand and whirled around to protect her back.

Scateen, pistol in hand, was running across the cantina toward the billiard room.

"Mateo!" Bert yelled from somewhere in the gambling hall, and Madero's pistol flew in over Scateen's head and Madero snatched it on the fly.

"Stop!" Madero boomed, the Remington already cocked and aimed at Scateen's stomach before he had even made it through the doorway. "Or die gut shot."

Kaney's pistol was empty, but she spun around to face any new threat to her man.

Scateen stopped as if he had hit a row of spears.

"Did you think that hurting a boy would end it?" Madero said, still straining for breath.

Scateen said nothing.

"Clear this trash out of here and tell your *patrón* that it's just begun."

Scateen laid his weapon down and came in and grabbed the body by the legs and hauled it across the floor. He labored as if he were dragging a dead buffalo.

For a few moments after he had gone, Kaney and Madero stood alone by the billiard table and just rested. Then a swarm of gamblers rushed into the room to snatch a closer look at the wild woman who had swept through their midst like a gale from Hell.

Kaney ignored them as Madero draped his arms over her and pulled her to him.

She sagged against his body. "A small gesture," she murmured as her head rested on his shoulder and she began crying softly.

<u>27</u> RECKONING

LIFE AND DEATH

SON OF RANCHER ASSAULTED

JUSTICE VISITED UPON ASSAILANT

This journal is distressed to report that Buck Stone, son of Harlo Stone of the Lazy S, was seriously wounded in what is alleged to be a case of mistaken identity. While rounding up strays at dusk, he was shot by a purported range detective, one Evan Hardin Kelliride, a man of the most questionable antecedents, who was engaged just recently by the Bar Double B. When a friend of the Stone family, Mateo Madero of Sonora, made of Kelliride what have been described as pointed inquiries about this tragic folly, the latter attempted to kill him. Witnesses inform us that Kelliride was decisively checked in this effort by a pistol-wielding member of the fair sex, whose identity this journal declines to reveal in the interests of propriety.

"Well?" Kelly asked.

"An inventive summary from someone who wasn't there," Madero said, laying down the sheet on Kelly's desk. "But isn't that always the case with newspapers?"

He smiled. "I did what I could."

"What witnesses did you speak with?"

"The other players in the billiard room. Bert, too. How's Kaney?"

"Still shaken."

"Naturally everyone in town knows by now it was her, but I had to maintain the niceties."

Kelly went to the stove and poured some coffee for both of them.

"Thank you," Madero said, taking a cup and sitting on the edge of the desk.

"And the Stone boy?"

"I was on my way out there when you waylaid me."

"Some of the Bar Double B hands are saying Barbicane pulled the erstwhile stock detectives off the range. At least for now."

"Why the change of heart?"

"I'm sure they're still ready to raise sand when the opportunity presents itself. Or if they can force the issue. But Barbicane is no killer."

"I never thought he was. But they're expensive just to have sitting in the shade and eating tortillas."

"It seems that most of Barbicane's men resent those four—three now, I guess. A few of them told me on the quiet that he was planning to fire them outright until Maart convinced him that you were the aggressor."

"Well, that cold-eyed *cabrón* is right—if you ignore the fact of a sixteen-year-old boy in bed with a bullet hole in him."

"Supposedly Barbicane isn't sure right now just how to use his prime negotiators."

Madero smiled. "He's like the monkey who was clever enough to open the tiger cage. Now he's confused and chattering at the top of the tree while the tigers are loose on the ground."

Kelly dropped into his desk chair. "I thought you might like to know that I sat up late last night with my Pinkerton hat on while you were engaging in all those theatrics."

"Does the hat still fit?"

"Like a bishop's mitre."

"Show me."

"Suppose what you suspect is true—that the Leek boys found some stashes of the Glanton blood money from years ago. . . ."

"All right."

"And suppose they haven't found all of it yet but are still searching. All the land around here is owned by Stone or Barbicane or Kathy. If it's not hidden somewhere on Kathy's spread or on Barbicane's—let's say that just for the sake of argument—then where is it?"

Madero sipped his coffee and said nothing.

"Let's say, too, that you don't really want the land because you already have more than you need, but you do need cash because you're a gambling degenerate who couldn't resist trying to buck the tiger a hundred times too many."

"If the Leek boys found the money, why wouldn't they just put it in a bank?"

"I don't know, but some people are strange about banks and don't trust them. Or maybe the Leeks found only a little bit of it so far and are still looking for the rest."

"On Harlo's spread?"

"Yes. And they don't want to risk their secret until they've found all of it."

"Where, under a pile of *mierda*?"

"How the hell do I know?" Kelly said in exasperation.

"What were you smoking last night? I think you stayed up too late."

"Don't you see what I'm saying?"

"*I'm* saying you might have taken too many pulls on the opium pipe." Madero set down his cup. "But, then again, maybe your pipe dreams really *are* telling us something."

"It certainly answers the question of why Barbicane is willing to squander money from his second mortgage on Sutorius and his crew. Look at the potential payoff. Who knows how much silver we might be talking about?"

"Well, maybe, but at night things always seem shrewder than they do in the morning."

"At least it makes sense as a working hypothesis. The important thing is that it answers your question, so we can—."

"Which one?"

"How two completely separate oddities—the Leeks with their forty-year-old silver and the Barbicane push—can actually be connected. And it explains why Sutorius and his two courtiers are still here. " Kelly smiled. "Doesn't that make you feel better now?"

"Oh, yes. *Estoy totalmente encantado.*"

Kelly looked like he was about to say something but then turned away.

"Don't be timid," Madero said.

"I was just thinking . . ." He took a sip of coffee and glanced over at Madero. "I was just thinking that the afterclaps haven't really hit yet . . . and that I'm glad you're here."

Madero said nothing.

"These are good people in this town," Kelly said. "They need someone who —."

"They need an honest sheriff, not a bandit."

Kelly laughed softly. "I guess you'll have to do."

"They have you to watch over them. And I think they know it."

"What are you talking about? I'm just an unemployed detective."

"If so, then where's the silver?"

"I can't answer that yet."

"Well, people are being shot," Madero said as he stood up. "You'd better answer it soon."

Madero went out and mounted Buddy in front of *The Clarion* office and smiled when he saw Diablo hitched before the mercantile down the street. Hoofbeats behind Madero caused him to turn. Holden was riding toward him from the opposite end of town. The Texan gestured, and Madero pivoted Buddy and trotted over to him.

"Can you come out to the ranch for a bit?" Holden asked.

"I'm on my way to the Lazy S."

"Just for a short spell. Kathy needs to see you."

"Couldn't she tell me that herself?"

"She had a bad night."

"Is she ill?"

"No, but she didn't sleep at all and she asked me to come in for you."

"Head out."

Holden said nothing all the way to the Callaghan spread, and Madero respected his silence.

When they arrived at the ranch, Kathy was already outside the house and waiting for them.

"I'll water your horse," Holden said as they dismounted.

Madero handed him the reins.

"Thank you," Holden whispered, and Madero was certain he was not thanking him for the reins.

As Holden led away the horses, Kathy walked over. "Thank you for riding out."

Madero smiled and flicked the brim of his hat so the hat fell down his back.

"Let's walk," she said in a sore voice as gritty as boot heels crunching a gravel road. "Please forgive how I look. I didn't sleep much." They wandered past the corrals and out toward the pasture. "I heard what happened at *la Luna*."

"I think everyone has heard what happened at *La Luna*."

"You could have died for nothing."

"There had to be a reckoning. Besides, I have my own guardian angel."

"Yes, I've learned that," she said with an intensity that surprised him. "You must really care about that boy."

"I know what it's like to feel abandoned."

Kathy pointed to the shade of a mesquite. "Please sit with me."

They rested under the tree, and Madero waited for her to speak.

"It's been so long, Matthew, so long," she said at last.

"Five lifetimes it seems."

She sighed and shook her head. "Then why can't I think of what to say?"

"Do you really want to know?"

That obviously surprised her. "I do."

"Because there's nothing important to say. Not now. Isn't there a line in the Bible about letting the dead bury their dead? The past is dead. Bury it."

"I can't," she said, lowering her head.

"*¿Qué pasa?*"

She looked back up. "Don't worry, I'm not going to cry. I'm all cried out." She reached behind the fabric of her apron belt and pulled out a *carte de visite*. "Please," she said, handing it to him.

Madero examined the photographic image pasted onto the stiff little card. A young man, appearing serious and composed in a rather ill-fitting rented suit, gazed off to the right in a three-quarter profile.

"Have I met him?"

"No, he's been dead a long time. That's Brian, my late husband."

Madero glanced again at the picture. "A nice looking young man." He handed the card back to her. "You should have kept it out of the sun and not let it fade like that."

"It's been in the dark in a drawer for sixteen years. Along with a cabinet card from our wedding."

Madero took the card back and examined it again.

"It's not faded," Kathy said. "His hair was the same color as mine."

Madero looked up from the picture.

"Oh, God," she said and jerked her head away. "I'm so sorry."

She had been wrong. She was not all cried out.

Madero laid the card gently onto her lap and stood up. He turned away and felt as if he were trying to breathe with an anvil on his chest.

"Black Irish," he said softly. "Like the legend."

"Please don't look away from me."

He turned back toward her. "Why would I do that?"

"For what I've done."

He sat down but remained quiet.

She seemed bewildered. "You're not angry?"

"How could I be?"

Her eyes filled with tears again. "I'm sorry, I can't seem to stop crying today."

"Have you told her?"

"I'm afraid."

"Then why did you tell me? Why now?"

She looked away. "I was shamed into it."

"How?"

"I'd rather not say."

"Dammit, Kath, tell me."

"By your guardian angel."

"*¿De qué demonios estás hablando?*" Madero blurted as he suddenly misplaced his English.

She looked confused.

"What the hell are you talking about, Kath?"

"Kaney."

"*¡Por de Dios! ¿Cómo es posible?*"

222

"How is what possible?"

"Kaney!"

"She's an amazing woman. She saw right away what I see every day of my life. The smile in Collie's eyes. It's your smile."

A long silence followed.

"Don't tell Collie, Kath," Madero said at last. "There's no point now."

"I'd love not telling her because I'm scared, but don't you think she should know?"

"No."

"Why not?"

"She needs a real father. Let's be honest, you and Kelly are going to walk down the aisle eventually and — no, no, don't even try denying it. And that's family enough. He'll be a great father to her."

"But half of her is *you*. The best half."

"Don't be ridiculous. My whole life has been an *audición* for the graveyard."

"Do you think she cares about that?"

"She should."

"She won't. She never will."

Madero looked off at nothing. "How can a good thing make you feel like you've just been nailed to a cross? My God, my God, why have you forsaken me?"

"Oh, Matthew, he hasn't. He's given you Kaney, and she's a blessing. She believed you deserved to know. She loves you more than you realize."

He looked into Kathy's eyes. "No she doesn't."

"She doesn't love you?"

"No, I mean she doesn't love me more than I realize. Believe me, I realize it." He pushed himself up from the grass and gazed off toward the mountains. "I'm sorry for yelling at you, Kath." He turned to her with a sad smile. *"De verdad te lo digo."*

She smiled back, and it looked like the first smile she had enjoyed in a long time. "I know." She stood up.

"There's one thing more I have to do right now," he said, spreading his arms.

She stepped toward him, and he pulled her close. She was shaking as he held her.

223

"I have to thank you for making me, for even just a moment, the happiest man alive."

Kaney was riding Don Luis's buckskin as she approached Madero along the road back to San Miguel.

Madero clicked to Buddy and he trotted off and then stopped beside her. She seemed uncertain, and Madero waited for her to speak.

"I saw you ride away with Rake, and I knew where you were going. And why."

"You're a hell of a detective," Madero said with a look as stern as the face of the Stygian boatman.

"Are you angry with me?"

"Don't you think I should be?"

She hesitated. "Perhaps."

"I agree." Then he could hold back no longer and his booming laugh startled even Buddy.

Kaney stared at him in confusion.

He leaned over and gave her the most sensuous kiss since Adam fell from grace.

She reddened.

"Really, woman, you're so much older than I that your experience in these matters has to be greater than mine. So how did you fake the blush of a frightened virgin?"

Kaney laughed until she cried. "Maybe it's because a first kiss never came to me before from *un pistolero Mejicano* on horseback," she said, still struggling to control her laughter.

"Well, Buddy is mature about these things, but I'm not so sure about that young mare of yours."

Kaney's smile faded gently. "You had to be told, Mateo, and she had the obligation to tell you."

"I know," he said, as they both rode back toward town.

"Remember what you said to me? How Collie looked familiar to you? Of course she did. You were looking at yourself. It was so obvious to me."

"A man can never truly see himself. In anyone. Sometimes he pretends, but that's all. We're born speechless and we grow up sightless."

"Are you glad I did what I did?"

"I am. And yet . . ."

"What?"

"I'm shamed by all this, too. All those years . . . that little girl without a father."

"But what could you have done? You never knew."

"I *should* have known. And it's going to haunt my dreams. I'll never escape it. But . . . well, that's Heaven's fair judgment."

They rode along quietly for a while.

"But you can do something about it now," Kaney finally said. "Something for her."

"What on earth can we do?"

"We?" she said, turning toward him in surprise.

"What could I hope to do for her without you? We're a team, aren't we?"

She quickly looked away.

"*¡Ay!*" he said. "No tears. I've had enough female crying for today."

"You're impossible!" she answered, turning back to him and smiling through moist eyes.

"Being *incorregible* is my special appeal."

"So what do you propose?"

"I'm not familiar with that word."

"*Señor*, you have the most convenient lapses in English when you want to."

"My education has certain gaps."

"But proposal? That's an easy word."

Madero shrugged.

"*¡Propuesta!*" she shouted in mock anger.

"*No comprendo.*"

"You're such a rogue. What can I do with you?"

Madero laughed. "*Never* say that to a man."

28 SPECTERS

Kaney was helping Sally stock the humidor when she saw a familiar figure step out of the dying storm and into the shelter of *La Luna*.

The rain had kept the usually small afternoon crowd even smaller, but now in the early evening they were beginning to drift in. Kaney watched the lean man as he carefully removed his dripping gray slicker and laid it across a chair and placed his dark hat onto the empty table beside it. A handsomely tooled black rig holding a nickel-plated Colt on his right hip rode high on his waist. He swept his gaze around the room and then toward the bar where Kelly stood with Luis.

"Odd looking, isn't he?" Luis said to Kelly.

"He has liver disease."

The stranger walked toward them with a weary stride, as if he had ridden a long way.

"Gentlemen," he said in a voice that sounded like it had been scored by too much Indian liquor.

"Sir," Luis said.

The man rested against the bar. "Do either of you know someone named Kelliride?"

"I do," Kelly said. "*Amigo* of yours?"

"Him?" he answered with a grating laugh. "He didn't even like his friends. He owed me money."

"Sorry," Kelly said. "He cashed in."

Kaney watched as the man's gaze flitted back and forth between Kelly and Luis. "Not natural causes I guess."

"I'm surprised you haven't heard yet," Kelly said.

"Well, obviously I wouldn't have come such a long way if I'd known he was dead. But—."

"I didn't say he was dead," Kelly answered. "If you believe as I do, he's somewhere else right now."

The man's eyes narrowed. "You didn't like him then?"

"Even his friends didn't like him."

The man smiled, but it seemed fake.

"You can check with Lawton Barbicane of the Bar Double B," Kelly said. "Kelliride worked for him. Maybe he left some cash."

Kaney stepped away from the humidor and stopped beside Luis behind the bar.

"This is fate, I suppose," the man said to Kaney with the most revolting smile she had ever seen.

"This gentleman was asking about Mr. Kelliride," Luis said.

"He's not a gentleman," Kaney answered.

The man looked like he was struggling to keep his smile.

"Tell them about the tough *hombre* who cut your cheek like that," Kaney said, nodding at the half-healed wound. "Or was it a woman?"

Still smiling, he said, "All real men should bear at least one slash from a wildcat."

"Kelliride bears his. I shot him through the face. Keep it in mind."

The stranger glanced at Kelly and Luis again and then went and got his things and left the cantina.

Kaney pressed her hands together to stop them from shaking.

"What was that, *bonita*?" Luis asked, obviously stunned by Kaney's verbal slaps at the stranger. "Who is he?"

"The one who pawed me in Tucson. They say he's a killer. His name is Cord Wilson."

Kelly frowned. "I think I know that name. . . ."

"Mateo might have mentioned him to you," Kaney said.

"Maybe," Kelly answered, but he seemed troubled.

"What did he want?" Kaney asked.

"He claimed Kelliride owed him money," Luis said.

"It's an odd feeling, that name." Kelly still looked uncomfortable. "It doesn't sit right. . . ." He pushed himself away from the bar. "See you fine people later."

After Kelly had gone, Luis turned to Kaney. "I haven't seen Mateo all day."

"He has a great deal on his mind right now."

"Bad things?"

"Good things, but . . . " She turned away.

"Cristina, what is it?" Luis said, laying a hand atop hers on the bar.

She turned back to him. "Is it possible to do something right and still have it be wrong?"

"You sound like an old philosopher," he answered with a smile. "I'm not wise enough to know that."

"Well, if Don Luis is not, what hope is there for any of us?"

"Love is the only hope for any of us."

"Oh Lord," she said, looking away. "Do I wear it like a banner?"

"*All* women wear their love like a banner. It's one of the beauties of womanhood."

"I can't even breathe without thinking about him."

Luis rubbed her hand gently. "Then all is right with the world."

"No," Kaney said. "It's not. He thinks he's going to die soon."

"But we're all going to die soon. Life is brief for every man. No matter."

"Don Luis Dámaso," she said with a tired smile, "you make me feel better even when I'm not sure exactly what you're saying."

Luis grinned. "Obscurity always makes an uncertain man seem profound."

"There," Kelly said, handing the sheet of paper to Madero.

"I've already read this," Madero said as he sat on the edge of Kelly's desk and held the first page of the Pinkerton record of Kelliride.

"Did Kaney tell you about Wilson coming by this evening? He was looking for Kelliride."

"She did. He's the one who got her fired in Tucson."

Madero smiled. "Thank God."

"I'm serious."

"You might try being clear instead."

"Wilson isn't here to collect a debt. At least not from a corpse. Read that again. Who was Kelliride's partner?"

Madero glanced down at the sheet. "*¡Híjole!*" He looked back at Kelly. "You're a lot sharper than you look."

"Why is it that even a compliment from you has a rough edge on the back of it? Like a goddam fish scaling knife."

Madero laughed.

"Well, it's him. I'm certain of it."

"Wilt Corson?"

"Robber and killer. The name Cord Wilson sounded familiar when you first told me. Remember? And ever since Kaney said it again tonight, it's been boring like a deathwatch beetle in my brain."

"It's a clever twist on the name."

"Criminals are strange. Sometimes they create the most outrageous aliases. Other times they just flip a few letters around. I've seen this many times."

"Well, I guess we can assume he isn't here to collect money."

"He's here to kill Kelliride's killer."

"Kaney? I've known some rotten bastards—on both sides of the law—but I've never known one who'd shoot down a woman."

"No, I mean you. You're the one who cracked Kelliride's face like an egg."

"So?"

"And maybe he's even here to take Kelliride's place with the other three choir boys. And idiot me sent him straight out to Barbicane."

"What does it matter?"

"Aren't you concerned about this?"

"Should I be?"

"I wired the Denver office this evening for more information on him. He's killed four men. In straight up fights. He's no back shooter."

"Then I'll make sure I keep my back toward him."

Kelly sank into his desk chair. "You're not a normal man. Do you know that?"

"Did I ever claim to be?"

"I've just never known anyone who didn't worry."

"Sorry, but I've never mastered agonizing. At least about myself."

"For God's sake, it's not some acquired skill, it's natural. Like breathing. It helps us stay alive."

"No it doesn't. It just shortens a man's life. And mine promises to be short enough."

"So what do you think?" Kaney said as she snuggled next to Madero on the sofa.

"Kelly is probably right about Corson looking for his partner. And maybe even working for Barbicane, too, if the pot is sweet. And the Mexican silver is making it sweet."

"Do you think he'll come after you?"

"He might. But he'll play it cautious for a while."

She hooked an arm around his and pressed her head against his shoulder. "Well, coming after you would be the biggest mistake he ever made."

Madero smiled. "So far, I think meeting *you* was."

She laughed.

"Now that poor ailing killer forever bears the Mark of Kane. An embarrassing badge to wear when he finally walks the streets of Hell."

"Let's not talk about him anymore."

Madero wrapped an arm around her. "Let's not."

"Why don't you sleep in the bed tonight? You look tired. I'll use the sofa."

"I'll be fine here."

"Do you ever agree with me about anything?"

"Why set a precedent?"

She just sighed.

"Get some rest now."

"All right," she said, slowly standing up. "I need my beauty sleep."

"Like hell you do."

She bent down and kissed him lightly on the lips.

"Hmmm," Madero said. "Rather chaste."

She straightened up. "That's so I can continue to be chased," she said with a smile and hurried off to bed.

Madero smiled after her and got up and put out all the lamps but one and turned that one down low. He poured himself some cognac and settled back into a corner of the sofa in the darkness.

He had deliberately not told Kaney that he felt physically restless and emotionally uneasy this night. For the first time in more than a year, he craved the laudanum that would grant him release. More than anything now, he wanted to reach for the cruel nepenthe and erase his mind of everything that had ever happened in his life, though he knew that was a fool's errand. So, with growing dread, he sipped the cognac and drowsed. Finally he set down the glass and stretched out on the sofa and drifted off. He later wished he had died. As he would tell Kaney in the morning, he felt as if he were both an observer of and a participant in a horrid unfolding.

In his slumber, he found himself in the aisle of a vast cathedral. He was sitting on a bishop's chair carved from ice. Looking up almost casually through the roofless church, he could see millions of stars flickering in the black void. Yet the serenity of the heavens was suddenly shattered by a ghastly upheaval. Without warning, the North Star convulsed and died in the sky, and the grieving planets lowered it like a corpse into a limitless abyss. The sun, rising at midnight, sizzled and fell, while the moon whirled and fled like a runaway wheel. Behind where the sun and moon had hung, there now glared two dead holes, sightless sockets in the vanishing face of a dying universe. And then the planets, deprived of their guide, tumbled and crashed into a bottomless tomb, gorged with the weeping ruins of ravaged worlds.

Madero groaned in horror. His flesh was painfully cold, but he was powerless to rise. Melting but never shrinking, the ice chair held him. It seemed to him impossible that a man could endure such cold and survive. But he had to live, for he was expecting someone. He could not recall who it was—the face receded just beyond the edge of his memory. But for eons he must wait for this elusive phantom. From far away, he heard a clock ticking off every second of the millennium. With a mindless monotony the tick-tock tyrannized him in its relentlessness. Yet he remained locked in place for the faithless friend who did not come, as he teetered on the brink of a frozen infinity. What was the despairing cry of the King of Addicts?—"An eternity not coming, but past and irrevocable."

Still shivering in the cathedral, he stared in revulsion when, without warning, an obscene duality grappled within his own mind. He twisted and recoiled as a succubus, scaly and serpentine, sought to draw within its coils his better nature in a mating of indescribable perversion. His finer qualities howled as they were entwined with the appalling drives of his darkest self. Two incompatible natures, each one repulsive to the other, locked together in a monstrous embrace. Like a pair of hate-filled animals coupling in an unnatural frenzy, this foul fusion revolted the heavens and struck loathing even in the infinite tolerance of God.

Madero wailed for release, but all he heard in response were mocking whispers in the darkness as they laughed and conspired in the downfall of his reason.

Behind him, footsteps echoed in the emptiness. Unable to turn, he was strangling from fear as they approached. A pair of woman's hands, bloodless and cold, slid around his upper arms. He moaned without hope.

Inexplicably, he found himself in a musty crypt beneath the church. No source of light could be found, and yet somehow he could see. The floor was strewn with rotting corpses wrapped in winding sheets. Little space showed among them, and he had to walk across reeking cadavers in order to escape. His foot crushed a stomach and it exploded in putrefaction. The mouth gaped in a silent scream and spewed rank gases, and he gazed in terror at the decomposing face of Colleen Callaghan. He yelled in protest and leaped away but fell with even greater force onto another carcass. That, too, burst with the miasma of decay. He turned toward it fearfully and saw again the face of Collie, bloated and black with dissolution. He wrenched his eyes away, but now he saw before him hundreds, thousands of rotting Collies. Unburied and unmourned, they would foul forever this secret crypt in the Church of the Pariahs.

He longed to fall to his knees and pray, but there was no space to kneel. He hurled himself against the dripping walls to break them down with his own body. Finally, after centuries of this useless torment, he lowered his head and wept.

"Sh, sh, sh," came a voice from the edge of the abyss.

Madero opened his eyes and saw the blessed face of Kaney as she knelt on the floor beside him in the half-light and cradled his head. She curled her arms around his neck and pulled his face against her. "I've got you," she whispered. "Don't be afraid."

That night, the most feared man in all Sonora sobbed without shame and finally sought solace in the safest place on earth, the soft valley between a loving woman's breasts.

<u>29</u> AMONG THE RUINS

A half-hour before sunup, Madero stood with one foot hiked up on a chair and savored some coffee from Don Luis's kitchen as he thought about life and death.

Kaney was curled up asleep in the corner of the sofa. Madero stepped away from the chair and leaned over and kissed her on the thick swath of hair that had fallen across her cheek.

She gave a start and opened her eyes.

"I'm sorry. I didn't think that would wake you."

She smiled sleepily. "As if a kiss from you wouldn't wake every woman."

He took each of her hands in his. "What I owe you is beyond imagination."

She squeezed his fingers.

"I'm going to go for a ride to clear my brain. I won't be long."

She released his hands and wrapped an arm around his neck and kissed him roughly.

"So there," she said with a smile.

"You tempt fate, young lady."

"I'm trying!"

Madero picked up his pistol from beside the statue of the Blessed Mother and grabbed his hat.

"Lock the door behind me."

Kaney winked at him, and he went out to the barn. Buddy came in from the outside pen when he heard the footsteps. Madero entered the stall and rubbed his horse softly on the forehead. He hooked an arm over him and then just leaned against that broad neck for support. With the preternatural intuition of horses everywhere, Buddy sensed his leader's unease and remained still but watchful.

Madero stroked Buddy's neck and spoke to him gently, and the horse cocked a hind leg and relaxed. Then Madero brushed him and picked his feet and saddled up.

Long ago in Sonora, Madero had been out riding in the evening when a friend had caught up with him to tell him that his favorite horse was ill back in Magdalena. The short return journey had been the longest of his life. The ride had been a blur then and still was, like the smeared image of someone running unexpectedly in front of a photographic plate. Now as he crossed the grasslands with Buddy, he suffered the same grotesque distortion. In a landscape soundless but somehow threatening, sights seemed flat and unreal, empty of detail. He struggled to bring his senses into focus, but finally he despaired and just rode on, deadened to the dead world around him.

But Buddy was there, vibrant and alert, caring now for the master who had always cared for him.

After a quiet trot of what could have been ten minutes or a week, Madero saw the tips of some buildings come into view beyond a ridge in front of the rising sun. He brought Buddy down to a walk, and man and horse took in their surroundings as they approached. Unlike in San Miguel, extra timber had been used in the confident construction of this fallen town, but to no lasting purpose. More wood but not more will.

Madero rode past a tiny graveyard of a dozen forgotten souls and entered a main thoroughfare that some optimists might once have called an avenue. An abandoned mine cart rusted at the edge of a cross street. Then the saddest irony of all appeared as he and Buddy rounded a corner. A split and faded sign over a doorway proclaimed the *Esperanza Observer*. A newspaper of hope in a tumbled ruin of splintered hopes and shattered dreams.

Madero rode up to a trough fresh with water from the summer rains. He let Buddy drink and scanned the area. Fresh hoof prints along the main street showed that other riders had passed through, probably to water their mounts. Even an occasional squatter might have been living in some derelict shop, although Madero saw no signs of life anywhere except basking lizards and squawking birds startled by the approach of strangers.

When Buddy raised his dripping lips from the trough, Madero laid a rein against his neck and they moved off. Madero hugged the eastern edge of the street, and the long shadows from the buildings cooled horse and rider as pleasantly as an early morning mist.

One thing that had always puzzled Madero about ghost towns was how so many of them seemed to have halted in mid-breath. After a slow and gasping decline, they seemed suddenly to stop, as if their few remaining inhabitants had just realized that they had pressing business elsewhere. In front of the desiccated husk of the newspaper office, a long low bench still held a checkerboard and a few pieces. Madero nudged Buddy over toward the boardwalk and then dismounted and grabbed his canteen. He loosened the cinch and let Buddy rest in the shade.

The pasteboard of the old black and red battlefield had so often caught windswept rains and then dried that it looked like a shriveled roofing shingle. For no sensible reason, Madero picked up some of the scattered checkers and returned them to the board. Sitting down where only specters sat now, he pulled off his hat and leaned back against the wall and thought about love and longing.

A turkey vulture circled in the blue heavens beyond the western edge of the shattered town. How carefree it seemed as Madero watched it soar upon the updrafts. So many people envied the great stalking carnivores of the world, with their ominous strength and penetrating intelligence. Yet each of those muscled marauders was nailed to the earth, a powerless prisoner of its own hulking mass. There in the sky lived real freedom. But not down here, where every captive was shackled to the ground like the chained predator that a fanciful newspaperman liked to call Madero of Sonora.

The vulture swooped low enough for Madero to glimpse its scarlet head and then the bird flew off, perhaps for something enticing that only its sharp eyes could see. Madero felt sad when it wheeled away and soared out of sight.

He opened his canteen and took a sip and threw some water on his face. The splash caught Buddy's attention, but then the horse suddenly swung his head to the side and Madero followed his gaze.

A dog was walking up the street toward them. Red-coated and about fifty pounds or so, he looked well fed for one who might be the last citizen of Esperanza. He stopped in the middle of the street about twenty feet away and inspected man and horse as if he had done this many times before. Long accustomed to dogs, Buddy turned away and his eyelids drooped.

When Madero stood up, he thought the dog might run, but the animal stayed where he was. Madero went to his saddlebags and pulled out a piece of *charqui* wrapped in brown paper. He turned and dropped to one knee.

"The *gringos* call it jerky," he said to the dog, "but I'll bet you know better." He smiled and extended his hand.

The dog hurried over and took it, retreated just a few paces, and then lay down and dined.

Madero went back to the bench and watched the dog tear into the meat much faster than human teeth ever could. As he gazed at the contours of the handsome red mongrel, he suddenly remembered a book the sisters had shown him when he was a child. It was a volume of engravings of Roman ruins, and among its treasures was an image of a street in Pompeii with one of the many feral dogs that lived there among the wreckage. This dog before him looked like that earlier one's reincarnation. It startled him to think of that now, and yet somehow it comforted him as well.

When the dog was finished, he came over and stood at the edge of the boardwalk and gazed at Madero with a soft eye. Madero tossed his hat upside down onto the planking and poured some water from his canteen into the crown. Without hesitation, the dog walked over and took a long drink.

"It makes me thirsty, too," Madero said.

He dreaded when the dog would finish and leave, but without warning the sated animal jumped up onto the bench and began licking Madero's chin. Madero caressed his face, and then the dog lay on the bench and rested his head in Madero's lap. Madero laid an arm across him, and the dog shifted his position a bit and then sighed and relaxed as fully as if he were stretched out for a nap on a feather bed.

Madero reached down and dumped the water out of his hat, and the dog never moved despite being jostled. Then Madero leaned back and closed his eyes. He felt that he could happily stay like this for eternity.

Yet God was not so merciful. Madero realized he must have been dozing when he gave a start and snapped his head up at the dog's growl. A rider was coming along the street from the south. Madero felt the warmth of the pistol on his hip.

The dog jumped off the bench. Ears back, he stepped to the edge of the boardwalk and stood between Madero and the stranger.

Madero heard himself sigh. That awkward horseman was an embarrassment to his Spanish blood. Even Buddy seemed to be eyeing him with despair.

"Next time try a wagon," Madero said as the rider came up.

Don Luis dismounted beside Buddy. He pulled off his straw sugar loaf hat, and Madero stood up and handed him the canteen as he came over into the shade. The dog looked at Madero and then back at Luis and evidently decided to allow this.

"What brings you to the shadow of Vesuvius?" Madero said.

Obviously puzzled by that, Luis shook his head and dropped onto the bench. Madero sat, and the dog took a sentry position between the feet of the two men.

"I didn't realize you were an Apache tracker," Madero said.

"I couldn't track a pig through a mud wallow," Luis answered and took a sip of water. "But I suspected you might end up here."

"Why is that?"

"All who are lost or adrift ultimately come to Esperanza."

Madero suspected he might be making a joke about the town's name, but Luis's eyes said otherwise.

"I didn't even know this town was here."

"It doesn't matter. The Almighty knew."

"A Spanish mystic," Madero said in exasperation. "That's what I need today."

Luis held out a hand to the dog and allowed him to sniff it. The dog seemed to approve and then relaxed, but he remained alert.

"Children play here, lovers love here, outlaws supposedly hide plunder here. And the despairing pray here. It defies explanation." Luis raised an eyebrow. "But it's true."

"Plunder?"

"That's the rumor."

"How long has it been like this?"

"¿*Una ruina*? More years than I've been here. Nobody can move in because Harlo owns most of the land in the area."

"Even the town?"

"That, too. And he bought up all of the old mining claims so he could have access to the grasslands nearby."

"Are there ever any squatters here? In the town?"

"Squatters?"

"*Okupas.*"

"There probably have been."

"Did you ever see the Leek brothers around here?"

"People see them around here all the time."

Madero leaned his head back against the wall, and for a while the two men just sat quietly and enjoyed the soft breeze.

"So why are you here today?" Madero asked after a few minutes.

"Concern."

"For?"

"You, of course."

"¿*Por qué*?"

Luis hesitated and then said, "Kaney told me about Colleen. I don't think she wanted to. But she was happy for you and it just came pouring out. Señor Kelly was there, too. Don't be angry with her for telling us."

"I'm not angry."

"I thought that perhaps today was not a good day for you to be alone. That maybe you wanted to talk to a friend."

"A man with an honest horse and a loyal dog is never alone. Besides, I simply had a bad night. That's all."

"And Colleen?"

Madero said nothing.

"Will you —?"

Madero silenced Luis with the wave of a hand.

Luis turned and leaned against the wall, and both men sat quietly.

After a while, Luis said, "May I speak now?"

Madero could not help smiling. "I don't think I can stop you unless I shoot you."

"Catalina should tell Colleen."

"Would *you*?"

Luis said nothing and looked away.

"A lie is just a lie in the beginning. After a week it begins to fester." Madero reached for his canteen and took a sip. "After a decade, it's a cancer."

"Do you think her husband ever knew?"

"I'm sure he did. Kathy would have told him the truth. Especially since it happened before they met."

"And the others in town?"

"Some must have suspected when they saw that black-haired baby. But apparently not many people had known her husband anyway. And by the time Collie was born, he was dead and all that most people would think about would be how to help the widow lady rear her little girl. The *Miguelanos* are good people."

"Yes, they are."

"So I suppose Kathy thought it was just a simple little lie to tell her daughter. No harm in that." Madero failed to control the bitterness in his laugh. "Is there?"

"Don't be angry."

"I'm angry only with myself."

"But now you can—."

"It's time for me to step aside."

Luis looked as if he had just been struck in the face with a bullwhip. "Aside?"

"To go."

"Leave San Miguel? You're already fitting into his place."

"I've never fit into any place." He smiled. "But I do love that little town. Yet Kaney and I have to leave."

"*¿Por qué?*"

"Isn't it obvious? Kathy and Kelly are going to be a couple. A one-eyed man could see it with his dead eye."

"So?"

"Colleen needs one mother and one father. No ghosts from the past lurking in the shadows."

"Catalina is a fair woman. She'd understand if you wanted to stay."

"I won't make a demand on her like that. The past is too —."

"You speak too much of the past."

Madero reached down and stroked the head of the dog. "It's the pointless habit of a man with no future," he said good-naturedly. "Nothing to be upset about."

"Of course it's something to be upset about!"

Madero smiled. "*¡Relájate!*"

"How can I relax? Listen to me. Just make each day count. Be happy. Believe in God. Dream of the past if you will but don't live in it."

"I wish I'd known you in my youth."

"You know me now."

"And I'm the better man for it."

Luis shook his head from side to side. "I can't believe you'd leave. Not while this whole bag of nails —."

"You and I will always be partners. I like *La Luna* too much to let that go. Besides, I'm not leaving right now." Madero stood up and stepped to the edge of the boardwalk with the dog walking beside him. He laid a hand against one of the poles holding up the roof over the boardwalk and stared into the distance. "Kelly is a good man. Tough, too. And Holden is no slacker. But these naïve *yanquis* aren't up to this."

"You say that as if there's more to it than most people see."

"I'm certain of it." Madero gazed off at another vulture circling in the blue. "I know that it's more dangerous than a squabble over cattle and water. There's death on the wind. Too much for the Pinkerton man and the Texican to handle." He extended both arms straight upward as high as he could and groaned as he stretched his tight muscles. "So I can't go yet. Not when there's so much killing to be done."

Buddy dipped his lips into the stream running off the High C just as the red dog barked at something in the distance. Madero turned in his saddle and saw Collie on Diablo resting in the shade of a mesquite about a hundred yards away. She twisted around and waved when she saw him. There was something so happy and exuberant in that wave that Madero instantly made a decision that he knew would change his present life forever. And, in effect, end it. He decided to take the bullet in the heart right now and be done with it.

He turned Buddy around and trotted toward Collie with the dog enthusiastically running alongside them. Collie closed the distance and met him about halfway, which, Madero thought, was much more than most others had ever had the courage to do.

She smiled, but dark circles under her lovely eyes pointed to a restive night.

"You're not supposed to be out here alone," Madero said, but he was finding it difficult to be stern.

"I'm not alone now," she answered in a tone that was weary but happy.

"Aren't you feeling well?"

"Do I look that bad?"

"You seem tired."

"I had a bad night. Terrible dreams."

Madero dismounted and Collie did as well, and they loosened their cinches a notch and let their horses wander off to graze.

The dog hurried over to her and Collie dropped to the ground and petted him while he licked her.

"He's a great judge of character," Madero said as they wandered back to the shelter of the mesquite.

"Where did you get him?"

"He's the mayor of Esperanza." Madero tossed his hat onto the ground, and they sat across from each other on the grass.

"I was coming into town to see you today," Collie said. "So this is a nice coincidence."

But Madero had stopped believing in coincidences long ago.

"I wanted to show you something that my mom gave me last night. It's a picture of my father. I'd never seen it before."

243

The pain that suddenly flooded Madero was so intense that it somehow seemed to expand far beyond normal torment into some sort of anguished delirium reserved until now only for his nightmares.

Collie went over to Diablo and pulled a small cloth pouch out of the saddlebag. Then she came back and knelt beside Madero.

At that moment, Madero knew that he lacked the courage to do anything but continue living the lie.

Collie handed him the little red velvet sack, and he reached inside and pulled out a tiny mirror and saw himself gazing back from it.

Stunned, he looked into Collie's desperate eyes.

She smiled, but half fearfully, and then in an instant her arms were around his neck as she wept with a primal joy such as no man could ever dare imagine.

When finally she collapsed on him in exhaustion, his shirt was soaked from her tears. Hesitantly, he slid his arms around her, and for the next thousand years they sat on the fresh Arizona grass and held each other tenderly and in silence.

30 DESTINY

"Who's this handsome fellow?" Kaney said with a smile as she dropped to one knee.

The red dog jumped up and placed its paws on her shoulders and begin licking her face.

"I call him Pompey," Madero said. "After that fated town."

"Is he yours?"

"I think I'm his."

"Where did he find you?"

"A ghost town east of here."

She rubbed vigorously behind the dog's ears. "With a bath and a brushing, he'll be quite the dashing rascal."

"I've always had a soft spot for waifs who clean up nice."

She looked up at Madero from beneath an arched eyebrow. "Lucky for all of us," she said with mock sarcasm.

"Has Kelly been here today?"

"He's having breakfast in the dining room." She stood up. "I spoke with Luis today . . . about Collie."

"I know. It's all right."

A look of relief swept across her face like a splash of sunlight. "I never knew a man who never got angry. Thank you."

"I save my anger for my own follies." He pointed toward the reading room.

She led the way, and Pompey followed them into the quiet shadows among the books.

Madero reached down and picked up a small ring of delicately braided horsehair that had been looped over the hammer of his pistol.

"Left hand," Madero said.

She extended her arm toward him, and he slipped the little black hoop over her ring finger.

She stared at it and bit down hard into her lower lip.

"Please," Madero said. "Don't drown me again."

She struggled to keep her composure.

"Buddy provided the raw material. I braided it on the ride back. I'll get you a proper one when this is all over."

She seemed as if she were about to speak, but then just shook her head from side to side.

"I own a silver mine in Sonora, so we can do better than this."

"No, we can't," she whispered. "Nothing could be better than this."

She slid her arms around him and he pulled her close. Suddenly she began laughing softly.

"¿Qué?" Madero said.

She took a half-step back and looked him in the eyes. "A homeless widow, a stray dog, and the Dark Archangel. Now *there's* a family made in Heaven!"

Madero laughed with her. "Where else could it be made *but* Heaven?"

"I love you more than you know," she said so only he and Pompey could hear.

"Oh, no. It's *not* more than I know." He kissed her on the forehead.

"You saw Collie today, didn't you?"

He looked at her in disbelief. "Yes."

"And she knows." It was not a question but a statement.

"You scare me."

"It's in your eyes. There are no secrets there."

"That's not what others say."

"I'm not others. And it went well. I can see that, too."

"Yes, I—."

She placed a finger on his lips. "You don't have to tell me now. Another time."

"Kaney, Kaney, Kaney . . . "

"What?"

"You're a gift from God."

She smiled but said nothing.

"I have to see Kelly now."

"Go," she said, still smiling. "I'm not leaving town."

Madero left the reading room and went into the dining area with Pompey following quickly behind.

Kelly was seated near Madero's table against the far wall. He looked up and sipped his coffee as Madero came in.

"Montero of Sonora," Kelly said.

"*Madre de Dios*," Madero sighed and sat across from him. Pompey lay down by his feet.

"I spent last night working on your biography."

"I spent my night elsewhere."

"Who's your friend?" Kelly asked, gesturing toward Pompey.

"A specter from my past to brighten my present."

Kelly nodded, as if to himself. "I have to jot down these strange phrases of yours. For authenticity. To give the book the proper flavor."

"You'll need more than that to get anyone to sympathize with someone like Madero."

"Now who said anything about sympathizing?"

Madero smiled. "How far along are you?"

"Oh, I don't know. Maybe a hundred and fifty pages."

"You write quickly."

"Not too quickly for it to be accurate, I hope. And I'm assuming you'll read the final draft to correct it."

"Why? Your Pinkerton *fantasías* will sell much better than truth."

"On the contrary, my melancholy friend. The truth is far more outrageous than anything I could ever hope to concoct."

"Do you have a final length in mind?"

"Did Moses for the Pentateuch?"

Madero laughed. "Hardly a sensible comparison. And you're beginning to answer a question with a question. Where did you contract that irritating disorder?"

"From consorting with fallen angels."

Madero took off his hat and threw it onto an empty chair. "The stash of silver is in Esperanza."

Kelly's coffee cup stopped midway to his mouth. "What?"

"Were there any tough words in that?"

"What's Esperanza?"

"A ghost town. The one Collie told you about where the Leek brothers have been seen."

"And the silver?"

"The Leeks are still around the town. They're probably living there. And this morning I saw four or five sets of fresh hoof prints in the dried mud. The boys are probably being followed."

"By Sutorius and his charmers?"

"Who else?"

"But why would Sutorius care about the town?"

"Hold onto your hat, detective. Harlo owns the town. What's left of it."

Kelly set down his cup. "Indeed."

"You were right. Barbicane doesn't want land. He's trying to buy the land so he can get the town."

"So you're convinced the Mexican money is buried there?"

"Or somewhere nearby. Eli was heard around San Miguel bragging about his silver stash when he was drunk. And both of the boys always seem to be in Esperanza. Why? Just looking for a hovel?"

"Doesn't esperanza mean hope in Spanish?"

"It does."

"Well, well, so now Esperanza is Barbicane's last hope." Kelly smiled. "Now *there's* an irony."

"There's no way to know if the Leeks have found all the silver yet. Barbicane can dig up the whole town once he owns it. But he can't go looking now and tip his hand. I doubt that he knew that Sutorius scouted out the place. The Dutchman was careless."

Kelly leaned back in his chair. "I guess we should pay a visit to Harlo and tell him about his good fortune."

"There's no good fortune here. Least of all for him."

"Why not? What do you mean?"

"His son was almost killed over Mexican blood money. Where's the good fortune? And you know the man—he's subtle as a blind bull. Tell him about Esperanza, and he'll probably do something foolish."

"I don't understand. Harlo isn't stupid."

"Don't deal him into this game now. He'll overplay it. There are times in a poker hand when a player should raise, but those are easy to know. It's when a player should check and doesn't—that's when he stumbles. Trust me—we're in my *terreno* here. "

"I thought we were supposed to act rather than react."

"That's finished. All the cards are face up now, and the only aces Barbicane is going to get are the ones Harlo hands him by being foolish."

"Then what do you think he should do?"

"Wait to see if Barbicane keeps trying to play his weak hand or if he folds."

"And do you think Barbicane will?"

"Not if Harlo gives him reasons to keep tossing in chips. And Sutorius will try to make reasons out of anything. Barbicane is naïve, but those *malparidos* he hired are not. They're killers. The safest thing now for Harlo is just to wait them out. Sutorius knows they can't stay here forever. Barbicane can't afford them."

"And you don't believe Harlo will wait?"

"*¿Un ganadero tan rico?* What do you think?"

"Maybe not."

"Harlo should just sit back with his cards and observe the other players. He has the luxury of time. But he's a fat and arrogant cattleman, not a clever gambler. And a bully as well. Bullies usually pick the wrong thing to do and the wrong time to do it."

"But certainly he has the right to hear what we know."

"What right? He didn't exactly exert himself to find out anything on his own."

"Does that matter?"

Madero's laugh was almost cruel. "Of course it matters."

"But he's probably in danger now. More than he thinks."

"What's that to me? If it didn't mean that Buck would end up an orphan, I wouldn't give a damn if Harlo lived or died."

"How on earth can you say something like that?"

"Have you seen how he treats his son? Detective, I've *killed* better men than Harlo."

Suddenly Kelly looked bewildered. "Just when I think that I've got at least a part of you figured out . . . I don't know."

"Disillusionment is a harsh elixir."

"You could disillusion a Hebrew prophet."

"Sorry, but that doesn't matter to me in the least."

"No, I guess it doesn't."

Madero reached for his hat.

"Wait a minute," Kelly said before Madero could stand up.

Madero dropped his hat back onto a chair.

"I want to give you an example of my labors. Especially tonight. After what you just said."

"What labors?"

"From my biography. Of Montero."

"*Un hombre siniestro.*"

"Sometimes. I've learned that."

"All right, but I expect no kindness from a writer — or even a journalist."

Kelly's gaze drifted away from Madero and he seemed to be gathering his thoughts.

Madero remained quiet, and then Kelly began speaking in a tone as soft as though he were talking to himself.

"*If the winds of destiny had shifted but slightly, this alarming wanderer might have become a desert hermit communing with beasts, whose serene silences he seems to prefer to the murmurings of men. But other tempests blew and cast him onto troubled shores hostile to those gentler gifts he should never have been given.*" Kelly turned back toward Madero with a rare look of sadness. "*Dark he is, and scarred, like the history of human travail.*"

"For a journalist, you're a shrewd man," Madero said as he stood up. "Whatever you write needs no correction from me."

"Well, it's good to know that there's at least some value in the reality of it."

"No," Madero said so sharply that Kelly flinched. "Its reality is the damnation of it." He drilled Kelly with his eyes. "Montero is what is *worst* in men."

Then he picked up his hat and walked quietly away with Pompey at his heel.

31 PUTREFACCION

A sharp afternoon storm had washed away the heat, and Maribel must have thought that steaming Mexican coffee would not be out of place in the sudden cool of the early evening. She poured some for Harlo and his two guests as they sat at the mesquite table on his veranda.

"Please leave that there," Madero said, as she was about to pick up his hat from the table.

She snapped her hand away as if she had almost touched a rattlesnake. Madero had never been able to understand why his voice so often startled people.

Maribel set down a plate of empanadas and retreated to the safety of the house.

"That's an interesting theory," Harlo said, holding his cup in both hands. "But I'm skeptical."

"Why?" Kelly asked.

"Well, first of all, it can't be the Glanton silver, because Esperanza didn't exist when Glanton and his murderers were killed. Did you know that?"

"I thought it was an older town," Kelly said.

"About twenty years—but not forty."

"Then this must be another stash."

"What do you think, *señor*?" Harlo said, turning to Madero.

"Listen to Mr. Kelly."

"But what are your views?"

"It's common knowledge that the Leek boys are tossing around old silver, and they're almost certainly holed up in Esperanza. Barbicane doesn't need land, and yet he hired four expensive men to intimidate you to sell your land and that land includes Esperanza. There's something in that town that he wants, and it's not Eli and Ned's underwear."

"You make it sound simple."

"Greed is never complex."

"Well, if you're right, then I should clear out the Leeks and start looking for silver—and tell Lawton what I've learned and that he can give up his fool's quest."

Madero gazed at Kelly with a weary smile and spread his arms in mock helplessness.

"Why not sit on it for now?" Kelly asked. "You're in command, not Barbicane."

"Lawton wouldn't do anything rash," Harlo said.

"He's already done it by hiring those three," Kelly answered.

"It's four again," Harlo said. "I heard that Barbicane has taken on Kelliride's old partner. Someone named Wilson."

"Wilt Corson."

"One question," Madero said.

Harlo turned to him.

"Your son was an inch from death because of a careless move. Do you think those killers would hesitate to swat you down if you gave them an excuse?"

Harlo gazed at Madero for a moment and then looked away.

"Don't let him provoke you into anything," Kelly said. "Soon his roaches will move on to where the feeding is better."

"I want to throw this in his face. I have my pride."

"Oh, yes," Madero said. "Pride—the last cry of the damned."

"Wait!" Kelly said as Madero was about to get up. "Please."

Madero eased back into the Mexican pigskin torture chair.

"You have a son to consider," Kelly said, looking back at Harlo.

"So?"

Kelly sighed and turned to Madero. "You're right. You can't protect people from themselves."

"Maribel," Madero said in a gentle voice, and she appeared almost in an instant.

"*Señor?*"

"Would you ask Master Buck to join us?"

She looked at Harlo.

"Go ahead, Maribel."

She was gone just briefly before she returned with Buck. He grinned when he saw Madero.

"*Compadre,*" Madero said.

"*¡Hola!*"

Madero smiled. "We have to work on that accent. How are you feeling?"

"*Muy bien, gracias.*"

"*¿Me estás diciendo la verdad?*"

"*Sí, en serio.*"

"Good. I just wanted to check in on you." He stood up.

Buck seemed crushed that Madero was leaving so soon.

"Can you hand me my hat?"

Buck picked it up, and a gleaming new Colt lay beneath it. He made an indescribable sound and quickly looked at his father.

Harlo nodded yes.

"It's a man's weapon," Madero said. "Treat it that way."

"Yes, sir."

"Is it loaded?"

"Yes, sir."

"How do you know?"

"Because I haven't checked it for myself."

"Very good," Madero said, smiling. "We'll fire it in when all this is over." Madero stood up and held out his hand.

Buck smiled and shook it vigorously, and that handshake clearly meant more to him than all the Colts in Hartford.

"Our usefulness here is ended," Madero said to Kelly.

"You go on ahead. I'll stay a bit longer. I'm a born optimist."

"And you'll die one as well." Madero took his hat and winked at Buck and headed out.

Summer storms slashed through southern Arizona so swiftly in the late afternoons that the sun often had time to reappear just before dipping at last below the horizon. As

Madero rode back toward San Miguel, a wash of crimson flowed across the wisps of lavender clouds adorning the western sky. When he had traveled abroad, he had often thought that the European painters struggling to create God's own effects in their dim garrets had unfortunately chosen the wrong hemisphere in which to set up their easels.

Buddy's ears pivoted left, and the horse swung his head around toward a rider coming from the east. In the way that a horse's eyes and brain intuitively sought out and analyzed distant silhouettes in a continual search for danger, Madero had trained himself since boyhood to evaluate far-off outlines long before they were within firing range. Maart Sutorius was loping toward him on a handsome sorrel.

Madero brought Buddy down to a walk as Sutorius slowed. Other than a carbine in a scabbard, no weapon was visible, but Madero assumed he had a sidearm as well.

"May I ride with you?"

"You may," Madero said.

"Heading back to San Miguel?"

"I am."

"It should give us plenty of time to talk."

"I prefer to listen."

"Even better. Because I have much to say. . . ."

"Go on. The evening is young."

"I want you to know that what Kelliride did was on no orders of mine."

"You mean the Stone boy?"

"Yes."

"So it wasn't an accident?"

"Or course not. Did you think it was?"

"No, but I wasn't sure, which is why I didn't kill him outright."

"You'd have risked the noose for that boy?" he asked in surprise.

"Certainly."

"You must care about him more than his own father does. I never had a father who cared about me like that."

"I never had a father at all."

"Just remember that Kelliride acted on his own."

"He was under your authority."

"So I do bear some responsibility. I admit it. But he was always a wild card. You know that."

"All right, I'll accept that."

"And the Callaghan family has no part in any of this. The fact that they're in the way is just an accident of fate."

"I stopped believing in accidents a hundred years ago. Why are you interrupting my beautiful evening with tales of fate?"

"Because I know who you are. I dropped in to see Pat this afternoon. Did he tell you that?"

"No."

"I asked him about you. So he handed me your file. I think he did it to warn me off."

"And were you warned?"

"Pinkerton records always have a great deal to say."

"That they do."

"Señor Madero, you're a very disturbing man."

"I try for the opposite, but I often fail."

"And a dangerous one."

Madero said nothing.

"I've sought no quarrel with you. Until recently I was happily unaware of your disquieting existence. . . ."

"Well, all happiness must end."

"You said that Miss Callaghan is a special friend of yours."

Madero stopped Buddy and turned and stared at Sutorius.

"I don't know what she is to you," Sutorius said, halting his horse. "But I —."

"*Eso no te incumbe,*" Madero snapped.

Sutorius looked confused. "My Spanish isn't the best."

"It's none of your concern."

"Even so, her wellbeing is as important to me as it is to you."

"I know that."

"You do?" he said in surprise.

"Yes. Because if she so much as bruises a toe on a stone that one of your men drops in her path, you know that I'll kill that man and then I'll kill all the others. Without a second thought."

Sutorius removed his bowler and frowned toward the setting sun. "I always suspected it, and now I know that. From reading your file." He turned back to Madero. "That's why I'm speaking with you now."

"And you'll join them that very day — shoveling coal in the furnaces of Hell."

"Mr. Madero, I deny the existence of Hell."

"No matter," Madero said. "Denying its existence won't deny you admittance."

Sutorius's eyes narrowed as he seemed to be trying to read Madero's being. "You're an alarming man."

"Draw off."

"I can't do that."

"Then accept the consequences."

"I will. But I also want you to realize here and now that even I can't control Corson."

"And he'd harm a girl?"

"He'd smash a kitten with a rock after he set it on fire."

"And yet you hired him."

"Barbicane hired him."

"Why?"

"You've seen how weaklings are always enthralled by savage men."

Madero sighed. "Yes, I have."

"Well, Corson carries that to the limit — if there is a limit. And he can't be bribed or seduced or cowed. He's a man without appetites. Hungers and yearnings have no meaning for him."

"Then why is he here?"

"I doubt that even he knows. Other than that his only friend died here."

"Well, I learned long ago that a passionless man is an unreachable man. And if he's evil, he has to be ignored or he has to be killed. There's no third choice."

"I want you to know that Corson and Kelliride brutalized women in the past. Either for their own pleasure or held them for ransom. So I'm warning you about Corson now."

"To absolve yourself just in case?"

"You can call it that."

"And the women?"

"Some disappeared. Others were never the same. You know what I mean."

Madero squeezed Buddy gently, and they moved off.

"I've never harmed a woman, *señor*.

256

"Other than the ones you made widows by smashing skulls."

"Yes," Sutorius said. "Not including those."

"But Corson admits no such delicate distinctions?"

"Corson is a dying man. He has nothing to fear. Nothing to lose."

Madero understood the sentiment well. Until not so long ago, having nothing to lose had shielded him, too. And yet now he knew he had so much to lose he could barely comprehend it.

"How can you even breathe the same air as creatures like that?" Madero asked.

"Surely you know. I'm a surgeon. To excise dead tissue sometimes you have to apply maggots to devour the rotted flesh."

"And how do you handle maggots without becoming like them yourself?"

"Does the doctor become the disease he treats?"

"Sometimes he catches it."

"I'm too strong for that."

"And yet the Pinkertons cut you off like a canker."

"They did," he said in words that he seemed to bite to death in his mouth.

"Why?"

"One of my informants was bleeding me like a tick and giving me piss and lies in return. I had to rough him up quite vigorously to convince him of the error of his reasoning."

"But you were never brought to account for it?"

"For a tick?"

Madero nodded and rode on in silence.

"Yet the Pinkertons let me go. The physician was too cruel on the cancers."

"*¡Qué compasivo!*"

He looked at Madero.

"How compassionate of them."

"Weak is the word. Ever since I was a boy, I'd hoped to earn a living by making the world a more enlightened place. A cleaner place."

Madero smiled to himself but said nothing.

"Empty of strikers and anarchists and hooligans," Sutorius went on. "Swept clean of . . . of many kinds."

"Of people like the diabolical Madero of Sonora."

Sutorius seemed suddenly wary. "Yes."

"I understand."

"You don't despise me?"

"I'm indifferent to you."

Sutorius seemed disappointed.

"Ah," Madero said, "is there anything so sad as unrequited hate?"

"And now after a lifetime of struggle what have I achieved?"

"You tell me."

"Nothing. I seem to have spent my whole life sucking on the hind tit."

"And despite all those cracked heads and fallen men, here you are," Madero said, scouting ahead the purple-shadowed landscape.

"Yes, here I am. In this rectal smear of a town on the ass end of Arizona."

Madero turned toward Sutorius. "I was right."

"How is that?"

"You've wallowed with maggots so long that's all you can see around you. San Miguel is a nice little *pueblo* in its own little Eden and all you can smell is decay."

Madero was startled to see a look of sadness in his eyes.

"You can't anger me, Mr. Madero, no matter what you say. No one can anger me with truth."

"You're flattering yourself. You're not important enough for me to try to anger."

He shrugged. "In any case, my hopes have shriveled to dusty ash and totter on the edge of the grave."

"There's always the chance to step back from it."

"No. As a man of the world, you know that there's a rotting of the spirit different from the usual reek of decomposing flesh. It's a dry rot—and once it starts, it's unstoppable."

"So why did you bother to come here at all?"

A long silence followed, and then Sutorius finally said, "What else on earth is there left for me to do?"

Madero lay in the dark and breathed heavily after wandering lonely streets in strange and pitiless dreams. Desperate to find his way home, he could locate not so much as an alley that looked familiar. Every corner he turned greeted him with another thoroughfare of looming buildings that led him nowhere. The atmosphere seemed thick and almost unbreatheable. Struggling for air, he opened his eyes and realized that fifty pounds of dog flesh and bone were pressing onto his torso. Pompey's chin rested on Madero's chest as the dog stared at him with the infinite concern only a dog can show.

Madero smiled and stroked his head. Pompey licked Madero's chin, and now all was right with his world.

Madero pushed him over onto the cushion and sat up. Pompey curled beside him and dozed off with the ease unique to dogs' tranquil souls.

Madero went and got a cheroot and lit up and then returned to the sofa and smoked in the darkness.

After a few minutes, Kaney's door opened and she came out in her nightdress.

"I could smell the cigar," she said.

"Was I crying out?"

"A little." She reached down and slid Pompey over and sat beside Madero. "Are you all right?"

Madero hooked an arm around her. "I'm fine, but the world isn't."

"Oh, don't worry," she said, resting her head on his shoulder. "It's always in chaos."

"Is this the best that the Creator can do? *This*, for God's sake?"

"What do you mean?"

"This race of fools."

Kaney rubbed his arm gently but said nothing.

"There was a *capitán* in the *Rurales* who wanted nothing more ferociously than to run me and my men to ground. I respected him immensely. He wasn't corrupt. Among the Mexican *policía*, that's as rare as a unicorn. He was about forty at the time. By accident we ran into each other once in Tucson." Madero smiled. "Neutral ground. We drank half a bottle of tequila together. We talked long into the night about the follies of man. You'd be surprised how *El Tesoro* can be a great leveler. . . ."

"Maybe the two of you were more similar than you'd thought."

Madero looked down at her face against his shoulder. "What makes you so wise?"

She smiled. "Age."

"That night he said something to me that I've never forgotten. I was feeling . . . oh, what's the word . . . *lúgubre*. My English is failing me tonight."

"Morose maybe?"

"That'll do. I said to him that I just couldn't accept how foolish people can be. Unlike every other animal, man never learns from his mistakes. Do you know how long it takes a horse to learn from a bad experience? Once."

"I think if men and women were more like horses, it would be a better world."

"And it doesn't even matter if a man is wounded and beaten. He'll *still* take a sick pride in refusing to listen to the wisdom of others." Madero smoked in silence for a minute. "My new-found *amigo* smiled at me and offered me an Italian cigar. Then he said . . . let me get it out in Spanish first. That's the way I remember it. The way I'll always remember it. He said, '*Mi amigo, el hombre protege su independencia por encima de todo lo demás. Siempre prefiere su propia estupidez en lugar de ser guiado por el juicio de un hombre sabio.*'" Madero paused for a moment. "That means, 'My friend, a man guards his independence above all else. He'll always prefer his own foolishness to being guided by the judgment of a wiser man.'"

"I think that's true."

"I guess I didn't realize that until I thought about it later. I was about to argue with him, but he held up his hand and stopped me and said, '*Esa es la gran verdad del Jardín de Edén, y la tragedia. No está en la selección de la fruta, sino en la soberbia, el desatino, y el fracaso.*' It means, 'That's the great truth of the

Garden of Eden. And the tragedy. Not the picking of the fruit, but the pride, the folly, and the fall.'"

After a brief silence, Kaney said, "He's sounds like an exceptional man."

"He was."

"And can his wisdom help you now?"

"It only makes me despair."

"Why?"

"There's no hope for these people. Kelly thinks this is over. So does Harlo." The cheroot glowed more brightly in the darkness as Madero took a long draw. "It's barely even begun."

32 DESESPERANZA

Madero set the hot iron coffee pot onto a Mexican tile on his reserved table in the dining room and took his usual seat against the wall. Pompey settled in by his feet.

Madero always kept several cups on the table for visitors, and now he stood up and turned over a pair as he saw Collie coming through the doorway.

"Good morning," she said with a grin as the dog ran over to her. She dropped down and gave him a good jostle as he licked her face.

"Say hello to Pompey."

She scratched him behind the ears and then placed her hat onto an empty chair and sat at the table.

Madero smiled as he poured her a cupful and slid it across to her and sat back down.

"I was hoping you might be here, even though it's late. Do you usually sleep this long?"

Madero filled his cup. "I didn't sleep very much at all. I was in a far off land."

Collie looked puzzled. "I just wanted to stop in and say hello. I have to pick up a few things in town."

Madero saw Kelly come in and take a table in a corner. He glanced over at Madero, and his annoyingly smug expression was that of a novice card player with a pat hand.

"Are you here alone?" Madero asked, looking back at Collie.

"Rake is at the feed store."

"What's wrong?"

She stared down at her cup. "You always read my mind, don't you?"

"Sometimes."

"I want to ask you something, but I'm afraid." She looked back up at him.

"Ask."

"May I . . . may I tell everyone who my father is?"

"What does your mother say?"

"She said she'd be proud if I did."

That stunned him. "You wouldn't stretch the truth with this old *bandido*, would you?"

"No, sir. But my mom said I could say it only if you approve."

"If?" Madero answered a bit too loudly. "My God, Blackie, of course."

Collie slid Madero's cup aside and took both of his hands. "Thank you," she whispered.

"If you were a boy, I might have said no. A boy would be tempted to wield it like a club. Madero of Sonora and all that nonsense. But girls are different." He smiled. "And Blackie is *very* different."

She cleared her throat. "I don't know what to call you. . . ."

"*Afortunado*."

"Oh, stop," she said, laughing.

"Call me Mateo. And call me when you need me. Always."

"Always?"

"Of course."

"You mean you're staying in San Miguel?" she said in surprise. "Please don't tease me."

"How could I ever leave?"

She gazed at him as her teeth sank into her lower lip.

"I have to speak with Kelly now, and you have chores to do." He stood up.

She leaned across the table and kissed him on the cheek, but still she gripped his hands.

"I need you to know one thing," he said so softly only she could hear. "No matter what happens—and some bad things might happen—I want you always to remember that you . . . you and Kaney . . . are my treasures. Two indestructible gems glittering out of the ashes of an incinerated life."

Her eyes reddened in an instant.

He squeezed her hands tightly. "I'm here with you until here ceases to exist."

She turned away before the tears fell, and then she snatched her hat and was off.

Madero picked up his hat and cup and walked over to Kelly's table with Pompey by his side.

"Don't ever play poker," Madero said. "Not with that face."

"Please join me."

"Why the self-satisfied look?" Madero asked, still standing as he sipped his coffee.

"It's finished—the whole mess. Harlo insisted on talking with Barbicane last night, so I went along. Smooth as cream gravy. Harlo told him the whole business—that he knew about the silver and Esperanza and the reason for Barbicane's offer. Everything. And Barbicane just wilted. The bid is off the table. Done."

"He told Barbicane he knew about the silver?"

"He did. And Harlo gave you the credit for figuring it out."

"What about Sutorius and the other three?"

"They were there. They—."

"He told them, too?!"

"Well, they were there. Corson said they should have come to you from the beginning about the silver. I think he believes you know where it's hidden. Sutorius said you would never have told them. Corson sneered and said there are ways of dealing with that. Then Barbicane paid off all four and sent them on their way."

"Jesus Christ!" Madero shouted and slammed down his cup. "Do you know the Leek boys? What they look like?"

"No, I've never seen them. What's—?"

Madero bolted out the door with Pompey right behind him.

Madero searched the street. Collie was putting something into her saddlebag on Diablo in front of the mercantile.

"Blackie!"

She spun around at Madero's voice and ran toward him.

"What's wrong?" she said, hurrying up.

"Do you know what the Leek brothers look like?"

"Oh, yes. I've—."

"Mount up. Do you have your carbine?"

"I do."

"I'll get Buddy. I need you now."

She smiled with pride and ran back to Diablo.

Madero raced to the stable and quickly brushed off Buddy's back and tacked him up.

Collie was mounted and ready when he loped Buddy onto Angel Street with Pompey running beside them.

Madero pointed toward the east. "Let's ride."

The sun was high when they reached Esperanza. Madero had spent the time explaining the entire story to Collie. He had always made sure his *pistoleros* knew as much as he did.

Pompey trotted ahead of them on the main street like a prince returning to pay a royal visit to his old haunts.

"Harlo should have posted this place," Madero said.

"Posted?"

"Set up sentries after he told Barbicane and the others about the silver."

Madero and Collie stopped in front of a trough to water their horses.

Madero dismounted and whistled to Pompey, and he came bounding over. Madero scooped a hatful of water from the trough and placed it on the ground for him.

Madero looked around.

"Mateo, did you notice all the fresh prints?"

He nodded. Three or four horses had recently cut up the dried mud from yesterday's rain.

"All right, boys!" Madero shouted. "Come on out. We're here to take you to safety."

Birds fluttered off, but there was no other sign of life in the fallen town.

After Pompey had drunk his fill, he turned away and wandered up the main street. Madero dumped the rest of the water from his hat and remounted. He gestured to Collie and they followed Pompey.

"There's something on the wind," Madero said, watching his dog. "He's tense. That's not him."

With an intuitive grace that surprised Madero, Collie silently swept her Winchester from its scabbard and chambered a round.

He smiled at her for a moment and then looked away. Perhaps she had inherited more than just black hair.

When Madero scanned the town again, Pompey was gone. Madero clicked to Buddy, and they trotted up the street. Collie and Diablo followed.

Madero spotted Pompey on the boardwalk in the shade of the overhang in front of an old hotel. Ears back, the dog was staring through the open doorway.

"Wait here," Madero said to Collie as he dismounted.

She stayed in the saddle but swept her gaze around in a smooth arc and then back down the street the way they had come. Madero smiled again. His flanks and rear were secure.

Madero peered through the doorway of the hotel. A dark mass lay in front of the main desk in the half-light. He flipped his hat down his back and walked in, Pompey at his heel.

Madero bent down before a corpse with a rope looped around the upper torso and digging deeply into the armpits. The face and clothing looked like they had been worked over with a giant wood rasp.

Pompey sniffed the body cautiously.

"Blackie," Madero said.

She hurried inside and dropped to one knee before the carcass.

"Can you identify him?" Madero asked.

She laid down her carbine and studied the shredded face. "Ned Leek." Her tone was as hollow as an open grave.

Madero flipped over the cadaver. It was still limp and warm.

"He must have hit a rock when they dragged him," Madero said, pointing to a large dent deforming the back of the skull. "Maybe before he talked."

"You mean about where the silver is?"

Madero nodded.

"Who would have done it? Sutorius?"

"Maybe."

"Is Eli still here, do you think?"

"Possibly. But we'd never find him now."

Madero rose from the pile of nothing that had once been a boy.

"He's only my age," Collie said, taking her rifle and standing up. "I never liked either of them. Now I feel guilty."

"Don't. They rolled their own dice. Goddamned *imbéciles*."

267

"I'll see if I can find a shovel."

"We can't waste time with that." He grabbed the string on his hat and pulled it up and on. Gazing at the body, he said, "When I was a boy, the sisters taught me never to despair. Yet they also told me about a Greek historian named Herodotus. A very wise man who said, 'Of all man's miseries, the bitterest is this—to know so much and to have control over nothing.'"

Madero turned away and left the hotel. Pompey was already out in the middle of the street and staring far off. Madero walked out and stood beside him. The dog was focused on a rider heading toward the western horizon. Madero went over to Buddy and took a nautical spyglass out of his saddlebag. The three-draw scope easily pulled in the distant rider and his dapple gray, but horse and man were unknown to Madero.

"Blackie," Madero shouted, but she was already running up to him.

He handed her the glass. "Any idea who that is?"

"Wilt Corson," Blackie said as she studied the horseman.

"You know Corson?" Madero asked in surprise.

"Kaney pointed him out to me." She handed the glass back to Madero. "He scares me."

Madero collapsed the scope and slid it into his saddle bag.

"Do you think he killed Ned?" she asked.

"Yes." Madero looked to the southern sky where the thunderheads were building. "Mount up."

They rode in silence back to San Miguel. When they arrived at *La Luna*, they watered their horses at the barn, and Madero unsaddled Buddy and brushed him off and turned him out to his pen.

"Are you headed home?"

"Yes, but I'll be back later. My mom is treating us to dinner in town tonight." She dismounted.

"Are you coming inside now?"

"No, but my mom told me to make it a point never to talk down to an adult from horseback. She's very proper that way."

"I understand."

"And I wanted to thank you . . . ."

"All right," Madero said. "About what?"

"For trusting me today with your safety . . . with your life."

Madero smiled. "You trust me with yours."

"Oh, Mateo, I'd trust you with my *soul*."

Stunned, Madero looked away and stared off down the alley behind the cantina.

"What is it?" Collie said after a long silence.

"In my improbable life, I've had people entrust me with many things . . ." He turned back slowly to her confiding eyes. "But never with everything."

She stepped toward him, and he pulled her close. Before this, he had been almost afraid to hold her, but now he knew there was no shame in touching this being who had drawn half of her life from him. His fingers could feel the strong muscles of her back through her cotton shirt and camisole, and her soft and peaceful sigh at last brought him the hope for which he had so often cried out in vain and in darkness.

33 THUNDERHEADS

A clean shaven man with skin the color of old candle wax sat alone with his back to the wall about halfway down the cantina. Madero lit an Italian cheroot and leaned against the bar and watched him dine indifferently on a plate of beans, a piece of bread, and a glass of water.

Luis came up on the other side of the bar.

"Wilt Corson," Madero said. It was not a question.

"I thought of keeping him out—for Kaney's sake. But she'd have none of that." Luis smiled. "She's a proud woman."

"Where is she now?"

"I believe she's doing some shopping at the mercantile."

"Have you seen the other three today?"

"I've heard they've taken rooms at the hotel. Did Barbicane let them go?"

"Yes."

"Maybe we'll have some peace now."

"Not until we bury them."

Luis groaned.

"Ah," Madero said, "the moan of disapproval."

"He has an odd way about him," Luis said, staring at Corson. "Like he sees and hears nothing. And doesn't want to."

"He's seeing everything. Don't let the fish eyes fool you."

Thunder rolled in from the south, and the threat of an early evening storm started chasing people in from the street.

"*Amigo.* . . ."

Madero turned toward Luis. "Collie told me that her father no longer has to be a secret. A few people already know. She couldn't hold it in."

Madero heard the office door close at the back of the reading room, and Kaney came hurrying out.

"I know I'm late, Luis."

He smiled. "Ladies have their ways."

"Sorry I'm a little disheveled."

"As if you ever could be," Madero said with a smile.

"Rogue!"

Heavy footsteps pounded across the floor, and Madero turned to see Harlo walking into the cantina. He was carrying a shotgun.

"I've never seen him armed before," Luis said.

The Remington suddenly felt warm in the sash against Madero's hip.

Harlo walked slowly, as if he were very weary or had been drinking too much. He lumbered up the middle aisle and stopped about ten feet in front of Corson's table.

Corson gazed at him like a bat eyeing a bug and continued eating his beans.

"Weren't you supposed to leave?" Harlo asked.

Corson set down his spoon. "Leave what?"

"San Miguel."

Corson took a sip of water and said nothing.

"I found a body in my town. . . ."

"What town is that?"

"Esperanza."

"Then bury it."

"I will."

Corson went back to his beans.

"You murdered him. Or one of the others did."

"Why would we do that?" Corson swirled a crust of bread around in his beans and took a bite and seemed too bored even to look up.

"You didn't mean to, but you were careless."

"As you're being right here." He poured some water into his glass from the pitcher beside him.

By now, everyone in the cantina had stopped what he had been doing. Even some diners from beyond the Chinese screen had come over and were standing and watching from the opening to the dining room.

"I've been patient," Corson said and then drained his glass and set it aside. "Now lower that weapon and walk away."

Like all false toughs, Harlo seemed suddenly unsure of what to do. He had confronted without purpose, goaded without thought, and now found himself standing on quicksand.

"Move," Corson said.

Harlo failed to budge, although whether from fear or defiance no one could be sure.

Corson slid his chair back and stood up. Without taking his eyes off Harlo, he glided to his right. Corson now commanded a clear line of sight and movement between the two rows of tables. Even the youngest and most naïve in that room could see that he had done this a hundred times before.

Luis began to say something to him, but Madero held up a hand for him to stop.

"But, Mateo," Luis whispered, "he'll kill Harlo."

"Of course he'll kill him."

In the graveyard silence, the snapping of Madero's fingers split the air like a whip crack.

Even Corson turned toward him. His nickel-plated Colt glittered against the black rigging.

With the imperiousness of a Roman emperor, Madero gestured with two fingers for Harlo to step aside.

Harlo melted away.

Madero tossed his cigar into a cuspidor. As he strode down the center aisle, his gaze swept the area. He saw Collie and Kathy and several other diners watching from the doorway of the dining room. Collie stared at him with a mixture of terror and awe. Madero nodded to her and moved on.

When he came abreast of Corson, Madero swirled to his right with the ease of a man walking on clouds.

Corson seemed mystified, as if no one had ever before dared to look him in the eye, let alone face him armed.

Madero's bearing conveyed a nonchalance, even an indifference, that was lost on no one in the room.

"You disturb people," Madero said. "Your manner disturbs them. Your face disturbs them. And your *existence* disturbs *me*."

"What's the remedy?"

"Time to move on."

Corson hesitated.

"And when you do," Madero said, "be careful with that right hand. There are people on the other side of the screen

273

behind me who are having supper. Families. Children. A stray round will go straight through that screen. If I even imagine a move toward your sidearm, you'll suck down your last breath in a pile of cold beans."

The man of wax was no fool. "I've finished my supper anyway." He picked up his hat and glared at Madero. "But that doesn't mean I'm finished with everything."

"Nor I."

Keeping his right hand far from his pistol, Corson eased his way among the tables and watched as Collie raced into the room toward Madero. Then the killer turned and left the cantina.

When Collie came up to him, Madero slid an arm around her shoulders. "It's all right."

She smiled into his eyes.

"Go back with your mom now. I have some things to do." He gave her that tender squeeze on the shoulder that meant so much to her.

"Can we come by later?" she asked.

"You and your mom go to my rooms after you've eaten and we'll relax together."

She grinned and went to rejoin her mother.

"Lock the door," he shouted after her. He looked at Harlo. "Go tend to your son." Then he turned around and saw Kaney smiling at him. There was no fear or tension in her eyes, just pride.

"Why don't you take the night off?" Luis said to her.

"I'm fine."

Collie had heard Luis and now gestured for Kaney to join her and her mom.

"All right," Kaney said with a smile. "I'm a bit shaky at the moment."

Then she went with Collie and Kathy into the dining room.

"Good Lord, this is a wild place," said a smooth voice behind Madero.

He turned toward the entrance. A stranger was standing in the doorway.

The man pulled off his hat and slicker as he came in.

"Well, I'll be damned." Madero said.

Jack Tarn looked years younger than he had just a few weeks earlier. His beard was gone, and his neatly trimmed silver moustache imparted a restrained elegance that many would have thought impossible not so long ago. A new gray suit of the finest material graced his lean form.

"This is such an uncivilized establishment," Tarn said in a gently mocking tone.

"Bert!" Madero said. "Remy."

Bert produced a bottle of cognac and a pair of glasses, and Madero and Tarn retreated to the reading room.

Madero poured and set the bottle down on a side table, and then the two men relaxed across from one another in comfortable chairs.

"Storms blow in many strange visitors," Madero said.

Tarn saluted Madero with his glass and sipped the cognac.

"You seem well," Madero said. "You look five years younger."

"I feel *ten* years younger."

"Religious conversion?"

He smiled. "In a manner of speaking. I got job as a dealer—an *honest* dealer—at the Congress. As you said I could. And since then . . . my God, it's as if I've drunk from the Fountain of Youth. I haven't slept this well since I was a child."

"Honesty has its rewards."

"I've come back to thank you."

"It's a long ride. You could have written."

"No," Tarn answered, suddenly serious. "I want to thank you in another way. I owe you at least that much. I want to repay you with some information, and I didn't want to write it down. Letters have no discretion—they'll yammer to anyone."

"All right. Go ahead."

"You took an interest in the Mexican coins I'd won from one of those Leek boys. It seemed serious to you at the time, although you didn't explain. Are you still interested in that?"

"*Sí, seguro.*"

"I guess the boys were telling people they'd found some scalp hunter stash. That was the rumor up in Tucson. Well, they were just drawing the long bow with that one. They'd stolen a coin collection from their uncle in Tucson. He's a faro dealer at the Congress."

Glass in mid-air, Madero simply stared at Tarn.

"Those boys were just puffing themselves up with talk of blood money." Tarn sipped his drink. "Just a fairy story.

"*Madre de Dios*," Madero said softly.

"Is it still important?"

Madero set down his glass. "The youngest one died for it."

"How?"

"Dragged to death for something that doesn't exist."

"Sutorius?

"Corson. The one who just left. As to the whereabouts of the older Leek, *¿quién sabe?*"

"Well, that I do know. I saw him riding on the road back to Tucson. He looked terrified. He didn't recognize me, but I knew him. I remember everyone I've ever fleeced."

"What about the uncle?"

"I think he felt sorry for them. They're orphans, so I guess he assumed they'd eventually come back. Maybe even with some of the coins."

"So it's all been for nothing. All this horror." Madero gazed off toward infinity. "Like so many men's lives . . . all for nothing."

"Can you tell me about it?"

In a voice that sounded distant even to himself, Madero patiently related the entire tale of greed and folly and death.

"But something good has come of it," Tarn said gently when Madero had finished. "Your daughter."

"Yes," Madero said barely above a whisper.

The two men sat in silence for a while.

"Will you stay for now?" Madero asked.

"That's my plan. I have a room at the hotel."

"Good. Wait for me here. I'll buy you supper." He stood up. "Thank you, Jack."

Tarn nodded and raised his glass. "*Compadre.*"

The horror of human wickedness scarred Kelly's expression like a fresh burn.

"The boy's death is my fault, isn't it?"

"To a small degree," Madero said. "And Harlo's. But there's no point in whipping yourself over it."

Kelly was seated on a stool beside his printing press. "And now we know it was all in pursuit of a mirage."

"That was my mistake more than yours."

"But not the boy's death. I'll have to live with this forever."

"That's what comes from being 'reasonable'."

"But what else was there to do?" He seemed desperate for absolution.

"Exactly what I said to do—nothing. Instead you wanted to be 'fair' and tell Harlo what he had no business knowing yet. And then Harlo decided to taunt Barbicane with it. This whole thing would have collapsed of its own weight very soon. It was too expensive for Barbicane to run these cards indefinitely. But a quietly folded hand wouldn't satisfy an arrogant ass like Harlo. He had to throw the cards in their face."

"But Barbicane—."

"This has nothing to do with Barbicane. This is four ruthless men with no reason now to hold back. The scent of silver is in their nostrils."

"But we know it's a false scent."

"Go tell them and see if they believe you."

"But—."

"But? But on a dirty floor in a derelict hotel in a dead town the body of a boy is rotting in the dust."

"You're a harsh man, Madero."

"Only if truth is harsh."

"What do you advise we do now?"

"We? You're not drawing any more cards in this game. You have to stay alive to watch over—."

"But *you're* here, too."

"We don't know how long that will be. So I'm counting on you to be with Collie and Kathy no matter what happens to me." He pulled on his hat. "This hangfire is about to blow."

"Listen to me," Kelly said as Madero walked to the door. "You can't deal with all of them alone."

"I've always been alone."

A horseman was dashing down Angel Street as Madero stepped outside.

"What the hell?" Madero said.

"Who is it?" Kelly asked, running up.

"Jack Tarn. A gambler." Rain had begun falling and thunder was rumbling in the distance. "He's racing into the head of a storm. Grab your pistol. Let's find out what he's running from."

The two men dashed back to the cantina.

A small crowd of stunned diners had gathered at the far end of the dining room.

"Mateo!" Collie yelled and rushed up to him with Pompey right behind her. "They're chasing Kaney!"

"What?"

Madero spun around as Kathy raced across the room toward him with a pistol in her hand.

"They were trying to get Collie," Kathy said. "Sutorius and the others. Kaney went into the cantina for a minute and then came running back in here. She said she overheard them talking about coming for Collie and taking her as a hostage. She—."

"Hostage for what?" Kelly said.

"Until Mateo tells them where the silver is." She turned to Madero. "Kaney grabbed Collie's hat and slicker and then pushed both of us into the back room. She gave me her pistol and then she said she'd ride out on Diablo to decoy them until you could come."

"Where did she go?" Madero asked.

"I don't know. Luis is getting some men together to hunt them down."

"Bert!" Madero shouted.

The bartender came running in from the cantina.

"When Luis gets back with his men, tell them to stay here. I don't want them blundering into this. I'll handle it."

"All right. I'll tell him that."

"Oh, Mateo," Collie said. "She did it to save me. We can't let her die!"

"Relax. They can't afford to hurt her. Not yet." He pointed to the floor. "Who's the blood from?"

"I heard a growl and a scream when we were in the back room," Kathy said. "I think Pompey got one of them on the leg. I came out shooting, and I might have winged one, but I'm not sure."

"When we came out," Collie said, "a man in a gray suit was running in from the cantina and asked what happened. When we told him, he said to tell you he went after them."

"Tarn?" Kelly asked Madero.

"He went alone, for God's sake?" Madero said to Kathy.

"He did. He said he owed you at least that much."

"Mother of God," Madero said in disbelief.

"He said he'd signal you with gunshots so you could follow."

"All right, come on." Madero led the way out the door and back to the stable. "Blackie, tack up Buddy for me," he said as he passed Buddy's stall.

Madero and Kathy and Kelly went into the living quarters.

"Sit and relax." Madero tossed his hat aside and crossed the sitting room to his bedroom.

He opened a dresser drawer and removed the leather bandolier he always kept full and draped it over his left shoulder and down to the right across his chest. Then he picked up his other Remington and made sure it was loaded and slid it into the sash at his left hip.

When he went back into the sitting room, Kathy was sitting on the sofa and Kelly was standing next to it and checking the cylinder on his Colt.

"Mateo," Kelly said, snapping shut the loading gate, "if you don't let me go with you, I'll never be able to live with myself."

"Better to live with yourself than die in the rain," Madero said as he got his slicker from a clothes pole near the door.

"Oh, stop it!" Kathy shouted as she jumped up.

Madero looked Kelly in the eye. "Pat, you're a man of courage. And a man of honor. I need you here for my daughter."

"But we can negotiate with them to release Kaney," Kathy said. "Can't we?"

"With what?" Kelly asked.

"I have some savings. And I can try to get a second mortgage on the ranch. I'll pay whatever I can to bring her back. I'll—."

"There's no dealing with these men," Madero said. "I have more than enough money to buy them off, but they're not taking anyone's promises. These are criminals. They trust no one. They'll hold Kaney until they see the silver stash." He reached for his hat.

"But there isn't any silver!" she said hopelessly.

"No there isn't. And they're not waiting for any mortgages. What they want they want *now*."

"But there are four of them! If we can't bargain with them or reason with them, what can we do?"

"*We* can't do anything," Madero said, putting on his hat.

"Then what can *you* do? What — ?"

Madero's raised hand silenced her. "What I was born to do."

A look of great sadness fell across Kathy's face like a shroud.

"Now listen to me," Madero said to Kathy. "I need one last favor. If I never walk through that door again, come and get Buddy. He won't be far from me. Treat him as well as he's treated me." Madero dropped to one knee and jostled Pompey. "And give this fine fellow the happy home he's always longed for."

Pompey gazed at Madero and whined with a dog's infallible intuition that all was not well. Madero stroked him under the chin, and Pompey reached out and licked his face. Madero smiled at Pompey as he stood up. "A man who hasn't been blessed with an honest horse and a faithful dog can never be a complete man."

A splintering thunder crack made Kathy and Kelly jump, but Madero barely heard it as his focus had already begun to shift.

Kelly turned toward the window and the storm. *"When beggars die there are no comets seen."* He looked back at Madero. *"The heavens themselves blaze forth the death of princes."*

"Well, well," Madero said as he pulled on his slicker. "You don't look like Caesar's wife."

Kelly stared at him in surprise.

"My literary friend, you're not the only one who was taught Shakespeare." Madero held out his hand. "Pat, it's been my very great pleasure."

Kelly shook his hand as if it were the last time.

"And make sure you get these ranchers to appoint you sheriff," Madero said and then turned to Kathy.

280

Looking terrified, she reached out and touched his cheek. "God bless you," she said, battling back the tears.

He took her hand and kissed her fingers. "Don't be afraid. *Of all the wonders of which I have yet heard, it seems to me most strange that men should fear, seeing that death, a necessary end, will come when it will come.*"

With an expression as blank as a steel plate, he turned and walked out the door.

Collie was waiting with Buddy by his stall.

"All set?"

She nodded but seemed unable to speak.

For a long moment they just stared at each other.

"Can I . . . ?" she began but then just slumped against him and gripped him as desperately as if he were about to slide into an abyss.

"Can you what?" Madero asked, slipping his arms around her.

"Can I ask one favor?"

He smiled. "What?"

"Will you promise me that you'll come back to me? Please?"

Madero reached up and brushed his thumbs softly along her black eyebrows. "You came back to *me*, didn't you? Can I do less?"

She shook her head no.

"After all," he said gently, "not a sparrow falls from the sky without God's knowledge."

"I love you so much," she said, clutching him even more tightly.

"As I love you." After about a minute, he eased his arms from her and bent down and kissed her on the forehead. Then he stepped slowly away.

"*Vaya con Dios,*" she whispered.

On a sudden impulse, he reached out and squeezed her shoulder tenderly, as he had done that first evening in the cantina.

Now her tears fell.

Madero turned quickly away, and he and Buddy went off to their destiny.

34 DOWNPOUR

Madero judged he had about twenty minutes of light left. The full storm had not yet struck, and the jumble of hoof prints was still easily visible on the way out of town toward the east. After Madero had ridden about a mile from San Miguel, he heard a gunshot in the distance in the direction of Esperanza. Again Don Luis had been right. As though pulled by some inexplicable force beyond conscious control, the desperate always fled toward the town without hope.

Darkness had closed in by the time Madero reached Esperanza. The storm now battered horse and rider as they cut their way through the rain down the main street. Bursts of gunfire from several pistols sounded from somewhere, and Madero watched Buddy's ears pivot to the right. Madero touched him with a gentle heel, and they loped off to the right down a side street for about fifty yards until Buddy's head turned toward a break in the buildings on the left.

"Ho," Madero said, and Buddy halted, sure-footed even in the mud.

It was the classic box canyon. About fifty feet square, the open space was sealed on three sides by dark buildings and had a single entrance—the place where Madero and Buddy stood. The structures to left and right were galleried along their upper floors with railed walkways serviced by stairs leading up to them. This self-contained cluster of dead husks might once have been a group of saloons and bordellos.

Toward the left side of the plaza sat a rotting shed comprised of a frame, a tin roof, and the back wall. Inside the shack were a few large crates and kegs, along with a steel drum with a fire blazing in it. Madero guessed that a vagrant or two had been using the shed as a sheltered cooking area, away from the tinder box buildings, and then had quickly fled from the horses and gunfire. Despite the almost blinding rain, the fire under the roof suffused the entire area with a flickering orange glow.

Madero heard snorting off to the right, and he nudged Buddy toward the open doorway of a long-abandoned stable.

Diablo and another horse were tied inside to a pair of hitching rails to the left, while another four horses had been placed in some derelict stalls off to the right.

Madero rode in and dismounted. He looped his reins around his saddle horn and then took a towel from a saddlebag and wiped some of the rain off Buddy.

He tossed the towel aside and examined Diablo and the other horse. They seemed fine but winded. Quarter horses had speed but little stamina, and these needed a rest. He walked over to the four stalls, and those animals seemed just as tired. Madero pulled the four carbines from the saddle scabbards and set them into a dark corner. Then he untacked the animals and took their saddles and bridles and blankets to a back doorway and dropped them outside into the mud and rain.

Madero returned to Buddy and spoke softly to him and stroked him on the withers before he went back to the doorway and reexamined the flooded square.

He thought he saw the glow of a lamp on the ground floor of a building at the opposite side of the plaza. Or it might have been light from the drum fire reflected in the windowpane. The windows of all the other buildings were as black as the eyes of the dead.

Madero turned back to Buddy. "Stay," he said and held up his hand. Then he turned away and walked out into the plaza.

Slashing rain hit him like steel rods as he trudged through the black lake. He scanned right to left and back again but found no signs of life. As he passed like a spirit through the eerie light, he saw that there was definitely a lamp glowing in the room at the opposite side of the court.

He snapped around as a door creaked to his left. A dark figure stepped out onto the wooden balcony.

"Who the hell are you?" the man shouted.

Madero strained to see through the rain. The silhouette looked like Scateen.

"I need shelter."

"None here. Get out."

"Wait," another voice said.

Madero turned to the right and tilted his head so his line of vision cleared his hat brim. On the balcony at the right side of the plaza loomed the cadaverous figure of Wilt Corson, distorted in the wavering light from the drum fire.

Madero looked back to the room where the lamp burned. Peering from the window was a quarter of the face of Jack Tarn.

"Well?" Corson asked, still not recognizing him in the storm. "What do you want?"

"Only one thing—for you to die an ugly death."

Madero bounded toward the room where Tarn watched. The door flew open and Madero dived straight through. A futile shot boomed behind him as Madero slid across the floor on his stomach and the door slammed shut.

Madero looked up and saw Kaney and Tarn sitting on the floor beside the door. A short-barreled Sheriff Model Colt rested in Tarn's hand.

Kaney grinned and slid over to Madero and pulled him close without a word.

"She was certain you'd come," Tarn said with an ironic smile. "No matter what. I've never seen such serenity in the face of folly."

"Thank you," Kaney whispered in Madero's ear.

"*¿Estás bien?*"

"*Sí.*"

Madero pushed back his hat and looked around. He found himself in a bare room about twelve feet square. The sole window looked out onto the plaza.

"Where's that go?" Madero asked, pointing to a door on the opposite wall.

"I don't know," Tarn said. "It seems to be boarded up and nailed shut from the other side."

The only furniture was a rectangular table and four chairs.

Tarn stood up and took the cloth from the table and hung it over a few nails above the window. "There—now we can move around."

"It doesn't say much for your tactical ability that you got run up a blind ravine."

Tarn gave him a sour look.

Madero turned to Kaney. "Fill me in, *mi amor*."

"I tried to reason with them. I told them that—."

"You didn't go out there, did you?"

"No, I stood inside the doorway. I shouted out to them that I was just a saloon girl. That your daughter was safe. I guess that confused them. There was a long silence and then one of them said that they'd wait and see if you came anyway. I think it was Sutorius."

"How did you end up in here?"

"That was my fault," Tarn said. "Our horses were tired and so we went into that stable to rest them. Then we heard Sutorius and the others right behind us. So we tied the horses and ran across the courtyard to hide in one of these buildings. I guess they saw our horses in the stable and closed in."

"What's the layout?"

"That was Corson at the top of the stairs on our left—on your right when you ran in. Scateen is sitting like a vulture in the room behind the opposite balcony on our right. Sutorius is in the building underneath Corson, and Craksi is below Scateen."

"What do you think?" Kaney said.

Madero went to the window and peered out from the edge of the makeshift curtain. "Well, we can't stay here indefinitely. Sutorius can send someone for water and food. All we can do is drink mud and eat those chairs."

"Do you think they'd deal?" Tarn asked.

"The only thing they want is what I don't have. Information that doesn't even exist. So, no."

"But why would they take the chance of killing us?" Kaney said. "Then the secret of the silver would die with us. They can't risk that."

"You're being reasonable," Madero said. "But these men are desperate. They're furious and they're frustrated. Trust me, they're killers, and if we don't give them what they want, they'll cut us down like crippled dogs."

"Do you think they'd fire at Kaney, too, for God's sake?" Tarn asked.

"I don't know. Sutorius . . . I'd say that with him it's unlikely. The others, I don't know."

286

"And they certainly couldn't come down here and try to beat any information out of you," Tarn said. "Even if it existed. Rushing this room would be suicide."

Madero gazed in silence out into the storm.

"Wouldn't it?" Tarn asked.

"No more so than leaving it."

Kaney slid next to Madero on the floor and curled an arm around him and rested her head on his shoulder. "Then we'll leave this world together," she said softly.

Madero turned to her and smiled. "I hope we do, my love, but we're not doing that tonight."

She looked at him in confusion.

He turned back to the window. "I've fought my way out of box canyons before."

"Do you really think we can?" Tarn said.

"One thing to bear in mind is that there's nothing more difficult than shooting down a running man with a handgun. In the dark. In the middle of a rainstorm."

Tarn checked his pistol.

"Do you have any talent with that?" Madero said.

Tarn smiled. "Hands of gold."

"I thought that was your heart," Madero said with a bemused look.

"I have no heart."

Kaney went over and bent down and kissed Tarn on the cheek. "Yes you do," she said with a smile.

Tarn flushed as red a chili pepper.

"Now *that* I never thought I'd see," Madero said.

Kaney sat down again next to Madero.

"That light isn't going to help us," Madero said, looking out at the fire blazing in the drum under the shed. "But there's nothing we can do about that." He unbuttoned his slicker to give him access to his bandolier. "Ammunition?" he asked, turning to Tarn.

"One coat pocket full."

Madero turned to Kaney. "Do you want to make a dash for it?"

"Certainly. I don't want to shrivel and rot in this room."

Madero smiled. "I've never known anyone like you."

Kaney smiled back.

"You know, Mark of Kane, Collie thinks you're a saint."

"And you, *señor*?"

"A goddess."

"You're such a rogue."

"Get your hat."

Madero turned back toward the window, and Kaney and Tarn joined him there.

"We have to make it to the shed unhurt," Madero said. "If any of us runs up against a pill and is bleeding even before he gets there, we'll never reach the stable." He looked at Tarn.

"Agreed," Tarn said.

"The shed is closer to our side of the plaza, so that's in our favor. But Scateen and Craksi are closer to us, too. And the water has to be three or four inches deep out there by now. Charging through it is going to feel like we're running in a dream. Once we—."

"You mean a nightmare," Tarn said.

"Yes," Madero answered softly. "A nightmare. Once we reach the shed, the roof and back wall and the barrels will give us some protection. We'll rest for a minute and then bolt for the stable all at once. The more targets to confuse them, the better."

"And once we get there?" Tarn said.

"We're home. I untacked all of their horses. And they probably wouldn't try to follow anyway—they know there's a whole town full of people back there eager to shoot them out of the saddle."

"But first we have to get to the shed," Tarn said in a less than optimistic tone.

Madero pulled up his hat and scanned the courtyard and eyed angles and distances. "That's the hair in the butter. And we'll never make it without covering fire. That means we'll have to go one at a time."

"I agree," Tarn said. "And I'm sure you're a better shot than I am, so I'll go first and you cover me. Then Kaney goes and we both cover her from different directions. You bring up the rear while I keep their heads down."

"Well, I see you have a feel for this sort of thing," Madero said.

"I've been keeping bad company lately."

Kaney reached out and squeezed Tarn's hand.

"Enough of that," Tarn said with a wary smile. "Before I lose my nerve."

Madero pulled the pistol from his left hip and loaded the empty chamber under the hammer and slid the weapon back into the sash. Then he loaded the sixth chamber of the other one as well but kept the pistol in his hand.

Tarn unbuttoned his slicker.

"Ready, Jack?" Madero said.

He nodded.

Madero cocked his revolver. "Go!"

Tarn sprang from the room and tore through the black swamp.

Madero's Remington spat flame in the direction of Corson, and then Madero spun to the right and fired at Scateen as he was coming through the doorway on the balcony. The bullet split the rail and Scateen leaped back. Craksi threw up the sash in the room below and Madero fired two more shots, shattering the glass and sending Craksi diving for cover.

Tarn flew through the water and mud with astounding speed.

Across the yard, Sutorius flung open a door and brought up his pistol, but a rain of .44 slugs drove him back.

Tarn dived headfirst over the row of kegs under the shed and disappeared.

Madero stood without breathing, straining to see through the distorting light.

Tarn popped up from behind the kegs and waved to Madero that he was unharmed.

Madero pulled back from the doorway and opened the loading gate of his pistol and ejected the empty shells.

"Ready?" he asked without looking at Kaney as he pulled fresh cartridges from the bandolier and slipped them into the cylinder.

"Yes."

Madero took his position by the doorjamb and scanned the plaza. The smell of the burning wood and the sulfurous gun smoke mixed with the ghastly light to create a vision ripped from the nightmares of Dante.

Tarn had his pistol out as he crouched behind the kegs.

Madero gestured toward the left of the yard and Tarn nodded. Sutorius and Corson would be Tarn's targets. Craksi and Scateen would be Madero's.

"Are you insane?" Sutorius yelled. "You'll all be killed."

Madero turned to Kaney. She was staring at him in silence and in love. He reached across and hooked an arm around her neck and kissed her so hard that she groaned. He gazed into her eyes one last time and then turned away.

He took a deep breath and pulled back the hammer to full cock. "Get ready. All right — go!"

Kaney dashed from the doorway as a bolt of lightning split the sky.

Thunder boomed and rattled the windows, but all guns were silent. Apparently confused about whether or not they should kill the woman, Sutorius's men held back. Then Corson sprang from the room on the balcony and leveled his pistol to shoot her down.

Tarn and Corson fired simultaneously. Neither hit anything as bullets flew everywhere. Then the other three killers let loose a barrage.

Madero blazed away at Craksi and Scateen, while Kaney ran on. She was a powerful runner and churned gamely through the morass.

Craksi and Scateen fell back to reload and Madero did likewise. Tarn's shots sent Sutorius and Corson retreating for cover.

Breathless but unmarked, Kaney closed on the shed. Pistols exploded anew but on she still ran. Then Satan sneered and threw out his leg, and she slipped and fell in the sludge.

"Kaney-y-y!" Madero screamed and flew through the doorway with a pistol in each hand.

Like a bounding panther, he sprang into the driving rain and drew the gunfire onto himself. All bullets converged now on the dark figure defying them in solitary rage.

He fired first with his left hand and then with his right and cries of agony split the air. His open slicker whipped in the wind and his hat flew back as he wheeled and drilled Craksi through the chest. Then he spun to the left and winged Sutorius and whirled to the right and struck down Scateen.

290

Tarn jumped up and fired at Sutorius, hunched in the doorway across from Madero. Tarn yelled in pain as a bullet from Corson tore through his gun arm. Tarn climbed over the barrels to get to Kaney, but a hail of bullets drove him back.

Scateen, twisted and bloody, had pulled himself to his feet on the balcony, and below him Craksi still lived despite terrible wounds.

Madero fired at Corson and he staggered back but kept his feet, and then a yell from Tarn brought Madero whipping around. A shot from Madero's left hand smashed into Craksi and a shot from his right tore the jaw off Scateen.

"Mateo-o-o!" Kaney yelled from the ground.

Wheeling again, with his extended left arm sweeping up under his right, he blew the charging Sutorius off his feet as he fired and fired in two-handed fury.

Corson fell halfway down the stairs, shooting as he fell, and a lucky bullet tore into Madero's leg.

"No!" Kaney screamed as Madero dropped to his knees.

Tarn scrambled over the kegs and threw his body over her as a shield as she fought to reach the man she loved.

By a demonic miracle, Sutorius still lived. Gut shot, he struggled forward, spewing blood from his mouth. Corson, too, came charging and shooting at the fallen bandit.

Madero's black guns roared and rocked and roared again, first one and then the other. Sutorius collapsed in the mud, and Corson took another hit but on he still came.

Corson suddenly stopped about thirty feet away and dropped to one knee and began ejecting empty shells from his pistol.

The hammers of both of Madero's Remingtons snapped onto dead cylinders.

With his left hand, Tarn threw his revolver to Madero, but it fell short and vanished into the swamp.

Madero jammed one of his pistols into his sash as he saw Corson pull a cartridge out of a loop on his belt. Madero quickly expelled two shells from his pistol and snatched a pair of cartridges from his bandolier as he cut loose with a piercing whistle as shrill as a shriek from the damned.

291

In an explosion of hoofbeats, Buddy thundered onto the battleground. Mud flew as he tore through the mire and raced toward his leader.

Startled, Corson snapped his head to the left for a few precious seconds. Recovering from his alarm at the charging horse, he slipped the cartridge into an empty chamber and swept the muzzle of his Colt back toward Madero.

A pistol spat fire and a .44 slug ripped through Corson's chest. Buddy shied to the side in the mud, spooked by Corson's hideous strangling cry that shot up even above the howl of the storm. Madero's second bullet sheared through Corson's face, and he crumpled into the blackness like a lost soul.

Madero pushed himself to his feet. He ejected all his spent shells and reloaded, but the fresh cartridges were no more necessary now than the final toss of dirt on a grave.

Tarn helped Kaney out from under him.

"Thank you," she said, kissing him on the cheek again and then rushing to Madero.

They just fell against each other as they both fought for breath.

Buddy stopped as he came abreast of them.

Kaney supported Madero as he limped over to his horse.

"Oh, *pícaro*," he said, throwing his arms around Buddy's neck and hanging on him. Then he leaned his forehead on those layered muscles and just rested there in silence and in love as the rain poured down.

35 REDEMPTION

Collie screamed and ran toward Madero as he walked through the doorway, but Pompey was faster. The dog jumped up against him, and Madero grunted in pain. Madero petted him, and he ran around in circles of joy.

Tarn came in behind.

Collie hugged Madero in a bear grip but looked frantic.

"Diablo is fine," Madero said.

"Oh, Mateo, where's Miss Kaney?" she said, looking beyond him to the door.

"Waking up Doc Briscoe," Madero answered and he kissed Collie on top of her head. "I should have gone over there right away, but I wanted to see you first." He squeezed her and just held on. "I *needed* to see you first."

"Thank you," she whispered. "For coming back to me." She touched his cheek and sanctified him with an adoring smile. *"Te quiero . . . papá."*

For one of the very few times in his life, tears burned Madero's eyes.

Kathy and Kelly hurried over, and Holden went quickly to the door with his ever present shotgun.

"Relax, Rake," Madero said and limped to a chair.

Collie sat on an arm of the chair and held his hand.

"Where are Sutorius and the others?" Holden asked.

"Exactly where they should be."

Kathy dropped to one knee and examined the crusted blood on Madero's thigh. "Is the bullet still in there?"

"Oh, yes, and eagerly waiting for the blade."

Kelly examined Tarn's wound under the makeshift bandage. "Just a graze."

"As long as I can still deal," Tarn said. "That's the main thing."

"I'll mention that to Briscoe." Kelly smiled. "Thank you for what you've done."

Tarn shrugged.

"I'll heat some water for you," Kathy said to Madero. "You can get cleaned up before you see the doctor."

"Yes, indeed. I have my standards."

Kathy grinned.

The door creaked open and Kaney walked in.

Kathy stood slowly and just stared for a moment at the weary woman enveloped in dried mud and peace of soul.

Kaney smiled at her.

Kathy stepped hesitantly forward. "Thank you," she managed to say. She seemed suddenly wobbly. "Dear God in Heaven, thank you."

Kaney held out a hand to steady her, and Kathy engulfed her in her arms and wept.

"That's the first time I've ever had an honor guard outside my surgery," Doc Briscoe said as he washed up.

Madero laughed and slid off the examination table. "Who's out there?"

"A lovely young girl saying a rosary, a red dog, and various others. Including a gambler showing people how to deal seconds with the left hand. And a priest."

"Father Gallo?"

"No less."

"Did he think I was cashing in my chips?"

"I believe he brought his holy oils in that event."

"The *Miguelanos* are lucky to have him."

"They know it." Briscoe wiped his hands. "Keep that dry for a few days and come back if there's any inflammation."

"With the gallon of carbolic you poured into this bee sting, I doubt it." Madero winced as he began to dress.

"You don't want any laudanum, do you?"

"No. I think Kaney told you why. With me, it's the robe of Nessus."

Briscoe pulled up a chair and sat down. "You're an unusual man."

Madero remained silent and finished dressing.

"Do you need anything else?" Briscoe asked.

"What would you suggest?"

Briscoe folded his arms and settled back. "Do you always answer a question with a question?"

"Do I?"

Briscoe laughed. "I hope Kristen knows what she's getting into."

"If she truly did, she'd run off screaming into the night."

"Well, many of us scream in the night, isn't that so? And what can be more comforting than a loving woman lying next to us in the dark?"

Madero looked at Briscoe as he buttoned his shirt. "You're a wise man, doctor."

"Just a country croaker, but I appreciate the compliment."

"Would you do a favor for me? Ask Father Gallo to come in here. There are nuptials to discuss. And tell him he can leave his oils out there but to bring his stole. I have some old accounts to settle and make good on at last."

Briscoe stood up.

"And one final thing. Please tell my daughter I'll be with her soon and we'll share a pot of coffee in the night and speak of great things."

Their wedding clothes, now slightly rumpled, lay draped across a chair as Madero and Kaney stood facing one another beside the bed in the darkness.

"Why is the lamp down to a flicker?" Madero asked.

She lowered her eyes. "I'm embarrassed."

"What on earth for?"

"I don't look the way I used to. I wish I were younger for you."

Madero slid his hands onto her soft shoulders.

"It's just that . . ." She looked up. "Parts of me . . . well, they're not what they once were." She laughed nervously. "They've descended over the years."

"And do you know why that is?"

She searched his eyes for meaning as she shook her head no.

"It's because now they're heavy with the fullness of womanhood."

"Oh, my God," she said and slid her arms around his neck. "I love you so much."

He pulled her close and he could feel her mature body trembling against him. "Are those the tremors of happiness you mentioned before?"

"Yes," she whispered. "I can't stop them."

"I'm glad, because I cherish every one."

And she continued trembling in his arms long into the night.

www.ingramcontent.com/pod-product-compliance
Lightning Source LLC
Chambersburg PA
CBHW021313250626
47155CB00002B/508